MASTER OF MATRICES AND DOMAINS . . .

Those gifted with *laran*, whether Comyn of the Domains or Tower dwellers, these were the truly powerfully on the world of Darkover. But how did these *laran*-wielders gain their special gifts, and how have these gifts been used for good or ill down through the Ages of Darkover?

In this latest collection of wondrous tales, Marion Zimmer Bradley and The Friends of Darkover explore much new territory in the Darkover landscape. From a Tower, matrix-trapped in time, to the early days of Regis Hastur's reign . . . from Ariada Aillard's pact with the chieren, the legendary sea people of Darkover, to a dragon that holds the land in a wintery grasp . . . here is an unforgettable new addition to the magnificent epic of Darkover.

A Reader's Guide to DARKOVER

THE FOUNDING:

A "lost ship" of Terran origin, in the pre-empire colonizing days, lands on a planet with a dim red star, later to be called Darkover.
DARKOVER LANDFALL

THE AGES OF CHAOS:

1,000 years after the original landfall settlement, society has returned to the feudal level. The Darkovans, their Terran technology renounced or forgotten, have turned instead to free-wheeling, out-of-control matrix technology, psi powers and terrible psi weapons. The populace lives under the domination of the Towers, and a tyrannical breeding program to staff the Towers with unnaturally powerful, inbred gifts of *laran*.
STORMQUEEN!
HAWKMISTRESS!

THE HUNDRED KINGDOMS:

An age of war and strife retaining many of the decimating and disastrous effects of the Ages of Chaos. The lands which are later to become the Seven Domains are divided by continuous border conflicts into a multitude of small, belligerent kingdoms, named for convenience "The Hundred Kingdoms." The close of this era is heralded by the adoption of the Compact, instituted by Varzil the Good. A landmark and turning point in the history of Darkover, the Compact bans all distance weapons, making it a matter of honor that one who seeks to kill must himself face equal risk of death.
TWO TO CONQUER

THE RENUNCIATES:

During the Ages of Chaos and the time of the Hundred Kingdoms, there were two orders of women who set themselves apart from the patriarchal nature of Darkovan feudal society: the priestesses of Avarra, and the warriors of the Sisterhood of the Sword. Eventually these two independent groups merged to form the powerful and legally chartered Order of Renunciates or Free Amazons, a guild of women bound only by oath as a sisterhood of mutual responsibility. Their primary allegiance is to each other rather than to family, clan, caste or any man save a temporary employer. Alone among Darkovan women, they are exempt from the usual legal restrictions and protections. Their reason for existence is to provide the women of Darkover an alternative to their socially restrictive lives.
THE SHATTERED CHAIN
THENDARA HOUSE
CITY OF SORCERY

AGAINST THE TERRANS
—THE FIRST AGE (Recontact):

After the Hastur Wars, the Hundred Kingdoms are consolidated into the Seven Domains, and ruled by a hereditary aristocracy of seven families, called the Comyn, allegedly descended from the legendary Hastur, Lord of Light. It is during this era that the Terran Empire, really a form of confederacy, rediscovers Darkover, which they know as the fourth planet of the Cottman star system. It is not apparent that Darkover is a lost colony of the Empire, until linguistic and sociological studies reveal that Darkovans are of Terran extraction—a concept not easily or readily acknowledged by Darkovans and their Comyn overlords.

THE SPELL SWORD
THE FORBIDDEN TOWER

AGAINST THE TERRANS
—THE SECOND AGE (After the Comyn):

With the initial shock of recontact beginning to wear off, and the Terran spaceport a permanent establishment on the outskirts of the city of Thendara, the younger and less traditional elements of Darkovan society begin the first real exchange of knowledge with the Terrans—learning Terran science and technology and teaching Darkovan matrix technology in turn. Eventually Regis Hastur, the young Comyn lord most active in these exchanges, becomes Regent in a provisional government allied to the Terrans. Darkover is once again reunited with its founding Empire.

THE HERITAGE OF HASTUR
SHARRA'S EXILE

THE DARKOVER ANTHOLOGIES:

These volumes of stories written by Marion Zimmer Bradley herself, and various members of the society called The Friends of Darkover, strive to "fill in the blanks" of Darkovan history, and elaborate on the eras, tales and characters which have captured their imagination.

THE KEEPER'S PRICE
SWORD OF CHAOS
FREE AMAZONS OF DARKOVER
THE OTHER SIDE OF THE MIRROR
RED SUN OF DARKOVER

Red Sun Of Darkover

Marion Zimmer Bradley

With

The Friends of Darkover

DAW BOOKS, INC.

DONALD A. WOLLHEIM, PUBLISHER

1633 Broadway, New York, NY 10019

First Printing, November 1987

1 2 3 4 5 6 7 8 9

PRINTED IN THE U.S.A.

Contents

INTRODUCTION
by Marion Zimmer Bradley 9

A DIFFERENT KIND OF VICTORY
by Diana L. Paxson 11

THE BALLAD OF HASTUR AND CASSILDA
by Marion Zimmer Bradley 32

FLIGHT
by Nina Boal 39

SALT
by Diann Partridge 53

THE WASTELAND
by Deborah Wheeler 66

A CELL OPENS
by Joe Wilcox 85

THE SUM OF THE PARTS
by Dorothy J. Heydt 108

DEVIL'S ADVOCATE
by Patricia Anne Buard 132

KIHAR
by Vera Nazarian 149

PLAYFELLOW
by Elisabeth Waters 174

DIFFERENT PATH
by P.J. Buchanan 187

THE SHADOW
by Marion Zimmer Bradley 209

COILS
by Patricia Shaw Mathews 233

THE PROMISE
by Mary Fenoglio 247

THE DARE
by Marny Whiteaker 269

And Introducing. . . .

The writing of an introduction to yet another Darkover anthology presents a greater problem each year; there is less to say without repeating myself. There's less to say without repeating myself. If I carefully explain where every story fits into the Darkover saga, for the benefit of new readers, I run the risk of boring old fans who already know the background of the stories. I try to walk a careful tightrope between overexplaining and arrogantly assuming the reader is already familiar with what I have written.

By now I am quite accustomed to the competence of young writers in the Darkover universe; and because these anthologies have been accepted as altogether professional, I no longer feel I must make allowances for amateurs.

To answer another question I've been asked: it's very rare for me to do more than the most minimal rewriting on these stories; I edit them in much the same way I would edit my own work in rewrite. Sometimes I break up an overlong sentence into two or three shorter ones (one of my own major faults as a writer), or correct punctuation to agree with proper style. But I do not usually do much "copy editing"; if a writer isn't fairly competent, I reject her work or ask her (or him) to try again.

One of the most frustrating things is that I invariably wind up with more stories than I can use and have to reject a good story I know my readers would enjoy.

In reading Darkover stories for these anthologies I look, first and foremost, for character—and for the ability to make the reader *feel* as if he or she were sharing some facet of Darkovan life. I don't look for slick professional writing, but I do demand good plotting—the ability tell a story and make the reader (in this case me) believe it while reading.

In general I look for one of three things:

1. a new or unusual use of laran,
2. an unknown or unsuspected sidelight on a favorite character, or
3. a character I instantly fall in love with.

With any of these I know I can hardly go wrong; because this seems to be why people read Darkover. And when I read Darkover stories by other people, that's what I'm looking for.

—Marion Zimmer Bradley

A Different Kind of Victory

By Diana Paxson

A few "amateur" Darkover writers have adopted certain periods and characters in the history of Darkover and elected to explore them in depth; and in consequence I have adopted them as "official" Darkover. Diana Paxson, in the first and second of these anthologies, has chosen to write about the period immediately post-Landfall, to explain to herself (and the rest of us) how the survivors of a technologically oriented spaceship crew could create for themselves a somewhat feudal society. One of these explanations includes

". . . there always seemed to be others who would rather prey on their fellows than wrest a living from the harsh planet on which their great-grandfathers had been stranded a century before . . ."

This is as true of Darkover as any other culture.

Diana has created her own series, the novels of Westria, of which there are now three, with at least four more contracted; she has also written a fine contemporary fantasy, BRISINGAMEN (Freya's necklace) and is in the process of writing an Arthurian novel centered upon the Tristan and Iseult legend. She is an educator who has taught at Mills College and in the Berkeley Adult Education program, lives in the well-known literary household at Greyhaven (which was explained fully

*in the anthology titled GREYHAVEN (DAW 1983),
and has two teenage sons, Ian and Robin.*

*By the way, a false impression was inadvertantly
given in GREYHAVEN that this famous old house was
my own home. Not true; I never lived in Greyhaven
except briefly while my family and I were househunting.
Greyhaven shelters my mother, my two brothers, their
wives, children, and occasional others who have passed
through as cooks, babysitters, or guests. My own
home, about a mile from Greyhaven proper, is called
"Greenwalls." Not, as some people thought, because
when we moved in, the front reception rooms were
painted a particularly revolting shade of avocado green—
sometimes called "Landlady green," but because of the
large garden, sheltered by green hedges on three sides.*

*But both Diana and I are also inhabitants of the
literary world of Darkover. . . . (MZB)*

By the time Darriel Di Asturien reached the top of El
Haleine's watchtower, the distant smoke was only a
smudge against the pale amethyst sky. Mikhael pointed,
the carven lines in his brown face deepening, and
Darriel measured its distance from the shining curve
of the Valeron.

It's too soon. He tried to blur awareness of what he
knew must have happened there. *We're still recovering
from the last raid. . . .*

No matter how often Darriel led the men of Valeron
out against the reivers, there always seemed to be
others who would rather prey on their fellows than
wrest a living from the harsh planet on which their
great-grandfathers had been stranded a century before. Darkover held too many dangers for men to
waste their lives in war!

"Are you sure? It's the middle of harvest—they
might have been burning stubble in the fields—" automatically he questioned, though he knew that Mikhael
was not likely to give a false alarm. Dominic Allart

clattered up the stairs behind him and he moved aside to let the boy see.

"There was more of it earlier, my lord—" said Mikhael implacably. "A plume of smoke, near as high as the cliffs. From the direction, I'm thinking it must have been Crawfield. Their hall is all timber, and the past week has been dry. I doubt there'll be more than charred bits left by now."

"Is that all you can say?" Dominic exclaimed. "What about the people at Crawfield? Don't you care what happened to them?"

Both men turned. Dominic's fair skin reddened to match his hair, but he stared back defiantly.

Once Darriel's hair had been as bright as Dominic's, but now it was threaded with gray. Tired as he was, Darriel could not shield himself against that flame of youthful indignation. He reached out to the rim of the tower, seeking strength from the cold stones. *El Haleine is proof against any enemy*, he thought despairingly, *but what use is that to those who cannot take refuge here!*

Mikhael moved between them, as if his body could barrier his lord from Dominic's emotion. Over the years, Darriel had become used to his men's odd protectiveness, though sometimes he wondered why they followed him.

"Aye, I care, and so does he!" said Mikhael in a low voice. "Too much, if anything, and I'll not allow ye to make it worse for him!"

Darriel felt Dominic's anger fade to a confused contrition, and straightened with a sigh. The sensitivities that were both his gift and his bane ran in the Allart family as well. Dominic was a good lad, but his emotions were uncontrolled. Darriel found himself avoiding him out of sheer self-protection. Perhaps he had been wrong to accept the boy as a fosterling—certainly there had been little time for his training this year.

"I'm sorry, then. I didn't mean to speak so hotly—" mumbled Dominic. "When will we start after them?"

"No doubt my lord will be gathering his men—" Mikhael began repressively.

"No, I'm going with you!" interrupted Dominic. "Please, my lord!" he pushed past the older man and dropped to one knee in front of Darriel. "My father sent me here to learn fighting, and for three months all I've done is walk the walls of El Haleine! You have to let me go!"

"Very well," Darriel found himself responding to the need in Dominic's gray eyes. "Get your gear ready. We should be on our way by midday!"

It was a little after the noonmeal when the riders departed, nearly two dozen men of Valeron on sturdy stag ponies, armed with short bows and bronze-headed spears and laden with supplies for a week or more. Darriel had not dared to take too many men from any holding, but Robard MacCrae and Mikhael and Dominic Allart and the others rode with him, good men all. Looking back along the line, Darriel saw their faces set in the grim lines of men who had done this too many times before—except for young Allart, whose eyes shone like *chieri* jewels. Darriel's stomach tightened uneasily as he watched him, but he could think of no reason to send the boy home.

They camped that night near the Valeron. The end of the next day brought them to the cold embers of what had been Crawfield Hall. This, also, was something that the men had seen too often. Under Robard's terse direction, they set to work to bury the charred and twisted remnants that had once been human. The ground told the story of a night attack—the reivers had stacked brush around the hall while the household slept, and no one had gotten out at all. Men tied their scarves across their noses to ward off the sickening scent of fried flesh, but Darriel scarcely noticed. As the odor tainted the air, the psychic atmosphere was tainted by resonances of anguish and a kind of malicious satisfaction that beat against his hard-won barriers.

But his defenses cut him off from the emotions of the living as well as those of the dead, and the shock was all the greater when Dominic began to scream. For a moment Darriel's control broke. Robard saw him stagger, picked him up bodily and carried him among the trees.

"Idiot—" said Robard, when Darriel's breathing had begun to calm. "You should have known better than to go in there!"

"I get tired of being babied—" Darriel sat up. "And I was all right until Dominic—" he looked back into the clearing, saw Mikhael lifting the boy, and gestured.

"I don't know how you put up with him! I'm sorry I wished the lad upon you, even though he is my own kin!" exclaimed Robard as Mikhael brought Dominic toward the trees.

Darriel looked at him quizzically. "You put up with *me* . . ."

Robard shrugged and grinned. "That's different. You *use* your gifts, and you don't spare yourself."

Perhaps that was true. A dozen years had taught him to accept the leadership Robard and the others had thrust upon him. He could only try to justify their faith. But this boy was a problem he had not faced before. As he looked down at Dominic's white, unconscious face, Darriel was reminded painfully of himself, twenty years ago. Young Allart had the same potential. Could he learn to control it?

"Well, if that's what I'm good for, I suppose I had better do something," he said finally. "Help the others finish back there. I'll try to pick up some sense of who the attackers were and where they have gone."

Darriel settled himself against the rough trunk of the silver-fir. With doubled senses he heard Robard's footsteps departing and felt his presence fade. He fumbled in his pouch for the soft leather bag where he kept the little starstone Robard had found for him on a trip into the hills. The lights that twisted within it had made him ill the first time he looked at it, but he remembered his mother's tales of the stone *her* mother had always carried, and he had persevered. After a time the sickness had passed; now he found that looking into the crystal could help him focus his powers.

Darriel settled the blue stone in the palm of his hand, focusing on the flicker in its depths. Then he let his breathing deepen, his eyes unfocus, his body relax against the tree. The spark of light in Darriel's palm glowed more brightly, pulsing in time with his heartbeat, drawing him down, down, and in . . . Abruptly the tenuous awareness within him expanded, and the dappled wood dimmed to a shadowscreen upon which a confusion of other images began to play. Darriel looked out upon a scene of fire and darkness.

Like a dream the events of two nights ago unrolled before him. He saw men's faces distorted by firelight and bloodlust like the demons from the *christoforos'* hell. Men carrying bags of grain and roots from the barns rounded up the herdbeasts, driving them away. Winter was coming, and they were harvesting. Gradually Darriel's awareness focused on one man who stood still in the midst of the turmoil—a big ginger-bearded man with one ear half gone. Almost as if he had felt Darriel's retroactive scrutiny the fellow turned, and Darriel flinched as eyes like winter seemed to meet his own.

And then, suddenly, another presence blurred the vision. It was familiar, but close—too close— In automatic self-defense Darriel thrust outward, and felt an anguished response on all levels that snapped him back to present reality. As his vision cleared, Darriel saw Dominic curled into fetal position a few feet away. Robard and the others were still digging—apparently the boy's cry had not been audible to physical ears.

When the world ceased its sick swirling, Darriel picked up the fallen crystal and put it away. Then he crawled over to Dominic. The boy was white and sweating, but still breathing, and after a moment the gray eyes opened again.

"Twice in one day! Poor Dominic!" Darriel forgot the furious words he had been going to say. "Lad— What am I to do with you? I told your father I would teach you to fight, but that's not what you need, is it? Your trouble, my boy, is that you're too much like me."

Dominic swallowed. "*You* do all right. . . ."

Darriel shrugged. Already he could feel a dull pounding behind his eyes. "More or less, though I don't always understand how. One thing I can tell you, though—I can't be disturbed when I'm working with that stone!"

Dominic shook his head. "It drew me. . . ."

"I suppose it would. Maybe we should get you one of your own. Meanwhile, try to develop some control. When the feelings around you get too strong, make a picture of a wall, and for my sake, put that wall up if *you* start feeling violent! I can protect myself from most people these days, but not from you!"

Dominic looked appalled. "I'm sorry . . . I didn't know!"

"Well, you do now! It wasn't your fault" Darriel added more gently. The two sons his wife Lionora had borne him got into the usual sorts of mischief, but he had never found himself at a loss to know how to treat them. He had not been prepared for a boy like Dominic.

But I should understand him—he's just like me at that age! Darriel felt an abrupt flare of sympathy for his own father, who had never known quite how to deal with him, either. A sudden appalled recognition shook him. *Dominic should have been my son!*

"I suppose we'll just have to learn to live with it," he said awkwardly. "Go on now and help Ewan with

the horses. I'm going to make another try at seeing
where those bastards have gone!"

Three days later they were winding steeply upward
into the hills. This was a new country. Human settle-
ments were scattered and poor, and the people hid
when the men of El Haleine went by. No one knew
where the reivers laired, but they knew a name, Rannarl
the Red, and when they said it, the Valeron men
could feel their fear.

They went on past crumbling walls that showed
them what Crawfields would look like soon, and Darriel
realized that it was the reivers that had made this
desert. They had exhausted the resources of their own
land and now they were moving in on the plains of the
Valeron. He shuddered, visualizing his own fields abandoned and the folk he loved fleeing in fear.

Driven by that vision, Darriel drove his men to
follow the fading trail. He had no eye for the beauty
of folded hills veiled with the pale mauve of mist in
the dawn, for the splendor of nut trees flaming among
the dark masses of the evergreens in the ruddy light of
noon, or the richness of purple ranges in the slanting
rays of the setting sun.

For him, the empty trail was filled by men scarred
within and without by years of preying on their fellows,
and always in the lead he saw Red Rannarl, the cold-
eyed leader with the missing ear. The days were still
pleasant, but there had already been several brief snow-
falls, and at night the pursuers huddled around their
fire. They must finish these outlaws before the snow
came to stay or wait until spring.

On the fifth day they came to the stronghold, not
the simple outlaw camp they had hoped for, but a
fortress almost as strong as El Haleine. Looking up at
it, Darriel felt an unwilling flicker of admiration, for
the kind of men they were following were not easily
bent to another's will. Darriel wondered how the en-

emy leader had compelled them to build such defenses as these? Remembering the wintry gaze he had seen in his vision, he guessed it was through fear.

That night the men of the Valeron made a cold camp in a hollow on the slope behind the fortress. The scent of roasting meat came faint and tantalizing on the wind. In the fortress the bandits were feasting on stolen chervine before a roaring fire. In the forest, their pursuers shivered and chewed on parched grain.

"Those walls are strong, but they're only wood," said Ewan. "We could stack brush around them and maybe set them afire—"

Robard responded with a short bark of laughter. "And what do you suppose the guards would be doing all that time? Didn't you see those fur caps moving above the edge of the palisade?"

"But at night—" the younger man protested.

"We set a night guard at El Haleine," said Darriel. "From what we've seen so far, this Rannarl must be a good enough commander to do the same!"

Ewan muttered something obscene.

"Yes, but he's a crafty one," answered Robard dryly. "Let's not underestimate him."

"We could wait for them to ride out and burn the place behind them," offered Ewan.

"Why should they go anywhere?" said Mikhael. "What they took from Crawfields will feed them till spring!"

"Snow's in the air." added one of the other men. "We'll do well to get home before the roads close."

"If we can't bring them to battle now, we'll have to go back. At least now we know where they lair," commented Darriel.

"Yes," agreed Robard. "But it makes my gut twist to leave them to gloat over the easy pickings on the Valeron!"

Darriel nodded. He felt a burning in his own belly

at the thought of leaving such an enemy unhindered here.

"If we can't break in from outside, can we get the place open from within?" Dominic's voice broke the silence, tremulous with excitement.

"What do you mean?" asked Robard, but even as Dominic answered, the massive gates were already swinging open in Darriel's mind.

"If a man said he was a fugitive seeking service with Rannarl they might let him in. He could go down at night and open the door. . . ."

The circle erupted into discussion. Would men like that accept a volunteer? How else did Rannarl get his band? If the story was good enough— But wouldn't they wonder how the man tracked them there?

"That's why they'd take him, because of that skill!" exclaimed Dominic. "And once he knew where they were they wouldn't want to let him go."

"Easier to just kill him," objected Mikhael.

"Oh, well," said the boy. "If you're *afraid*. . . ."

"I'll go—" Mikhael stiffened, but Robard put a restraining hand on his arm.

"Any man with the wits to carry out such a plan would have the sense to be afraid!" Robard said sternly.

"But it was my idea!" exclaimed Dominic, and Darriel felt a sudden pang.

"Time enough to take volunteers when we've decided on a plan!" interrupted Robard. He turned, and Darriel realized they were all looking at him now.

"I won't hazard any man's life on such a chance if there's any other way!" Darriel stared around the circle of faces, dim blurs in the gloom.

His other senses served him better. He could feel Robard's steady support, Dominic's excitement, Mikhael's subsiding anger and a cascade of mixed emotions from the other men. The discussion contin-ued, but every idea seemed to have some major flaw, and after a time it became apparent that the only one with any chance of success was the Allart boy's plan.

"It will work—I know it will!" said Dominic. "They'll never suspect me—"

"—of being any kind of desperado!" interrupted Robard. "Lad, lad, you can't go in there—they'd eat you alive! Look at you, with the fuzz on your cheeks and the sparkle in your eye! They'll never believe you've done anything deserving outlawry!"

"That's not fair!" The sparkle had become an angry glow. "The plan is mine. Don't you think I can act well enough to convince them?"

"It's not a question of what we think, Dominic," said Darriel gently. "You are untried, and the stakes are too high, both for the man who goes in there and for the rest of us, to make Rannarl's fortress your testing ground."

"But how can I prove myself if there is no danger?" Dominic stared around the circle. "It's not my fault I look young . . ."

"You *are* young," corrected Darriel. "And you'll have plenty of chances to prove your courage!"

"Will I?" came the bitter answer. "You've been avoiding me all summer, and I suppose you'll continue to keep me out of your way when we get home. How am I going to show you what I can do if you're not there!"

Darriel stared at him, appalled by the sheer force of Dominic's need as much as by the boy's words. Had he failed him so badly? In one sense, what young Allart had said was quite true. Darriel's own experience had shown him that one learned how to do the impossible thing by daring it. He knew only too well how many times he had led the way in fear and trembling, not knowing whether he would succeed, but forced by other people's need to try.

That, he supposed, was the difference. It was not his own need, but the knowledge that there was no one else who *could* do what was needed that had given Darriel the courage to take risks whose memory still made him tremble.

"It's not me you have to show, Dominic, but yourself . . ." he said tiredly. "If you feel this way, then I *have* failed you. I will not ignore you in the future—I swear! But I have to consider not only your needs, but the requirements of the task. Are you truly the best man to send into that nest of scorpion-ants?" His gaze went to Robard and the others in appeal. *Say something!* he thought desperately. *Don't make me take the responsibility for this all alone!*

"I'll go—" said Robard staunchly.

Darriel looked helplessly at his friend's solid strength and the unswerving integrity in his gaze, wondering how he could say what he felt for him without embarrassment.

"Rob, I'm asking for judgment, not volunteers," he answered softly. "I think you've been master in your own house for too long to play the outcast now. The same thing disqualifies me, and in any case, I don't suppose I look strong enough—" Darriel held out his arms, whose power came less from muscular strength than nervous energy, then looked around the circle.

"We need a man who looks as if he's been through a few battles, someone with a stone face who can hide his reactions if those banshees start boasting about their kills." His gaze moved from man to man, though in the dim light his physical sight was less use than that other sense for which he had no name. Young and old, dour and enduring, or vibrant with eagerness, they looked back at him.

"Maybe Mikhael?" said Robard finally.

"I'll go, *vai dom*, like I said already—" Mikhael echoed him. "Before you took me in, lord, I rubbed shoulders with every ruffian in Dellerey. I'd put all that behind me, but some things a man doesn't forget. I don't think they'll suspect me."

"Not if you're a traitor yourself! There's no way I can compete with that!"

Darriel bit back an astonished rebuke as he realized that Dominic had not spoken aloud. There was a little murmur and Darriel felt approval from the other men. He took a deep breath.

"Yes . . ." he said slowly. "I hate to send any man in there, but I think Mikhael has the greatest chance of walking out again. Try to get in tomorrow. If you succeed, we'll keep a watch on the Gate every night for a week thereafter. I don't think we can stay longer and get home before snowfall. If you can't get us inside by then, Mikhael, you'll have to stay, and escape as soon as you can."

"I understand, *vai dom.*"

Darriel could read the settled purpose in the other man and realized that was true. But Dominic's bitterness still throbbed in the darkness beyond him.

If they won't let me prove myself, what am I good for? came the soundless cry, and Darriel knew that despite his silence, the boy did not understand at all.

For five days the Valeron men watched Rannarl's fortress, patient as a two-toed cat waiting for a bush-jumper to come out of its hole. They were chilled by the nightly rain, but they were used to that. Twice they were blinded by snow-flurries, but the snow did not stay. By the end of the third day Darriel's head was aching from lack of sleep and strain. Rannarl the Red walked laughing through his dreams, showing him the tortured body of Mikhael. By day, he felt the pressure of Dominic's pain. Darriel knew that Robard was watching him anxiously, but he would not complain. Awareness of Dominic's anguish was his penance for ordering other men into danger.

Just before the sixth dawn, when the clouds had parted and frozen puddles glistened amethyst and aquamarine in the light of the setting moons, the Great

Gate moved. Dominic was the first to see it, and for a moment the others thought that eagerness had altered his vision. Then the dark crack widened, and the men of the Valeron slipped from shadow to shadow toward the opening.

Darriel paused as they reached it, whispering Mikhael's name. There was no answer, and he stilled, sending his awareness before him. He found emptiness, and his skin prickled with foreboding, but the men were pressing up behind him, willing him to go through. He told himself that Mikhael must be on guard and had gone back to his post to lull suspicion. If he wasn't waiting for them, at least no one else was either. For a moment intuition battled reason, then reason won, and he led his men through the door to darkness.

It was quiet. Too quiet? Darriel shook his head, reminding himself that even bandits slept soundly in the chill hour before dawn. He strove to suppress his inner awareness, knowing it would only distract him now. The shuffle of soft boots on stone seemed to echo as they moved cautiously across the forecourt. Buildings loomed up before them; a long low shed with the warm smell of animals and beyond it the sturdy log walls of the Hall. As they came around the end of the stables they found a larger courtyard of cobbled stone. There was a pillar of some kind in the middle—no, it was a stake with something tied to it. As they moved out from the shadow of the stables, the rags bound to the stake fluttered. Softly, as if it had distilled from the darkness, Darriel heard his own name.

Robard bumped into him from behind as he stiffened, inner senses opening abruptly to let in a flood of impressions that told him that a man was bound to that pillar, that other men were all around them, and the bound man's name, just as the pain-wrenched call came once more.

"Betrayed . . ."

Darriel's mind and body reacted simultaneously, evaluating distances and reading the positions of their enemies even as swift orders swept his men into a tight circle around the stake. He fought back a tide of anguish that was not all his own.

"Ewan, cut him down—we'll cover you!"

As his men scrambled into position around him, Darriel drew his sword, then nearly dropped it as a blast of raw emotion struck him.

Mikhael! My fault! I did this to you!

"Robard, get Dominic away from him—hit him if you have to!" Darriel gasped aloud. Dominic's horror resonated too closely with his own. With an effort he stiffened his barriers. How could he blame the boy? In a way it was true, but if the plan was Dominic's, it was Darriel whose choice had put Mikhael in danger, and the only reason he could bear it was because he had had to learn to keep going when his orders had sent men to their deaths before. And then there was no more time for guilt or grieving, for the darkness of the courtyard was suddenly ablaze with torches, in whose wavering light they saw a blur of movement as the reivers rushed them.

"A Valeron, a Valeron!" came the cry as weapons came up to guard all around him, but before its echoes faded another cry replaced it, deep-throated as an animal's snarl—

"Rannarl! Rannarl!"

And then the reivers shocked against them. Darriel thrust out wildly, missed and forced his body to obey him, struck again, and heard his opponent scream. A man fell beside him, Robard stepped quickly to fill the gap and the two of them found a defensive harmony that long practice had made instinctive. Robard's blows were heavier, but Darriel was quicker. A reiver struck by Robard MacCrae did not rise again, and those he missed often fell to a swift stroke from his lord's sharp blade.

But it was desperate work there in the flickering darkness. Darriel realized just how desperate only when the pale light of the rising sun showed him the battle-field. The bodies of several reivers lay still upon the cold stones. The rest of their attackers had drawn off for a moment, but the circle of Valeron men had grown smaller, too, and Mikhael was not the only wounded man it protected now.

"Who's down?" Darriel asked harshly. His arm stung from a long gash, but otherwise he was unharmed.

"Ewan's dead, lord. Paidro was pierced through the lung and may be dying—"

Darriel continued to stare at the foe as Robard went on with his grim tally of deaths and injuries. They had moved back to form a larger ring around the court-yard. He wondered what they were waiting for.

"And what about Mikhael?"

"Very bad—"

"They tortured him!" Dominic cut in, his voice crack-ing. Darriel turned quickly and saw the boy kneeling among the wounded. But he could see no sign of injury. "Lord—" Dominic went on, "Mikhael's asking for you."

With a muttered caution to Robard, Darriel picked his way to the center of the circle where Mikhael lay. His clothes were in tatters, and the angry marks of burns showed on the flesh beneath them. Darriel's own vision swam sickly as he realized that the reivers had put out Mikhael's eyes.

"Mikhael! Mikhael!" Darriel's throat closed and he carefully laid his hand on an unmarked spot on the man's arm. The skin was cold.

"Dom . . . failed you," Mikhael drew breath harshly. "Rannarl . . . recognized me . . . somehow. . . . I held out as long as I could. Should have let the boy go!

"No— I would have betrayed myself and the rest of

you as soon as they threatened me!" exclaimed Dominic, and Darriel realized that the boy had realized that guilt was torturing Mikhael worse than his body's pain. The wounded man's skin had gone even paler. It was shock that was killing him now, and the cloaks they had piled around him were no defense against it.

"Forgive me!" said Mikhael with sudden strength. Misshapen fingers groped blindly and Darriel slid his hand under that of the other man.

"It is you who must forgive me, Mikhael, for bringing you here!" answered Darriel painfully. Emotion had thinned his barriers, and from Mikhael's memory he received an image—the sneering face of a gingerbearded man with icy eyes.

"And me! And me!" This time Dominic's anguish did not trouble Darriel, for it matched his own.

"Always—Vai Dom!" Mikhael drew a harsh breath, then another, and then the contact broke abruptly as he went still.

Dominic began to sob brokenly, but Darriel got stiffly to his feet and turning, saw for the first time in the flesh the face that had haunted Mikhael's memory and his own dreams. Across the space of the courtyard their eyes met, and then, shockingly loud in the morning stillness, Rannarl laughed.

"A little exercise in the morning is always welcome! Stirs up the blood, eh? For valley rats you fight well!" The reiver laughed once more.

He was a tall man, big-bellied and solid with muscle, but it was the force of his personality that made him seem so much larger than life, standing there. He made the men around him look insignificant, and Darriel felt himself puny and helpless before him. With an effort he straightened, forcing up his barriers again.

"Are we supposed to thank you for the compliment? Come try another round, then. We would just as soon kill you here as at home." He answered stiffly.

"No, I don't think that will be necessary. My lads are ready for their breakfast now."

Darriel stared at him, wondering if this was the beginning of an attempt at negotiation, and mentally began to consider what the Valeron could spare. Despite his brave words, he knew that his men were outnumbered. He was willing to sell his life dearly, but it would be wiser to buy it if he could, and live to fight Rannarl again another day.

"I think—I think it is time to end it now!" The reiver's next words disillusioned him, but as Darriel reached for his sword he realized that instead of charging, their enemies were gathering around their leader, slack-jawed and staring. Rannarl fished something from beneath the neck of his tunic, and Darriel caught a blue flash before the renegade's great fist closed around it.

A starstone! Darriel was just beginning to take in the implications when all other thoughts were overwhelmed by a wave of pure fear. He heard a gasp behind him, and from someone else a low moan. This, then was how Rannarl had known!

A starstone focuses its owner's gifts . . . and this man leads by fear. . . . The thought came slowly, as if he had tried to lift a rock too great for his strength. Instinctively his barriers stiffened, as they had against Dominic's emotion. But the men around him had no such protection. He heard a terrified babbling; a little shiver went through the circle. In a moment they would break and run, easy prey for the reiver's hungry swords.

Rannarl was still gripping his starstone. His eyes blazed and his lips were drawn back in a fixed and terrible grin. In desperate imitation, Darriel fumbled for the pouch that held his own stone. He had no idea how to fight such a duel—had never imagined that the crystals could be used this way. But he had no choice now.

He looked into the blue stone and felt a momentary spasm of nausea as its twisting fires woke within. Then he was past it, one with the stone, struggling to build that flame into a barrier that would protect them all. He felt Rannarl's will like a blast of icy wind extinguishing his fragile flames. The sounds around him were faint echoes of the real battle. Dimly he sensed that Robard understood what he was doing and was trying to calm the men enough to support him. But Darriel's men gave him a willing loyalty—he had never needed to bind their wills.

His whole body throbbed as if he stood against a mighty wind. In a moment the pressure would grow too great, and he would be whirled away by a horror all the worse because he had tried to resist it. And still he held, while the strain grew more terrible. He held, and—

—and felt a sudden easing, as if someone else supported him, adding his strength to Darriel's own. The respite let him gather his forces, and in the moment of release he recognized the presence that upheld him as Dominic.

Perhaps his own anguish had been too great for him to notice the pain when the boy's mind touched his, or perhaps—and the thought came to him as a great wonder—their shared guilt over Mikhael's dying had linked them.

Whatever the reason, the power that had nearly overwhelmed one man alone was not strong enough to overcome two who were united.

With a joy that transcended his terror, Darriel poured power into the bright barrier and fed the pale fires he had drawn from the starstone until they were surrounded by a sphere of flame. Whether or not the other men could see it, they felt its protection, and as their fear diminished more energy was released for Darriel to use. Now the two forces were balanced.

Rannarl could not break through Darriel's protection, but the men of Valeron could not break free.

Could he send that fire against his enemy? Something within Darriel sickened at the thought of it, and it came to him that if he used his power for destruction it would be tainted forever. He thrust away a sudden, horrified vision of himself become another Rannarl, ruling the Valeron by fear.

But if he could not destroy, surely it was not forbidden to deflect an enemy's blows. Wordlessly, he opened more fully to Dominic and felt the boy's eager response blaze between them.

A shield! A shield! Make it so hard and smooth that all his fury will bounce back again! Now the flame was solidifying into a curve of burnished brilliance like a sheet of ice in the noonday sun.

Rannarl's hatred found no place to strike, and deflected, recoiled back upon its source again.

It seemed to Darriel and Dominic as if a great stillness surrounded them, as if they floated in the heart of a storm. And when the change came, it was no new presence but an absence of pressure that told them what was happening now. Carefully, delicately, they thinned the barrier. As if from a far distance, they heard cries and the sound of clashing steel. Dimly they saw struggling figures, and one taller than the rest among them who, even as they identified him, swayed and fell.

It took awhile, even then, for them to realize that they had won. But after a time Darriel found the will to dismantle the structure of energy that had protected them. As it wisped away, the nervous tension that had sustained him eased as well; he staggered suddenly and only Robard's strong arm kept him from falling.

"Dominic!" he turned, and saw that one of the other men had got the boy. Dominic's skin had gone white beneath the blaze of his hair, but his eyes were shining.

"We did it!" came the whisper. "We won!"

Straightening, Darriel looked across the courtyard. The last of the reivers were fleeing, but more lay silent on the stones. And among them was something that had been hacked to red ruin. Only the color of its hair identified it as Rannarl—only that, and the starstone that lay dull and lifeless in his outstretched hand. They had won indeed, and Darriel's mind still reeled with the shock of unsuspected power the starstones had unleased here. He wondered if he would ever truly understand or master it. Dominic was younger . . . perhaps he would be the one.

Darriel took a deep breath and looked back at the boy. Dominic had said *"we"* not *"I."* Remembering just how they had won, Darriel shivered, for he knew very well that without young Allart he would be dead now, or worse. The boy had shared all the strength of his soul in unconditional offering. It seemed to the older man then that this dawning had seen more than one kind of victory.

"Do you know now what you're good for, my son?" he said softly, and all the answer he needed was in Dominic's smile.

The Ballad of Hastur and Cassilda

By Marion Zimmer Bradley

Long before Darkover was Darkover, I wrote this "Ballad" to explain to myself some of the interplay of the ancient Gods and heroes of that world. Its literary antecedents, if any, are obscure: Chambers' "The King in Yellow," of course, and perhaps the ballad sung by Aragorn, about Beren and Luthien, in the Tolkien trilogy.

Many friends, knowing of my interest in folk (not filk) music, have asked me if music exists for this poem. No; one of "Bradley's rules for folk singing" is that any ballad with more than five identical verses, except when sung by Jean Redpath, should be punished by having the guitar broken over the singer's head; and that any song of more than ten verses, even when sung by Jean Redpath, *should be received by being dropped out of a fourteenth-story window. I have sat politely through Darkover folk songs almost as long as this; but would never inflict any such song on my listeners; especially in filking, brevity is the very soul and body of not only wit but also of endurability.*

I have been known to speak in the Darkover books of someone "singing" the Ballad of Hastur and Cassilda; but personally, I always hear it declaimed *rhythmically, to a background of minor arpeggios on a steel-strung*

Irish harp or even an authoharp—a sort of zither with an idiot-box—which is the only instrument I can play. (MZB)

Numerous versions of this ballad have survived, quoted and sung to many tunes by folksingers—some of these melodies being of great antiquity, others apparently originated by the singers. There is no proof which version is oldest or nearest to the lost original versions; the unreliability of folksingers' memories has been long proverbial on every planet in TE. The text here given is based on the most ancient sources available, some of them apparently dating from the Ages of Chaos to judge from their archaic casta forms. It is also the longest version known, raising the possibility of accretions over the centuries—accretions which might account for the irregular metrical patterns. Stanzaic divisions are guesswork.

> The stars were mirrored on the shore,
> dark was the vast enchanted moor,
> silent as cloud or wave or stone.
> Robardin's daughter walked alone.
> 5 A web of gold between her hands.
> On shining spindle burning bright;
> deserted lay the mortal lands
> when Hastur left the Spheres of Light.
>
> Then singing like a hidden bird,
> 10 Cassilda cast a secret word,
> beside the waters clear and cold;
> he heard her as he downward spun,
> and through the fields of stars he came
> 15 treading the night where shadows run
> till into water fell his flame.
>
> The song was cast into the night,
> the sun arose with doubled light;

he lay thrown up along the shore—
20 the sands were jeweled evermore—
and to the shores Cassilda came
and called him by a mortal name,
and at her heels Camilla fair
came flying in the glowing dawn,
25 a flowermaid with flaxen hair,
and found him when the mists had gone.

Cassilda paled and wept and fled,
Camilla knelt and raised his head;
he woke and saw blue eyes and gray
30 and saw the paler mortal day
and sheathed his sword's immortal fire
in mortal man's entranced desire;
a hand to each, he faltering came
within the rocky mountain hall
35 where Alar tends the darkened flame
that brightened at Cassilda's call.

White bread and wine and cherries red
brought by her doves through morning bright,
Camilla laid, and bowed her head,
40 he ate and drank by earthly light.
And as his brilliance paled away
into a dimmer mortal day,
Cassilda left her shining loom;
a starflower in his hand she laid,
45 then on him fell a mortal doom;
he rose and kissed Robardin's maid.

The golden web unfinished lay,
Camilla darkened day by day,
Cassilda brightened into noon
50 (for mortal love comes soon, comes soon);
They wandered in the shining wood
and in the mortal sun they stood,
and watched the waters ebb and flow

and saw the silver wheel retrace
55 the skypath in the waves below,
a glory mirrored in each face.

Camilla's tears, unshed aloud,
turned the gray waters into cloud;
where Hastur's steps on sand had shone
60 the flowermaiden walked alone;
yet by her sister's side she smiled,
and in her arms the golden child
the Son of Hastur, cradled bright,
wrapped in the web of tattered gold,
65 Cassilda's son, the child of Light,
Camilla's arms were first to fold.

The silver wheels of night had swung
where bright Avarra's sickle hung,
and on the shores Cassilda sang,
70 and bell-bright harps of Hastur rang;
but in the mountain hall the flame
rushed to the roof in frightened red,
and from the hall Camilla fled,
for Alar called on Zandru's name.

75 A fearful mist about him laid,
his eyes were darkened in the shade,
and Hastur's glorious face did seem
a wavering distorted dream;
for when the God had left the stars
80 he roused again the evil strife;
and in the Darkest Heart there grew
knowledge of Hastur's mortal life.

Into the heart of Alar fell
a splinter from the darkest hell;
85 and madness on him raging came;
he cried again on Zandru's name,
and in the darkened fire he made

a darkly shining magic blade,
an evil spell upon it cast
90 wound with the Terrors out of Night,
and runes he graved, darkly enmassed,
spells to put shadows into flight.

He saw no God, but daemon dread
in Hastur's fair and shining head,
95 and in Camilla's tears a sign
of evil thought and foul design;
he could not see the patterned plan
that gave a God to mortal wife,
that mortal love beyond a man
100 should bring down more than mortal life.
Silent he crept along the shore
where Hastur sang his mortal song,
and while Camilla trembled sore
Cassilda's joy blazed bright and strong.

105 The song was silent in the dark,
Camilla wept where none could mark,
but Hastur came, and bending low
raised up the maiden white as snow,
and on her pure and flowery face
110 a kiss of holy love he laid,
a blazing brother's pure embrace
for sister of his lovely bride.

And joyously she knew his kiss,
and more than a lover's was her loss,
115 and on the sands Cassilda smiled,
where smiling played her shining child,
then starlight hid her gleaming face,
and through the shadows Alar came,
and as they stood in long embrace
120 the witch-sword glittered cold with flame.

*   *   *

Evil was Alar's magic art!
Camilla fell without a cry,
and Hastur, shielded by her heart,
knew he could die as mortals die,
125 and rising into blazing fire
immortal was in spent desire.

The sword lay broken on the shore,
but no man saw Camilla more;
by Zandru's spells the sword was made
130 to banish only, not to slay,
and pierced by that accursed blade
to Shadow-realms she passed away;
and there she wandered long and drear,
and evermore they heard her cry
135 until the fading of the year
became a sadness and a sigh,
the silver leaves that fell like tears
the twilight dim with shadow-fears
dying upon a kiss to die.

140 Then Hastur son of Light had known
(for so had doomed his shining Sire
when first he fled the Realms of Fire)
once more his star must burn alone.
For on the earth he might not reign
145 if once he caused a mortal pain;
or in that hour he must return
to the far spheres that were his own;
for mortals many griefs do burn;
no more might be by Godlings sown.

150 And never to the misty lake
could shining Hastur come again;
nor did Robardin's daughter take
a husband from the mortal men,
but when his star was spun alight

155 over the towers of the land,
    she raised her mirrored eyes of light
    and from the starry-mirrored sand
    her songs from sphere of stars took flight.

    At last she brought her shining child
160 wrapt in the tattered web of gold
    high to the Tower in the Wild
    where Astra dwelt in days of old.
    And there they named him King and Lord,
    and bade him keep the tattered cloak
165 torn from the loom that day she fled,
    and all the shining fibers broke,
    and on his shield, the cherry red,
    and keep the doomed and fearful Sword.

    They set Cassilda's throne on high,
170 and Hastur's crown within the sky;
    they built a city in the Wild
    fit for his rule, the kingly Child,
    and singing of Camilla's doom
    they wrought for her an opal tomb;

175 And evermore the cloud waves break
    along the fringes of the lake,
    and tears and songs still whisper there
    upon the still and misty air;
    Cassilda singing in the light,
180 Camilla weeping in the night;
    Hastur a star enshrined above
    who mortal was for mortal love;
    and Alar chained in darkest night
    never again to know the light;
185 bound to the King by magic art,
    a she-wolf ever gnaws his heart.
    The shining King of Hastur line
188 became your forefather and mine.

Flight

By Nina Boal

Although in general I have tried to become a very methodical writer, it doesn't really come naturally to me; and when I sat down to write the introductory matter for this anthology, I discovered that I had misfiled or mislaid the biographical material I had asked for from Nina Boal. I remember mainly that I met her when I was last in the Chicago area, and I enjoyed talking to her. She appeared first in the anthology TALES OF THE FREE AMAZONS (the amateur Thendara House publication, now out of print, by the Friends of Darkover), and the DAW anthology FREE AMAZONS OF DARKOVER (DAW 1985). At that time she was a full-time student of mathematics, and a student of martial arts, published in such magazines as FIGHTING WOMAN NEWS. Her hobbies include raising and showing Siamese cats.

One on the most overdone plots in amateur Darkover stories is the basic rerun of THE SHATTERED CHAIN: "Escape from the Dry Towns and rescue by Free Amazons." In general, I think when I find this story that it's only a replay on Margaret Silvestri's "Cast off your Chains" (FREE AMAZONS OF DARKOVER) and reject it. Nina Boal's "Flight" struck me as having a new twist on the old story. (MZB)

* * *

A hawk slowly circles . . . circles and rises into the lavender-blue sky, toward the sun . . .

The picture flashed across his mind as he lay on his pallet. He was in the slaves' quarters of the Great House of Tarsa. Desperately, he closed his barriers against the image. His thin back raged with liquid fire. His sides heaved; he was gulping and gasping out the stagnant Drylands air.

I can't bear it any longer! his anguished mind cried out. *I won't!* A blinding, swirling rage arose within. *I only wanted to . . . to do his bidding. I . . .* The room began to spin, slowly at first, then increasing its whirl. *Laran,* a voice told him. A "gift," a curse from a time past—he had never been trained properly. *No! I must not think of such things!* he commanded himself. He reached into his mind and forced the spinning to stop. Rage was still churning inside his stomach.

He turned the rage against himself as he felt his back's pain shoot through his entire body. The visions had come to him earlier in the evening, while he had been polishing his lord's ancestral vases—one of his regular chores. In his confusion, he had broken one of the vases. For his carelessness, Lord Marek of Tarsa had punished him.

He sighed. His back was scarred with the marks of all his previous failures. He had always received many more punishments than any other servant in the Great House. The floors he polished to a burnished sheen were not shiny enough. The spider-silk sheets he had carefully arranged on the beds had a wrinkle in them. A tenday ago he had forgotten to sweep a small corner of the huge kitchen fireplace. Now his mind was betraying him with those pictures. . . . He lashed into himself again. *You are less than a man. Who are you to have these visions and idle daydreams?*

Shame crawled through him. He reflected on what he really was. He was Lewis-Gabriel with the exotic

name, the delicate features and silken red-gold hair—
who was his master's regular bedmate as well as his
house-servant.

He would never develop into a man. Before he had
been sold at Ardcarran, over five years ago, the traders had operated on him—made him *emmasca* to
make him more valuable. A wave of nausea jolted
him. The pool of his rage suddenly resurfaced.

Blank resignation chased his anger. *I let them do it!*
Who was he to rail against his fate? *A true man would
have driven a knife into his heart, or would have willed
his heart to stop beating before allowing that!*

His mind seemed to float above his body as he
assessed himself. His greatest reward was to be show-
ered with Lord Marek's favors. A shiver ran through
him. *What else can be expected from a contemptible
half-man?* a bitter voice demanded.

Tonight, he had been banished from his privileged
place by his lord's side. Lynette, not he, would be in
the bedchamber—Lynette, with her braided coils of
golden hair, her full, curved body. *A complete, whole
woman,* he thought, *not a creature like me.* A dam
within him broke. A flood of tears surged from his
eyes. He buried his face as loud, muffled sobs burst
out, resounding throughout the dormitory.

"Hush up there, Lewis-Gabriel!" came an impatient
voice. "I have work, plenty of it tomorrow—and I
need my rest."

A mocking voice laughed. "Poor pretty boy. He
weeps more prettily than any woman could."

"Why don't you leave him alone?" a third voice
interjected. "He has enough of his own troubles. He
tries, poor fellow."

Lewis-Gabriel, his cheeks burning along with his
back, stifled his sobs so as not to disturb the others.
Nausea roiled his stomach again as he pictured his
tear-stained face. *"Poor pretty boy . . ."*

Will I even be sent away? Fear gripped him as he felt

shame crawl though him again. Recently, Lord Marek
had been lending him out to guests at night; he had
submitted to them, enduring their ravenous hands on
his body. Would he be sold to another? He pictured
himself discarded, given up to an Ardcarran brothel to
be used up—or even worse. . . .

A shrill, screeching fury arced through his consciousness.

. . . *The hawk arises, flying high, over the Hellers.
Her cry rips the sky asunder . . .*

He slammed his barriers. With all his strength, he
stilled his body's trembling. Something was building
up inside; his head ached with its near explosion. *I
can't let it happen!* He tried reasoning with himself. He
would try to rest tonight. Tomorrow, he would work
hard to regain his lord's favor. Somehow, he would
learn to dam his mind against the torrent which was
struggling to escape.

He built a wall. It shut out the raging pain which
racked both his back and his mind. He forced himself
to sleep.

The dream seized him. He was enveloped by it.

*A verrin hawk slowly circled, the vermilion sun bath-
ing her feathers a burnished copper. Her amber eyes
searching, she gave a keening cry as she rose into the
clear sky, over the Serrais hills.*

*A youthful rider followed her, astride a midnight-
black horse, cantering up a wooded slope. His fine
red-gold hair blew in the crisp summer wind. His slender, beardless face smiled happily as his pale green eyes
followed the soaring hawk. She plunged down into the
underbrush. He flinched suddenly from the rabbit-horn's
terror. Then he felt the hawk's triumphant joy flooding
him. The hawk returned with the prey; he took it from
her and rewarded her. He gazed at the distant mist-gray
Hellers—beyond which lay the great deserts of the
Drylands. His soft, rippling laugh floated upward. He*

turned his horse and galloped down the fir tree-lined trail. . . .

Lewis-Gabriel awoke. He looked up; he was on his hard, narrow bed in the Great House's musty servants' quarters. Vivid red rays from the dawning sun were poking through the single, high window. *No more than a dream,* he thought, regret clutching at him.

The rider's youthful face flashed before him again—or was it an *emmasca's* face? A chill ran up his spine. The room spun. He felt himself begin to flow upward, out of his body toward the sun's rays which were now pouring down from the window. . . . *Laran,* his thoughts suggested again. Back when . . . *No! It is impossible!* He fiercely shoved the thoughts out of his consciousness; the spinning came to a halt. Once more, he had succeeded in controlling himself. *For how long, this time?* he wondered apprehensively.

Enough, he told himself resolutely. *Time to get up.* He was ravenously hungry, but he would have to wait for his own breakfast—until after Lord Marek and his family had eaten. He suppressed a groan as he tried to move his stiff, bruised body. He stoically forced himself to dress, then headed toward the Great House's huge, cavernous kitchens, where his morning duties awaited him.

It was after breakfast, and Lewis-Gabriel was in the kitchens, scrubbing the large cooking bowls. A burly, fur-covered *cralmac* came to him and indicated that he was to report immediately to Lord Marek in his study. Numbly, he left the cooking bowls behind and walked down the long corridor toward his lord's study. A new dread was assailing him. He felt his shirt brush against his stricken back. Had he committed yet another misdeed, was another of his shortcomings to be pointed out to him? *No!* his mind cried its silent anguish as he thought of the lash rising and falling on him yet again. *I can't bear it any longer. Please* . . . he breathed a prayer to whatever god would take pity on him.

He passed by other servants, and felt their sneers. *There goes Lord Marek's minion, his favorite he-whore, on his way to service him, no doubt!* He fought to control the shaking in his body.

He entered the austerely furnished study. He swallowed hard as he spotted Lord Marek bent over his desk in concentration. He did not want to interrupt. "My lord," he finally said, dutifully, struggling to keep his voice impassive.

The tall flaxen-haired Drylands chieftain looked up appraisingly at Lewis-Gabriel—and then his broad face broke into a genial smile. Lewis-Gabriel felt an immediate wave of relief wash over him. Lord Marek addressed him. "Lewis-Gabriel, I have something important for you to do. Pour me some *jaco*. Close the door and pull the curtain." Lewis-Gabriel hurried to pull shut the heavy wooden door, then closed the beaded curtains. His spirits lifted, he poured the hot drink into Lord Marek's earthenware cup. He kept his arm in the graceful arch that his lord so desired. He strove to conceal the unseemly curiosity that had been aroused in him.

Lord Marek took out a carefully folded piece of paper. "I need to have this delivered," he said with deliberation. "You must take this to Shainsa—alone. By yourself. No one else must know about it." Lewis-Gabriel felt his eyes open wide in wonder.

Lord Marek continued. "My enemies have spies everywhere, even within this Great House. I cannot be sure." His lord looked thoughtfully at him. "But you know nothing of a man's honor, his *kihar*. You know only complete devotion to me—even if I must occasionally chide you for your carelessness. And since you are originally from the Domains, you have no connection with any Drylands clan or House." Lewis-

Gabriel, without knowing why, began to feel a twinge of inquietude.

"I will provide you everything you need for your journey," Lord Marek explained, "a map, an *oudrakhi*, food, water, some coins. You should get into Shainsa late tonight to deliver the message. By tomorrow night, you should be back here."

Lewis-Gabriel numbly gazed at Lord Marek as Lord Marek placed a hand lightly on his shoulder. "You are perhaps afraid, Lewis-Gabriel?" Lord Marek asked gently. "I've sent you out to carry messages before—your gentle grace represents me well. But you have always been well-guarded—so that no other House would steal my favorite from me. I cannot afford that now. But I can give you this." Lord Marek handed Lewis-Gabriel a small, delicately curved dagger, its opalescent hilt bearing the crest of Tarsa's Great House. "This will identify you as mine. I don't think anyone will molest you—or they will have to deal with *me!*" he stated fiercely.

Lord Marek paused. He ran his hand through Lewis-Gabriel's hair while caressing him with his deep, sky-blue eyes. Lewis-Gabriel stood rooted to the floor. He wanted to feel the warmth, the comfort that his lord's affection had brought before. Instead he felt . . . he felt a blur of his unreasoning rage, coursing the length of his body. He slammed his barriers to shut it out, momentarily dropping his eyes. He looked up once more as his lord spoke again to him. "Take care, Lewis-Gabriel," he said softly. "Remember I am trusting you—there is no one else I can trust—with this important message."

A short time later, Lewis-Gabriel, seated on an *oudrakhi*, wearing a cloak and hood against the desert's heat, was on his way to Shainsa. The red sun blazed almost pastel, rising over the sands and isolated cliffs. He gazed at the distant, jutting forms of the

Hellers as he let his body rock to the rhythm of the desert beast's long strides. A gentle breeze blew against his cheek.

His thoughts were in turmoil, swirling around him. Last night, he had been in disgrace—punished for his carelessness. Even now, he still felt the sting on his back. Today . . . *I am my lord's trusted messenger. I carry his dagger, traveling alone on a mission of vital import.*

. . . Alone. He felt a pulse. A stray fragment struggled to burrow upward and outward. He shoved it down. *I will deliver my lord's message. That is all,* he told himself resolutely.

Alone. It resurfaced. He turned his head, craning his neck, glancing out at the flat, sere expanses that surrounded him. This time, no protecting guards accompanied him. A stab of sheer terror momentarily tore at him. *What if bandits were to suddenly swoop out and . . .*

Before he could stop it, the memory had reached out to seize him in its steel hold. . . . *He was riding, hunting among the fir trees in the hills of Serrais, ranging far from his father's estate. He had just turned fifteen, the age of manhood. His handfasted marriage was still unconsummated. But at least he could bring a rabbit-horn home to his bride.*

The bandits, Drylanders all, swooped out from behind a clump of trees as he vainly fought against them. "A delicate young Comyn lad," crowed their leader. *"He'll bring a good price at the Ardcarran Markets . . ."*

His heart was pounding. Cold sweat now covered his body, despite the desert heat. *Mutilated . . .* Neither man nor woman, he was something altered—manufactured for men's pleasures like a *ri'chiyu* from the Age of Chaos. Violent tremors coursed through his body in wrenching waves. He had willingly given himself to the man who had purchased him. He had not willed himself to die.

The blood-red sun hung aloft in the cloudless sky, its rays now bathing him in its noonday heat. His body continued to rock with the *oudrakhi's* steps. He saw a flitting shadow fly over the sun-drenched sands. A bird, a small, pale tawny desert falcon was smoothly gliding, riding effortlessly on a gust of wind.

His fears were strangely gone. Something else stirred; something struggled within. The wind's shadowy wisps brushed against him as it carried the falcon aloft in a gentle, rising curve. A voice whispered from within. A name, unspeakable—a name from a past life—was spoken to him. *Lewis-Gabriel Ridenow.* The voice, a glowing ember, then whispered its message. *You are alone, unguarded. He has given you all you need—food, water, some coins, a beast on which to ride.* The desert falcon's shrill cry pierced the sky—and his consciousness. The unthinkable thoughts sent rippling shock waves through him. *You can go home. You can be free.*

He was suddenly slammed with its opposite. *Miserable half-man*, it shouted, twisting his insides. *Would you also be a traitor?* Pitiless shame battered him with repeated blows. *The Comyn would never take you back—not some emasculated creature which would allow itself to be so used, something which eagerly seeks its muster's side.* The old resignation crawled through him. *Better to stay in Tarsa's Great House. Serve your master. You belong to him.* He felt for the small dagger that he wore, whose crest protected him by marking him as Lord Marek's property. *Do your duty for the one who trusts you. Do not shirk this time.*

Besides, he reminded himself. *You know what will happen to you if you try to escape and fail.* A memory flashed before him—the tortures that had befallen a stableman who had tried an escape, who had been dragged back by Lord Marek's guards. The entire Great House had been required to witness the punishment. Lewis-Gabriel cringed as he saw himself in the runaway slave's place . . .

He cringed at a different memory—a white light that suddenly flared before him, ripping a cover from his mind. He numbly moved his hands under his cloak, beneath his undertunic. He felt the myriad welts and scars that crossed and criss-crossed his still-raw back. He felt a smoldering force pressing from within, against his mind. He could see his future clearly before him.

. . . *Arriving in his lord's bedchamber where his scarred and mutilated body would be violated—over and over . . .*

NO!

The white-hot rage of his mind cried out. He had thought it cut out of him along with his manhood; for years, he had turned it viciously on himself. Now it erupted fully from newly-opened barriers—a scorching ribbon of flame clawing its way upward and outward from a dank barren pit blacker than Zandru's deepest hell. *Merciful Avarra, no!* he called to the Goddess of rebirth. *No! No! Not ever, ever again!*

He felt his bright rage, a seething torrent furiously rushing, a molten river flooding his mind. It had shattered all the barriers of his shame. *What am I? What have I become? Better to die, even to die by the worst tortures than to endure even one more minute of that . . .* To be a creature without honor, a Dry Town tyrant's beaten, whining possession . . . *No! I will not bear it any longer! He does NOT own me and I do not have to submit. I can leave that House of horror. I can go free.*

The river washed away, subsiding—leaving a cool lake of calm inside his soul. He gazed at the sky. He could see clearly now. His mind no longer spun with runaway images. He saw the form of the desert falcon as it winged toward the sun, blending into a blaze of crimson light.

His soul was not that of the falcon. It was a butter-

fly, emerging from a cocoon. Hesitantly, it spread and
dried its shining wings.

He recalled another—who had succeeded in escaping the Great House. It had not been a man, but a
woman, Rizelle, a concubine who wore fine linen.
One night, she had been found missing. All of Lord
Marek's troops had searched throughout the countryside, yet could find no trace of her. Lewis-Gabriel had
heard the underground rumor of her having somehow
survived the desert, making it to a Free Amazon Guild
House.

She could not bear it either, Lewis-Gabriel thought.
He felt a momentary doubt. There was nothing like a
Free Amazon Guild House that could shelter him. He
clenched his jaw as he felt the resolution harden again,
flowing within him. *There will be a place for me
somewhere—there must be. Because I will remain a
Drylands slave no longer.*

He hummed to himself as he urged the *oudrakhi* on.
Come, my friend. You will be free too, he smiled. He
stretched his mind out, finding he could still touch the
animal's mind, soothing it. He had once been Comyn,
a Ridenow. He still had a Gift. He found that he could
direct it; it no longer reeled out of control.

His mind working busily, he began to make plans.
He would deliver Lord Marek's message so that nothing would seem amiss. Then . . . He was supposed to
stay at Yusoph's inn in Shainsa tonight, as Lord Marek
had instructed. *No*, he decided. *I'll leave tonight and
ride by moonlight toward the Hellers*. He put his hand
on the hilt of the small dagger he wore. *And if any of
Marek's men come for me, I'll use this on myself—
before I let them capture me.*

The sun was dipping underneath the horizon, bathing the desert sands in its purplish lights when Lewis-
Gabriel saw Shainsa come into view. He approached
the ancient walled city, studying the map that Lord

Marek had given him. As he rode through the gate, he
saw merchants and craftsmen putting their wares away
for the night, some of them still haggling for one last
sale. Lewis-Gabriel approached a seller, a large beefy,
profusely bearded man who displayed loaves of nut-
bread. "My master needs bread for his House," Lewis-
Gabriel intoned, his eyes properly lowered, his thoughts
laughing, as he gave payment. He packed the precious
sustenance, needed for his own journey, on the *oudrakhi*
and began to follow the winding dusty streets toward
the city's interior.

Lewis-Gabriel had never before been in Shainsa by
himself. He checked the map over and over again for
the address Lord Marek had given him. Finally he
came to a small wooden door that hung weakly on its
hinges. He knocked on the door, and a wizened, bent
old man answered; he matched the description Lord
Marek had given. "From the Black Hawk," Lewis-
Gabriel murmured as he had been instructed. "From
the far East, where runs the banshee," the old man
answered. Lewis-Gabriel handed over the folded piece
of paper. The old man gazed at the message on the
paper, then broke into a broad grin. Without uttering
another word, he went back into his dwelling and
closed the door. *So much for the urgent message,* Lewis-
Gabriel thought, chuckling wryly to himself.

He turned away from the dwelling and remounted
his *oudrakhi. What would I have done if there had
been a return message?* he wondered suddenly. He
wrapped his scarf around his face as he felt the cold
breath of the desert night. Silently, he passed by the
torch-lit, bleached-stone houses, his eyes and ears alert
for sights and sounds. A child cried. His mother called
him, then snatched him up. Lewis-Gabriel winced at
the tinkle of her decorative chains—that every Drylands
woman wore by custom. *At least I was never forced to
wear those,* he thought. A man staggered out of a
tavern, singing uproariously. A donkey, loaded down

with sacks of grain, suddenly sat down as its owner yanked and swore.

Lewis-Gabriel came to a street-corner. To the right lay the way to Yusoph's inn, where he was supposed to spend the night—after which he would return to his lord who awaited him in Tarsa. The road to the left led to the city's Eastern gate—beyond which lay the vast steppes, extending to the Hellers. Lewis-Gabriel felt his palms moisten as his heartbeats quickened, thudding against his chest. The strains of a mournful desert air, played on a lute, floated out from among the blank walls. Lewis-Gabriel gazed in the direction of Yusoph's inn. His actions, once taken, would be irrevocable. He would now be a runaway, an outlaw whom any or all could drag back to his master. He shivered. They could do *other* things first, to a runaway woman or *emmasca*.

Resolve flowed back into him in a rapid rush, washing away his fear. His hand gripped the dagger's hilt again. He saw himself once more, back in Tarsa's Great House—Lord Marek's plaything, trembling and obedient, submitting always to his master's wrath. His stomach churned inside. *Better I face the dangers of escape than face that* . . . He had made his decision, now he would follow it. Swallowing hard, he turned his *oudrakhi* and took the road that led out of the city.

The indigo night was clear. A shimmery silver light was cast on the stony reaches of the steppe as lavender Idriel and pale green Kyrrdis reposed, embedded in a billowing river of stars. Lewis-Gabriel paused as he rode up a gentle slope. He faced the dancing lights and dense black walls of Shainsa. He gazed briefly in the direction where Tarsa lay, then turned and put it to his back.

He would travel by night, on little-used roads, using only the stars as a guide. He had traveled in the desert before, accompanying Lord Marek or acting as his courier. He knew the dangers which awaited him—sandstorms, bandits, banshee-birds, parching heat by day, bone-chilling cold by night. Ravaging hunger and thirst . . .

And what will my family say if I return to them? Would they welcome him with open arms—or scorn him as one who had stained the honor of Comyn by living rather than dying? He thought of Ruyven, his erstwhile *bredu* who worked in Neskaya Tower. *Will he, too, see me as one dishonored—or can he still welcome me?* A bittersweet sting of longing brought tears to the corners of his eyes.

Images then flowed into his mind—the images that he had tried to push out, that he had dammed during all the years he had been enslaved in Tarsa's Great House. He allowed them to surge freely forth.

. . . *Hills covered with pristine, fallen snow. Golden kireseth blossoms gently waving in a spring breeze. Banners and ribbons of Midsummer Festival, the gifts of fruits and flowers. Fir trees greeting the first autumn winds . . .*

. . . *The verrin hawk, as she slowly circles, her keening cry as she rises above into the lavender-blue sky . . .*

Lewis-Gabriel brought himself back to the desert. The distant Hellers, now misty gray shadows, lay before him. He heard the quiet flutter of a desert night-owl which whistled its low, cooing song.

His soul spread its wings and sang its own song in response as he rode into the night.

Salt

By Diann Partridge

Diann Partridge, under a slightly different version of her name, was a well-known writer for the first series of the Darkover Newsletter, and if memory serves me, appeared more than once in the winning columns of our now-defunct fiction fanzine Starstone. *At one time we ran a short story contest, and Ms. Partridge was one of the regular contestants; she may even have been a winner.*

None of her stories, however, made as much impression on me as "Salt," which contains a really new sidelight on the question, "The Aillard Domain transmits its lineage in the female line. Why?" Several theories have been offered for this anomaly in Darkover tradition; none of them really caught my fancy until now. I don't say this is the *answer; but it's worth considering.*

Diann spent two and a half years in the Army, stationed in Wyoming, then married a Master Sergeant, and spent five years roaming around the country. She has "been writing ever since I can remember," says she hopes that this story proves something to all the people who thought she was crazy "because I sat and wrote and didn't giggle and groan over boys." Since that was my own life story—sitting and writing, without bother-

*ing to giggle or groan over boys—I am perfectly sympa-
thetic; let's hope a day will come when "sitting and
writing" is a perfectly reasonable option for any of us.
It seems to me to make a lot more sense than giggling
and groaning over boys—or anything else. (MZB)*

Ariada Aillard walked along the shore of the sea of
Dalereuth, kicking the wet sand with her bare feet.
Her undershift clung wetly to her legs. There was no
breeze this evening. Blue Liriel hung full in the sky,
competing with the setting red sun. Waves advanced
and retreated around her bare feet and she walked on.

She picked up a shell and hurled it angrily out to
sea. Then another and another. There was no way that
Council would make her accept their chosen husband
now that Dom Arvel was dead. Having him on the
High Seat for most of her life had been bad enough;
never again would she accept another man's domination. The half-formed plan that had been whirling
around in her head since she received the Council's
statement began to take on sense and form. She *did*
have other options and planned to use them.

There was a rocky point ahead of her. A thin piping
sound sprang up from there. Her head snapped up and
she dropped the shell. It was an unmistakable sound.
Sand spurted from beneath her feet as she began to
run. She hadn't dreamed he would be on the beach
tonight.

She gained the point and scrambled up over the
rocks. Near the top was a small cave. A small fire
burned there, hidden by rocks piled around it. In back
of the fire sat a manlike creature. He was naked save
for a string of black pearls wound around his neck.

"alu!" gasped Ariada as she struggled over the last
rocks and threw herself into his arms.

He grabbed her and they rolled together. His thin-
lipped mouth found hers. She ran her tongue over his
sharp little teeth. Passion that had been denied in her

for the past few tendays flamed high and she used her *laran* to touch him with it. He fumbled with the wet shift to get it out of the way so as to take her quickly. The great bloody red sun of Darkover was the only witness to their lovemaking, then it plunged behind the horizon and left them in private.

Later on it became chilly in the darkness. Ariada stirred and sat up. The fire was almost out. There was driftwood that alu had brought and she piled some of it on, bringing the embers back to life. She watched the myriad of colors that the salt-soaked wood produced.

He seemed asleep, but she knew by now that it was a mistake to think him unaware. She searched out the bedraggled shift, dry in some spots and wet in most and covered all over with sand. Shivering, she got to her feet and shook it out over alu.

He rolled and was on his feet in between heartbeats. The speed and silence with which he moved never failed to amaze her. He grabbed the shift and whirled it around his head and let it fly out over the rocks.

"alu! No!," she cried out laughing, "I'm freezing."

He pulled his lips back in a toothy grin. She lost more undergarments this way.

His eyes were enormous in that flat round face and they glowed in the dark. She watched the firelight glint off his teeth.

"There is no need for such a covering. The Sea provides All and alu has brought you this." He held up a glimmering scaled cloak, more beautiful in the firelight than anything she had ever seen. He flipped it out and around her shoulders, then drew her down against him by the fire.

She knew better by now than to thank him. There were no words for "thank you" in his language. She drew the edge of the cloak around to look at it. The scales were tiny; blue edged with silver and the pattern shifted and swirled when she moved. The size of the cloak made her wonder what monster he had battled to win it. She shivered again, but not from the cold this time.

"It is beautiful, alu. It will keep me as warm as thoughts of you do."

Again that knife-edged smile. From the cave he pulled a woven bag and took out some fresh fish. His were eaten raw, hers were roasted over the fire. It no longer bothered her to see him eat as he did. He handed her a piece of hard salt and she crumbled it over the smoking fish.

They made love again after eating. As they lay together afterward, he held up his hand in the firelight. She laid hers against it. Both hands were similar, long and slim and six-fingered. Slight differences were the blunt points of his nails against her short trimmed ones and the fragile-looking webbing between his fingers. She moved her hand and caressed the gill opening in the hollow of his throat. His head arched back with pleasure that sang through her and he was ready for her again.

The rest of the night was spent as the first part had been—making love, eating, and small talk in between. He could sense the anger deep within her, but in the manner of his people allowed her to chose her own time to speak of it. Toward dawn he took up his bone pipe and called up a dozen gigantic sea creatures to jump and splash in the bay off the point where they lay. It was after this that she told him.

He listened intently. When she was through, he asked, "You would do this to your own people, Ari?"

She nodded. "You must understand, alu. If the Council in Thendara succeeds, it will mean I will have to marry some man of their choice. My husband, as such, would have complete control over me. He could lock me in a room and starve me to death and no one could stop him. There would be no more nights like this between my sisters and me and you and your brothers. And most important, no more children for your waves."

She had saved this for last. His lips drew back in a soundless snarl.

"alu would pipe any land-walking man who would own you in such a way to the sea and tear his heart out and feed it to the crabs!"

"I know you would, love. And your people would once again be discovered and hunted. It was difficult enough to keep the secret from my father. Now you are mostly legends to the rest of Darkover, not even remembered in the frozen wastes north of Thendara. I would not have this happen, just when your people are beginning to thrive again. And I won't have a home that my sisters and I have worked and cared for taken from us just because we are female!"

"alu is glad that you are female," he murmured against her ear. His hands slipped beneath the cloak and roamed. "And the *chieren* are your people also."

"Yes, my people, too. Since my grandmother's time. So I would make the Council accept me as a member instead of choosing a husband for me to fill their Council seat." His hands were driving her crazy once again and she lost herself to the rhythm of his body.

When she awoke this time, the sun had tinted the horizon a pale lavender. alu was awake also. He belted the knife around his thin waist. Then he unwound the pearls from his neck and rewound them about hers.

"A gift from ela first-daughter."

She pressed them against her skin. "And how does my first daughter?"

"She thrives and prospers with the Waves. We call her clever-fingers, for she has a gift for finding. Would that you could be with us in the Water."

These were always his parting words. And she wished it, too, but she could not live beneath his waves and he could not live for long upon her land. Even now she could detect how dry his skin had become during the night.

"We will do as you ask. I will leave you this," and he handed her the pipe. "If you need help, blow this and we will hear. Someone will come to help."

It was light enough to see by now and he had to go. She kissed him one last time and he scrambled awkwardly down the rocks and loped off into the sea. She stood watching the *chieren* until he was out far enough to dive. Each waved one last time and he was gone.

There was nothing left for her to do but go home. She left the cloak on the beach, though she doubted it would hurt to get it wet and waded into the sea to wash. Naked, she came out of the waves, draped the cloak around her and began to walk back to where she had left her clothes the day before. The fear that had held her in a clenched fist yesterday was gone. In its place was the fact that now she had a bargaining point and she skipped a few steps down the sand. The wind dried her body and left a faint tracing of salt on her skin. She licked the palm of her hand, tasting it.

Please, Avarra, she prayed silently, let this be my salvation.

Sunlight lay in colored splotches on the floor as it streamed in through the stained glass windows of the receiving room of Dalereuth Tower. Ariada Aillard waited in anxious impatience. Her auburn hair was elaborately braided atop her head, a string of rare black pearls entwined among the coils. She still carried the scaled cloak and stroked it gently. The *kyrri* that had shown her in had offered to take it, but as he went to touch it he had received a nasty shock. His fur had puffed out and he had jumped nearly a foot into the air. Ariada had been hard put not to laugh out loud, but the sensitive creature had felt her laughter anyway and stalked off.

She had dressed in the best she and her sisters

owned for this meeting. The heavy thistle silk dress
was dyed sea green and they had all taken turns em-
broidering the stylized waves around the hem in copper thread. The rings that covered her fingers were
also jointly owned among the seven sisters. Blazing at
her throat lay her matrix crystal, held in that hollow
by no other force than her own *laran*. Smaller starstones
glimmered at her ears.

Finally, the *kyrri* returned, with the Keeper of
Dalereuth Tower behind him. Ariada bowed low. He
was an ancient man, with dry, translucent skin and
tired, deepset gray eyes. There had never been another Keeper here in her memory. As to age, suppos-
edly he was her grandmother's uncle. She figured only
he knew for certain. All she knew was that he was
OLD.

Formalities were observed. He asked after her family and she inquired after his health. He knew well
enough that Lord Aillard had just died and that his
body was now on the way to Thendara City and then
to Hali for burial. She twisted the rings on her fingers
and mentally drummed her fingertips on the table.

"So, child," the old Keeper began, after the *kyrri*
had brought in a tray with glasses of cool cider, "there
must be something else on your mind that brought you
here in all this finery than how we do at Dalereuth. I
suppose it must have to do with the choosing of husbands for you and your sisters and who will occupy the
High Seat. Arvel was wrong to keep you unwed for so
long."

Ariada felt the anger brought by his words flame up
and try to escape her control. She cast her blazing
green eyes down and reached up her sleeve and brought
out a wooden tube. From it she took a parchment
document and handed it to him. He unrolled it and
began to read.

"You can't do this," he spluttered a few seconds
later. His voice had lost the pleasant tone one used

with a child and was now cold with anger. His mother had been an Aillard and his father an Alton with the then new thought-killing *laran* bred into the line. Ariada stiffened her spine and refused to let him scare her.

"I can do it, Uncle, and I will." She made her lips smile. "If that fat *grezilin* who sits on the throne in Thendara thinks he can marry me or any of my sisters off to whomever he pleases, he will find himself mistaken. I can and will cut off the salt trade to the other Domains and the oil from the fish will stop, too. How will they like that in Thendara and farther north, when their skins dry out in the midst of winter and there is no salt for their meat?"

"But this document demands full Council membership and the right to rule the Aillard domain in your own name and for any daughter you bear to inherit after you! King Ronalt will never agree to this. In all likelihood it will mean war between Aillard and the rest of Darkover. You silly girl, wherever did you get such an idea of ruling by yourself?"

She could not touch him mentally or physically, but she longed to knock him to his knobby knees. She was no girl, but a woman grown who had borne six children, even if they did swim beneath the waves of Dalereuth sea instead of playing in the Aillard courtyard!

"I have the right, Uncle. My sisters and I have had enough of male domination. My so-called father, though, thanks be to Avarra and Evanda both that he was no relation to me by blood, had just about beggared this Domain through his sloth and wanton gambling. We sent the last of his catamites packing before he had drawn his last breath. He refused to let any of us marry because it might endanger his profits from the salt trade and kept us dangling in front of every available Domain heir like so many worms on a hook. You are the only male Aillard of direct descent left. If you step down from your position as Keeper, I will burn this paper. Otherwise I want it sent through the relays to Thendara City today."

They both knew he would not step down. He had not been outside the Tower physically since before she was born.

He tried another tactic. "King Ronalt will bring troops down here and force you to marry. Even now he has picked out Carlyn Alton's eldest son to take you as his wife."

Mentally she spat and let him see it this time. Physically she sat back in her chair and folded her hands.

"Let him make war, if he can get his fat backside on a horse. There will never be another male warming the Aillard High Seat again. This I swear, Uncle."

She leaned forward and touched the sleeve of his robe with one fingertip. "If Ronalt the Unwise should come to Aillard, he will find every man, woman and child in this Domain ready to do battle with whatever weapon comes to hand. And there will be no more salt trade between our women and the *chieren*."

"Silence!" the old man roared. "That is a subject never to be spoken of and you know it."

"You old hypocrite!" she yelled back. "It was all right with your generation to sell the Aillard women in body to the *chieren* as long as no one talked about it. Or is the silence you want because the Aillard men were embarrassed to find out that their women preferred the *chieren* as lovers to themselves?

"I will speak of it, Uncle," went on Ariada in a calmer voice, "The time for secrets is over between us. I have their promise that there will be no more salt and that the *chieren* will drive the fish away from our nets if I or any of my sisters are married off against our will. I was given this to show you as proof." Reaching into the bodice of her gown she pulled out the little bone pipe.

He took one look at it, shuddered violently and averted his eyes. "Put that abomination away. I remember all too well the one he gave my niece when the bargain for salt was struck. She and her sisters had no choice in the beginning, but soon they were more than willing to trade their bodies for what the salt wealth brought into this Domain."

And for other things, too, my Uncle, Ariada thought, remembering alu's warmth.

"Believe me, Uncle, my sisters and I have stuck to the letter of that bargain. And we have no wish to go to war. Dom Arvel was the last male Aillard to be born in this Domain and he was Ardais on his father's side. If you don't do it, we will rule this Domain ourselves. You had better believe me when I say I will destroy the High Seat with my own hands and sow this land with blood and salt if the Council doesn't agree. There will never be another male to rule here.

"We want full Council rights for the female line, inheritance to pass from mother to daughter, the right to choose from among the third- and fourth-born sons of other Domains for husbands and we will not settle for less. Already, my sister Allna has taken a husband from one of Dom Arilinn's grandsons. He was a fosterling here when my mother was alive and came for Dom Arvel's funeral."

She sat back and waited for him to speak.

He closed his eyes and breathed deeply, searching for some semblance of control again. Then, in a shrewd move, he spoke.

"The Council will never agree to this, Ariada. To prevent war, I would tell them myself of the *chieren.* You have no idea of what war brings, child. I have seen the killing and deprivation and suffering that happens when war sweeps the land. I wish you would go back and think this over."

"I have thought enough, Uncle. We have had enough of deprivation and suffering here ourselves in the last twelve years. Who do you think ran this place while Arvel grew crazier and meaner, never taking any in-

terest in the land or its people except to show up when
the profits came in? You surely never lent a hand or
even advice! Then he would go off again, to spend the
money where he would and never a thought to what
was needed *here*. I did the accounts and we all took
our turn at the nets. I know well enough that Ronalt
dislikes war as much as he likes spice bread and ale.
And that for every caravan that makes it through from
the Dry Towns with a load of spice and salt, there are
eight that are lost to bandits. What will the common-
ers think when there is no more salt for their tables?
Ronalt won't keep his throne or his head long if they
revolt. As it is, no one except the wealthiest of the
Comyn can afford the Dry Town spices now.

"And think on this, Uncle. If you break the bargain
of silence about the *chieren*, they will pipe you out of
this Tower and into the sea to your death."

He knew she was right. And he doubted if the
Comyn Council would believe him about the *chieren*
anyway. He also knew, as she didn't, that even to step
outside the barricaded Tower walls would mean instant death. She had him and the rest of the Domains
by the short hairs and she did know that. He did not
want war at this time in his life. He had had enough of
war as a young man and had vowed then to die before
taking up a sword again.

In the end he agreed to do as she asked. There was
no choice, other than war. For he knew she could do
as she said; that the *chieren* would stop trading salt
and would pipe the fish away. The memory of the first
meeting between the men from the sea and the men
from the land was still vivid. Adan Aillard wanted the
wealth such a trade would bring him and elo wanted
the children his brothers would spawn on Adan's daughters. The *chieren* women had grown fewer and fewer
with each generation until their race was nearly extinct. Adan's daughters had produced an unknown
number of the creatures and passed the secret on to

the human daughters they bore. No male other than himself and Adan had ever learned of the *chieren*.

There was no sense in dwelling on the past. What was done was done. You could not put a chick back into the egg, as the old saying went. The Keeper picked up the parchment and without a word of farewell to Ariada, left the room.

Arvel Aillard's body arrived in Thendara two tendays after Ariada's declaration did. She had wished him good-bye with a curse for his soul to make a speedy trip to Zandru's ninth hell. His last remains were hardly noticed because of the uproar caused by the letter. Ronalt called a hasty meeting of all the Council members currently in Thendara. Carlyn Alton was ready to go to war. Serrais and the Di Asturiens were all for war, too. Lord El Halyn and Jan Ardais said no to war; El Halyn because he charged a tax on the salt that went through his lands and Ardais because he had twelve sons and could see a possible future for some of them now.

The Dalereuth Keeper's testimony that Ariada Aillard could in fact do what she threatened finally carried the vote in her favor. King Ronalt was indeed lazy and fat, more inclined to the spoon than the sword. El Halyn offered one of his daughters to Carlyn Alton's son and one by one, each Lord was talked or bribed into agreeing. With all of them in agreement, Ronalt could do nothing but grip the pen in his greasy, fat fingers and sign.

When the Council convened in the spring, Ariada Aillard would have a seat among them.

One of the Tower *kyrri* brought the message from the relay screens to Ariada. She read it aloud to her sisters. This was a cause for a celebration! Plus, Allna was pregnant already and Ariada suspected she was, too. This time, alu had promised the child would be human, one for Ariada to keep. This time there would be no secret pregnancy, even though it took only half the time to carry a sea child as it did a human one. No more midnight trips down the secret stair into the tunnel that led to the sea, where a form would be waiting in the darkness to take the squirming bundle. And no more worrying about the secret trysts kept between Aillard women and the *chieren* being discovered.

Ariada tucked the little pipe down inside her dress. It wasn't good to play it in the house; the music tended to set the dishes to rattling and made the dogs howl. She smiled to herself. Liriel would be full again in another tenday. And alu would be waiting for her for another night of love-making. Few human men could compare with him as a lover. Most likely everyone would believe that this child was started by Allna's new husband. But the seven sisters of Aillard would just smile at each other; they knew where babies came from in the Aillard Domain.

The Wasteland

By Deborah Wheeler

This particular story embodies one of the things I said in my introduction that I am looking for; an unusual use of laran, and a central character I can believe in.

Deborah Wheeler has appeared in all of the previous Darkover anthologies; this is the first story that has dealt more with people than animals. She is a chiropractor, a martial-arts expert, was at one time a Dean of a college, and is the mother of two delightful daughters, Sarah (now six or so) and Rose—a small and serious baby who has the habit of making, not aimless baby noises, but purposeful small sounds. (MZB)

Without warning, a huge man loomed over Rorie Leynier, blade edge glimmering in Kyrrdis' blue-green light. Rorie lashed out with one booted foot and reached for his sword as he rolled away from the banked fire. The attacker fell forward with a shriek of pain. Sparks flew beneath him as his beard burst into flame.

Even as he twisted into the inky night, Rorie's nostrils filled with the stench of seared human flesh. The big man rolled free, beating out the fire in his hair with oaths so coarse as to be unintelligible. Other voices answered him from the darkness. Rorie recognized enough of the dialect to realize that his assailants were outlaws, come ravening down from the heights in search of easy prey.

Rorie's horse, tethered beyond the perimeter of the camp, whickered and stamped her feet. His muscles tightened as he gauged the distance to her *Too far,* he thought, and his back bare to the jackals the whole way. He felt the others close in—*if only he could see where they were!*

Hands reached for him from the darkness, hands that only seemed human but tore like Zandru's demons at his throat and sides. Rorie wrenched away from them, slashing with his sword. He felt the blade tip catch, then rip through fabric. A quick, shuffling step brought him in closer, and this time there was an answering cry to his thrust.

Without consciously willing it, Rorie jerked aside a moment before a knife came humming out of the night, angled low to hamstring him. His sword slid along the shorter blade, barely stopping at the guard to slice through fingers and beyond to softer flesh.

Gods! How could they see him, when all his eyes brought him were shadows of blue and dimmest red? Then he remembered what Mirelle, his Keeper at Corandolis Tower, had told him when she sent him away as unfit—that whatever flawed his *laran* talents also diminished his night vision. Now he was fighting for his skin, dodging the short, deadly blades more by intuition than sight.

Worthless to Tower and family he might be, Rorie thought angrily, *but he was still Comyn and deserved a better fate than to fall before trail scum like this!* Without conscious thought he turned, slicing in a downward arc, and heard a burbling cry that marked the end of another attacker.

The slain outlaw fell slowly, as if death had given his flesh a curious lightness, and landed in the remains of the fire. Sparks leapt momentarily in puffs of singed hair that quickly died into stillness.

Rorie gathered his feet under him and tightened his grip on his sword. Without the fire's glow, the dim blue-green light of one small moon was not enough to give a significant visual advantage to his attackers. Now they were equally blind—and foolish enough to give away their positions by shouting at each other.

With adrenalin pounding through his veins, Rorie forced himself to move softly, angling away from the nearest outlaw and toward his mare. Now that he was no longer straining for vision, he could hear all four remaining assailants, the big chief thrashing about with his blade. One man, to Rorie's left, stood still and began fumbling with something—a flint to relight the fire?

He had no choice now, no luxury to inch cautiously toward his horse. Rorie sprinted across the remaining distance, praying that he would be able to scramble onto the mare's back before the outlaws dragged him from her.

The horse pranced as Rorie cut her tether line and grabbed a handful of mane with his free hand. Aldones be praised, she was sweet-tempered enough to stand still while he threw his right leg over her back and dug his knees into her sides.

The mare leapt forward even as the first of the outlaws reached her, hands stretching toward the dangling end of her halter rope. She shuddered as her rider's desperation seized her, screaming like a terrified child and lashing out with her front hooves.

Now they were in the open, running with a shared, almost demonic need for escape. Dry-throated, Rorie clung to his sword with one hand, the other entangled in the mare's wind-whipped mane. The muscles of her back and shoulders flexed and knotted, jumping in hard nodules beneath his thighs. Once she stumbled, going down almost to her knees, and the sharp bones of her withers dug into his crotch as he lurched forward.

Rorie could hear shouts from behind. They were

following, they must have had mounts of their own hidden nearby. Then the mare was on her feet again, once more a creature ruled by his own panic. Between the disjointed scramble of her gallop and the rampaging of his own heart, Rorie could hear nothing more.

He lost all sense of time and direction, barely aware of the changing terrain and shifting blue shadows. Idriel and pearly Mormalor rose to join Kyrrdis, and he became aware that he had left his pursuers far behind. Perhaps they had returned to the camp, content with its booty.

Rorie made no attempt to guide the mare with his knees or reach forward to grab the trailing stub of rope swinging from her halter. The passing terrain was no more than a swirl of shadows, and her night vision must serve for both of them. Eventually the mare slowed, her sides heaving like great bellows. The thin leather of Rorie's breeches was soaked with their mingled sweat, acrid with fear. Heat rose from their bodies like a cloud of steam in the cool night.

Rorie shifted his weight and the mare came to a weary halt, head lowered. He slid to the ground, looped his belt into a makeshift sling for the sword, and began to walk his horse to cool her down. He told himself doggedly that his present situation might be bleak, but it would be bleaker still if he lost her due to carelessness.

He remembered thinking, as he had made camp only a few short hours ago, that his life could not be much more dismal, being the extraneous fourth son of a family richer in heirs than lands, now being sent home as useless by the Tower that had once seemed like his only chance to find a place for himself. . . . Rorie snorted at his pathetic self-pity, and reached over to scratch the mare's sweaty ears.

Now look at the mess he'd gotten himself into! Like the game that walks from the trap to the cookpot, he'd lost his food, saddle, extra clothing—in short, everything but what he'd slept in, one sword without a proper sheath, and a loyal but tired mount. He still had his life, and he wondered if even a normally-sighted man could have done as well against the trail scum that had jumped him, grown bold by the disorder that still lingered after the signing of the Compact.

The night hung quiet and heavy around him, silent except for the occasional clink of halter ring or creak of the makeshift sword sheath. Even their footsteps seemed hushed, unnatural. Eventually the mare cooled and Rorie wrapped the halter rope around one hand and sat down, making himself as comfortable as he could. His head fell forward on arms crossed around his knees and finally he slept.

He awoke to pain, a cool, pulsating ache over his sternum. Rorie sat upright, blinking in the gray morning light. He put one hand to his chest, half-expecting to find his shirt slick with congealed blood, but there was nothing except his starstone. Even though he had wrapped it in insulating silk as he had been taught at the Tower, it throbbed insistently. He forced his eyes into focus.

The mare stood at his feet, nuzzling his boots as if considering their suitability as fodder. The severed rope had slipped from his fingers and lay trailing in the dust.

Rorie froze as his eyes took in his surroundings. Dust, gray and lifeless, covered the ground, the few withered skeletons of bush and tree, the low hills rising before him. He could spy not a single blade of grass, not a single buzzing insect. Except for the thunder of his own heart and the mare's soft breathing, they were two alone in a desolation of stillness and monochrome dust.

Bonewater dust.

He had thought himself safe in the hills, far enough from the lands blasted sterile by the unthinkably terrible *laran* weapons of the Age of Chaos. The wasteland had been marked on his maps, but sketchily, as if the cartographer had neither known nor wanted to dwell on its exact parameters. Somehow, in the terror of the night attack, in his blindness and the mare's panic, they had wandered so far into the wasteland that it now surrounded them . . .

. . . Surrounded them, the insidious particles already working their way through his body's defenses. Rorie gasped, then fought his breathing under control. Was he even now drawing the deadly stuff into his lungs where it would seep throughout his body, turning his bones to crumbling ash? Would his flesh melt into jelly even as his blood thinned to rosewater while his brain, functional to the last, watched in helpless, insane horror?

He shivered, drawing upon his fragmentary skills to monitor himself for the first signs of internal rot. Even though he unwrapped his starstone and gripped it tightly, he could sense no departure from the normal workings of his body. Nothing, neither in himself nor the mare. *Of course,* he thought bitterly, *what did he expect?* The few poor skills they had managed to drill into him at Corandolis were just that—useless yearnings.

He got to his feet, reflexively brushing the grit from his thighs. The mare, undisturbed, pricked her ears at him in mild curiousity. Slinging the sword through his leather belt, he swung onto her back, hoping against hope that from that vantage point he would be able to tell the direction from which they had come.

It was no use. Gray dust, gray hills, gray twisted remains of plant life stretched as far as his eyes could see in all directions. Nor did the shifting layers of powder-fine dust hold any trace of hoofprints from the night before. The red sun lay directionless behind veils of clouds, the air chill and sullen, unnaturally still.

Rorie grasped the end of the halter rope, but made no attempt to guide the mare as he nudged her forward. Her instincts might not warn her of the insidious dangers of the place, but surely, given her head, she would seek out water and grazing, a way out of this waking nightmare. Maybe there was still some slim hope. . . . But he did not believe it.

All time seemed suspended as man and horse traveled on through that unexpressibly bleak and silent landscape Rorie found his mind numbed and unresponsive, as if some essential part of him had already surrendered to the poisoned land. Even the mare's lack of concern struck him as hopeless, a token of her dumb bestiality rather than her animal intuition. The motion of her gait loosened the fear-tightened muscles of his back and thighs, gradually coaxing him into a hypnotic rhythm. He surrendered to it as he did to his own overwhelming despair.

Rorie was so caught up in the mesmeric certainty of his own doom, that he nearly toppled forward over the mare's neck when she came to an abrupt halt. He grabbed her mane and righted himself on her slippery back. They had come up to the top of a long, gentle rise and stood looking down over a river-etched valley.

At the exact center, cupped by the surrounding hills, stood a Tower.

And such a Tower as Rorie had never in his short life seen, or even dreamt. Corandolis, or even the great Tower at Hali seemed but a smudged copy beside its grandeur. Indeed, he thought as he felt a tremor run through the mare's body, such a Tower had not existed in the Domains for many a long year, not since the height of Comyn madness.

Even in the dispersed red light, it gleamed, opalescent and luminous as if its foundations were mixed with starstone chips. Its soaring lines spoke of grace and confidence, of building techniques far beyond mere human masonry. And it stood intact in its glory, untouched by the desolation which surrounded it.

Rorie let out his breath and the mare started forward at a brisk trot, her ears pricked forward. Without

any urging she broke into a jolting canter, sweeping
down the hill toward the gleaming Tower.

The gates stood before them, open and majestic. As
Rorie drew near, a slender figure clad in shimmering
blue darted forward, hands outstretched in welcome,
long red hair like a banner behind her.

A girl. A Comyn girl.

Rorie hauled on the mare's halter rope, drawing her
to a clattering halt just inside the Tower gates. His
eyes fastened on the girl, seeing that she was no child
but a young and beautiful woman. Beyond her a fountain played in a courtyard, and he caught a flash of
living green.

"Blessed Cassilda, you've come!" she cried, reaching up to steady the mare's head. She looked up at him
with wide green eyes set in a perfect heart-shaped
face, her cheeks delicately flushed with rose. She met
his gaze with a directness that could only come from
Tower training, and he caught the unmistakable tang
of powerful *laran*.

"I—I don't understand," Rorie managed to stam-
mer. His heart raced as much with her disturbingly
feminine presence as with the discovery of the Tower.
"What are you doing here?"

She shook her head, her hair rippling with light like
a glorious copper mane. "I was so worried while I was
alone, but everything's going to be all right now that
you're here to help. Please, get down. Can I get you
anything? Water? Food—fodder for your horse?"

Rorie responded to the subtle hint of command in
her voice and slid from the mare's back. "Water, I
think. To wash the dust away." His unspoken thought:
Would that do any good now?

She laughed, leading the way toward the fountain.
"I, too, feared so at first, but even handicapped as it is,
this Circle has great healing powers. Here I am as
proof, well and whole."

The mare plunged her nose into the clear water

without hesitation as Rorie rinsed his face and hands. Again he turned to the Comyn lady: "Who are you? What are you doing here, in the middle of this. . . ?"

"I'm Shani, originally trained at—but that was a long time ago. I won't ask you what Tower you're from. What matters, Rorie, is what we can do together. We are both needed so desperately."

Rorie looked away from the intensity of her eyes, realizing that her skill was such that she could pick up his name and his reticence to recount his expulsion from Corandolis. "What do you need me for?"

"You know what this place is?"

"A Tower—intact but apparently abandoned, surrounded by bonewater dust."

Shani nodded. "Only one of the many terrible *laran* weapons used by one Domain against another. But although this Tower, whose very name has been lost, was attacked, it was not destroyed."

"Yes, I can see—"

"The Tower Circle is still intact, along with its matrix screens."

"That can't be possible, not after hundreds of years!"

"I'll show you in a moment. But think—how else could these turrets still stand? How else could there be a fountain of pure water, and safe food for human and beast?"

Rorie could find no answer, but followed Shani through a graceful arched doorway and into the central tower. They crossed the common room with its comfortable furniture and generous fireplace, everything looking as undecayed and undisturbed as if it were inhabited. Rorie would have thought the Tower still in daily use, but there was an unnatural density in the shadows that told him it had been many long years since anyone had sat on those pillows or lit a blaze on that cold hearth.

The stairway was broad, as open and airy as the rest of the Tower. Built using *laran* forces, without the

constraints of human limitations, it clearly indulged
the Darkovan love of sweeping spaces and natural
lighting.

Rorie could feel the energies of the central Tower
room even before they entered it. It was like nearing
an immense battery in which barely-checked forces
surged and flowed. Even with his meager, barely developed talents, even with his starstone shrouded in
insulating silk, the stored power of the place clawed
hungrily at him. The hairs on the back of his neck
rose.

Shani turned back to him with sympathy in her
green eyes. "It's all right, really. Just a little alarming
at first because of the magnitude of the matrix, but it's
perfectly safe. The Circle has it well under control."
She swung aside the door and stepped back for him to
enter.

Rorie stepped into a wide, circular room, furnished
in comfort to the point of luxury. On a round table sat
the huge crystal, alive with blue and silver . . . and
nine men and women, robed in opulence and bathed
in flickering light. Their features bore the unmistakable stamp of superb *laran*, refined through generations of breeding and rigorous training. They were all
young and beautiful, their hair in shades of flaming,
almost arrogant red, rising and falling in gentle waves
as they gazed intently at the central pulsating gem.

"The Circle," Shani whispered. "Even as they locked
themselves out of time in that final, fatal battle. No
one knows who they fought, or why. All we can see is
the wasteland that is the result . . . and this little
island of safety they managed to carve out for themselves."

"I don't see that it's done them much good," Rorie
said. "Even if they could free themselves, how could
they escape the bonewater disease? Surely if they
could, they would have, long ago, without any pitiful
help I might be able to lend them." *And*, he thought,

how do I know they were the ones defending themselves and not the perpetrators of the desolation outside? Even if it were possible, could I dare risk turning loose telepaths of that magnitude with no loyalty to the Compact?

He thought of Mirelle, Keeper of Corandolis, and her perpetual caution, her insistence that *laran* be used only for safe, Compact-legal purposes, her underlying fear that would not let her acknowledge any talent she could not control. . . .

"Weren't you listening?" Shani scowled. The musical tones of her voice, even in scolding, shook him from his doubts. "They used the matrix screen to shield themselves, and to a lesser extent, the whole Tower. There's been no energy left over for any voluntary action. Here they've sat, locked into their own salvation. But with my *laran*—and yours—we can give them the edge they need to break free, to use the starstone to cleanse the land so it can live again. Isn't that worth taking a small risk for?"

"I don't know. Even if they could . . . even if *I* could—"

"Do you doubt my judgment?" Shani's question whipped out with the unmistakable authority of a Keeper. The starstone between her breasts blazed with power. "Or are you the proverbial blind man denying the existence of color just because it is beyond his own senses?"

Rorie shrugged. Just as he had not argued with Mirelle when he'd been dismissed from Corandolis Tower, so he felt he had no basis for denying Shani's claim. Her own trained talent was evident in her every gesture, and he was acutely aware of his own limitations.

She nodded, smiling slightly. Was there just the hint of satisfaction in that smile? *Are you going to doubt everything?* Rorie demanded of himself. *What a pitiful means of salving the remnants of your self-esteem.*

Shani gestured to him, brushing her fingertips so

close to his wrist that he felt a slight shock of energy, although no actual contact. He recognized it as a classical Keeper's touch—evanescent, suggestive, non-committal.

"There is your place," she said in a low, throaty voice, "there . . ." She nodded toward a break in the spacing of the entranced Circle workers. "And there is mine."

Rorie thought for a moment that the seat she indicated as hers must be the Keeper's place, but he immediately dismissed the idea as ridiculous. Shani, for all her obvious training, was not part of the original Circle, but a wanderer like himself, attracted by the concentration of *laran* power, and then held by the Tower's demanding need and her own compassion.

"We join the Circle, then?" he asked.

Shani stood behind him as if to help him take his seat. Rorie turned his head to see her eyes upon him like luminous green gems, like a falcon scanning the burrows of a rabbit horn. His palms felt suddenly chill and moist. Clumsily, he began to lower himself onto the padded bench, lost his balance momentarily, and reached out a hand to steady himself.

As his fingers passed through the outer edge of the energon rings, tremendous forces sparked along his nerves and Rorie gasped. He had known the matrix to be powerful, but had no conception of its true magnitude. No wonder it was capable of focusing enough *laran* to preserve the Tower workers through the years against bonewater dust and equally terrible weapons! Even its outer edge, casually touched, was strong enough to stop a man's heart.

He blinked, his vision darkening . . . and froze. For superimposed upon the images of the men and women of the Circle, frozen in timeless concentration and beauty, were the lineaments of horror. Those serene faces were but tissue coverings for leering decay, shreds of charred flesh hanging in obscene strips from grinning, whitened bone. Sickly blue light played over the eye sockets, faintly reflected within. Instead of graceful cupped hands, he saw skeletal claws, suspended in agony and greed around a pulsating maw of raw psychic hunger.

Through the borders of his awareness howled the traces of their death agonies—not, as Rorie had first suspected, sadness and defeat, grasping at a last, desperate hope for survival—but raw betrayal, the searing pain of souls forever condemned to a hell of their own making.

The Circle had not, as Shani had said, preserved themselves through the giant matrix stone. It had been an instrument of desolation for so long, focused on unthinkable evil, that in the end it had acquired a consciousness of its own, with only one goal—to survive. They had reached for its power in their last frenzied moments, only to be devoured, drained of their precious *laran* energies until only husks remained. Once they had been powerful telepaths, the best of a whole tradition of selective inbreeding and exhaustive training, these men and women of the unknown Tower. Their energies had fed the stone for many a long year.

Now its reserves had dwindled, its energy waned, and even the wasteland in which it lay like a perverted jewel gave it no sustenance. It had reached out and drawn Rorie into its web, even as it had caught Shani before him.

He had to warn her—get her out of there, get both of them out of there before it was too late! The appearance of the Circle was but an illusion, their need nothing but a thin veil for the ravening of the stone.

"Sh—Shani! I think—" he stumbled, fumbling for the words which would give him the time to warn her, yet not alert whatever parody of intelligence might lurk within the stone. "I need to rest a bit before we try. I'm—you know my *laran* isn't very strong, and I've had a hard night."

Rorie stood up, carefully avoiding any further contact with the energon fields of the giant matrix, and turned to her. . . .

He saw her beauty, and the subtle blend of feminine seductiveness and Keeper isolation she spun about herself. But underneath, pervading the whole image, lay corruption as rank and vile as he had seen in the Circle. Rorie knew than that Shani was indeed the Keeper of the Circle, and it had been through her that the others had been sucked dry. Twisted blue light flickered behind her eyes, and for a fleeting moment he caught the odor of a charnel house on her sweet breath. The mark of the giant starstone lay upon her like a veil of death. She opened her rosebud mouth, and he saw the rotten skull gape its jaws in anticipation.

Without thinking, Rorie grabbed her by the shoulders, dimly aware that he was committing the most unthinkable assault upon the person of a Tower-trained woman, a Keeper who should have been immune from even a thought of an unwanted touch. Desperately he pulled her over the bench, using his hips and thigh muscles to swivel around and thrust her into the very center of the matrix.

She screamed, a piercing, almost mechanical wail. Tentacles of coruscating blue fire leapt from the heart of the crystal, lashing toward Rorie's heart. He threw himself backward, but the padded bench caught him at the back of his knees, slowing his fall. The nerves of his skin shrieked in sudden agony as the energon fields seized him.

As the matrix dragged him within its surging core, Rorie could no longer feel his mortal body. He could only imagine the convulsions that shook his frame again and again. He experienced energy as a visual sensation, vivid as his usual vision never was, as it tossed him in its tumultuous sphere. He could sense shadows of the minds which had gone before him, thin echoes of once vibrant personalities now worn into ragged crusts by time and the relentless drain of the matrix.

The center of the thing loomed before him, a maw of blackness, pulsating and puckering as if already welcoming him into itself. Every fiber of Rorie's consciousness shrank from it, for it boded not simple oblivion but a mental slavery that would endure century after century until the last wisp of awareness departed from his spirit.

Even as he struggled against the pull of the matrix, Rorie wondered what use it could have for him. He could understand the crystal's lust for a powerful, trained talent such as those which had comprised the original Circle . . . or any of the Tower workers with whom he had studied so briefly. But he had been sent from the Tower as inadequate, unfit. Mirelle, his Keeper, had said so in no uncertain terms. How could he have enough *laran* to be of any value to the matrix?

Then he realized . . . The matrix was not a living, thinking being, but a mockery of one, and as such it was not subject to the delusions and preconceptions of a human mind. It didn't *know* he was no good; no Keeper had, for personal or political reasons, ever told it so. Therefore it had relied only on its own limited perception of him—and that perception had told it that within Rorie lay the force it needed to continue its parasitic existence. There must be something inside him, something his own Keeper had been blind to, even as he was blind in the darkness. Perhaps, the thought seeped through his draining consciousness, perhaps she had sensed it in him, but shrank from it in a reflex conditioned by fear and guilt.

Perhaps the same ability—Rorie could no longer consider it a flaw—that limited his night sight also gave him the true vision of the Circle corpses—also let him see the matrix for the evil thing it was—and would also give him the tools to conquer it. . . .

Anger flared up in him, hot and red in contrast to

the livid blue of the matrix. He fed it with his will to
live, the same determination that had refused to give
up when the bandits had attacked him the night before. How dare this thing, this mere inanimate mass of
crystal and energy ring dare to destroy a human mind,
feeding on precious Comyn talents without conscience
or reason—could there be any greater sin, and more
obscene insult to the Gods?

Machine! roared through Rorie's thoughts. *It's nothing but a Compact-banned machine!* If he had been in
his physical body, he would have spat on it in outrage.
But righteous indignation alone could not conquer the
vastly powerful starstone which held him into its core.

His physical body . . . he could feel it, half-crouched
against the padded bench. *Hand—he must move his
hand!* He thrust his will into the command and felt the
shadow-hand move toward the hilt of the sword still
strapped on his back. The white and blue energies of
the crystal crackled around him, protesting even this
small freedom.

Rorie hardened his determination. Whatever it was
the stone resisted, that thing he would do with all his
might. *Lungs—inhale! Heart—beat! Shoulder muscles—
tighten! Hand to sword-hilt!* Could he actually feel its
texture beneath his shadow fingers, or was it merely
an illusion born of his fevered desire?

Yes, he could see the sword sliding through its makeshift sheath, the glimmer of steel before his shadow-
eyes. Caustic blue light played reflections across the
blade's polished surface. *Other hand—grasp . . .
wrists—flex—*

In frenzy, the matrix tightened its stranglehold on
him, smothering him with the sheer weight of its power
as it drew him in. Rorie realized that with every effort
to control his physical body, he weakened his mental
defenses against it. He knew he could not defeat the
matrix on its own terms. His only chance for survival
lay in his unique ability to stay outside of its chosen

sphere of battle, to see the illusions it created as they really were—and then to use the physical dimension to his own advantage.

Rorie relinquished his psychic resistance to the crystal, throwing his strength and will into his real body. The muscles of his hands tightened around the leather-wrapped steel of the sword hilt. His abdomen hardened as he brought his weight to bear, slashing down, the tempered blade aimed at the center of the starstone.

Splinters flew in every direction, shattering the light at the heart of the demented crystal. For an eternal fraction of a moment, Rorie-within-the-starstone and Rorie-without were blinded, buffeted, ground to quivering fragments under the explosive assault. His ears brought him the frantic, keening death-wail of the thing and his pupils constricted in denial of the poisonous white nova before him.

Gradually sensation returned to him—tears dripping from his face, the heat in his hands as they touched his blackened sword, the trembling of his thigh muscles. He dropped the molten blade and sat back on the bench, aware of its unsteadiness but unable to support his own weight any longer.

Rorie's vision cleared with agonizing slowness as he made out details before him. The table which had supported the matrix crystal sagged crazily, tilting under its burden of lightless shards. Bones disjointed and crumbled into piles of grayish ash. From somewhere outside the Tower room came the frantic whinny of a horse.

Rorie gathered his legs under him as the bench collapsed into ruin. As he turned toward the stairwell, he saw cracks widening through the dull stone of the turret. Once the sustaining power of the matrix was withdrawn, time and decay would have their way at last.

But the courtyard was not a desolate ruin. Water still bubbled from the tumbled stone of the fountain, and healthy green still sprouted everywhere. Rorie grabbed the mare's halter rope and patted her sweating neck. She rolled her eyes and danced nervously at the falling chunks of stone, but followed him through the sagging gates.

Rorie had expected to see gray bonewater dust stretching to the horizon, but even the wasteland had been transformed by the destruction of the starstone. Devastation had wracked this land, certainly, but it had been far in the past, and now Evanda's bounty touched it once again, bringing little clumps of green.

Rorie halted the mare to look back at the Tower, still collapsing in on itself. He did not know why the crystal had maintained the illusion of death and devastation—perhaps as an additional defense against the re-establishment of Comyn rule? What human mind could comprehend its motivation? The mare pulled at the halter and bent her head for a mouthful of tender grass. Rorie let her graze as he unwrapped his own starstone.

Instead of its usual dim blue light, the gem blazed with a complex dance of reflected glory. Rorie realized that his confrontation with the matrix had activated his unusual latent talents, talents his own Keeper had been unwilling to recognize.

Willingly had the Towers participated in the obscene warfare of the Age of Chaos. Willingly they might have worked to halt the destruction, but the time was not yet when they might pretend it had never happened. It was still and everlastingly their responsibility to erase all traces of that evil from the face of Darkover.

And how do you know this? Rorie challenged himself. His *laran* might be, indeed, flawed or unusable, but he himself was Comyn, however minor his house. His caste had signed the Compact with their own blood and vowed stewardship of the Domains. And if some fear-blinded Keeper would not face up to her responsibility, by Aldones he would compel her!

But the Towers were not all weak and self-serving, and the telepaths who worked in them had a right to know of the thing which had laid its deadly trap in the wasteland.

Rorie focused on the glittering depths of his starstone, reaching out with an ease he had never known before.

Corandolis . . . he called.

The response came from the kindly middle-aged technician working the relay screens: *Rorie? Is that young Rorie?*

Rorie could feel the strength of his *laran* blasting along the pathways, ringing with urgency and command: *I have found something which concerns the honor of us all. Mirelle must come.*

Wait . . .

And then the Keeper's mind in his: *We will come in answer to a Comyn equal who calls us as his right. I will know where to find you* . . . Mirelle's telepathy bore no trace of surprise or dismay. As always, her emotions lay buried under unbreakable control, and Rorie knew he would never receive a hint of apology for the injustice done to him.

Rorie wrapped his starstone in insulating silk as Mirelle's mental touch faded from his mind. He did not know if his recent growth and trials would change her mind about his place in the Tower. He did not know if he even wanted it, but he was finished thinking of himself as something flawed, inadequate, and for the moment that was enough.

A Cell Opens

By Joe Wilcox

Joe Wilcox describes himself as a "native of Berkeley, variously uprooted and repotted in such places as Puerto Rico and Canada." Currently he's employed as a teacher of emotionally disturbed teenagers. His background includes psychology, education and "a dabbling in neuroscience"—whatever that is. His reading of science fiction began with Heinlein's R IS FOR ROCKET thirty-odd years ago (some, I suspect, very odd years), but "A Cell Opens" is the the first of his writings to be published. I somehow doubt it will be the last.

He also states, "My purpose in writing the story is to introduce a clear conflict between spiritual and secular forces . . . to portray the painful journey toward meaningful change. The 'vision' in the story is mythical in nature, and is no more an attempt to rewrite Darkovan history than the Eden myth is an attempt to rewrite Earth's."

I frequently think Darkover's myths are more interesting than its history—as note "The legend of Lady Bruna" in FREE AMAZONS OF DARKOVER, "The Ballad of Hastur and Cassilda," in the present volume, "The Tale of Durraman's Donkey" by Eileen Ledbetter in THE KEEPER'S PRICE—and I am sure there will be others. Myths, as Joe Wilcox says about his story,

are an attempt to "cast history in a different light."
(MZB)

The Fathers had never liked him overmuch; now they
had simply put it into words. He had been "heedless
as a boy, arrogant and headstrong as a youth, and
blatantly impious as a young man." The letter of dismissal on his table, flapping weakly in the breeze like
an uncertain bird, put it quite succinctly: "There is no
longer a place for you among us."

More than anything else, he felt relief. There would
be no more tongue lashings from his "spiritual" in-
structors, no more fasting "until the blasphemies have
been starved out," and no more false confessions,
cutting his heart in two. He knew his own way, as he
had always known. They were merely removing their
clumsy, brown-robed stupidities from his path. Unbur-
dened, he would reach heights of which they had
never dreamt, leaving their outworn notions lost in
churchly mist below.

Still, he had to admit, life among the *cristoforos* had
not been all bad. Father Luxor had taught him the
secret of the inner flame, showing him how to marshal
and conserve the warmth of his flesh. He could sleep
naked, without shelter, through a winter's night, and
awaken unharmed the following day. While most of
the initiates at Nevarsin learned to endure the cold
within their cells, only a handful had gone farther, to
true mastery of the fire. Of these, he was the most
adept; he felt it to be so, and had read it in the eyes of
the approving Father.

Perhaps there was a balance of sorts to the cosmos,
though he couldn't stomach most of the "good to outweigh evil" mush he had been force-fed from the age
of seven. But his gift with the inner fire seemed to
make up, in a way, for his total lack of *laran*. While
boys less able than he had been nursed through threshold sickness, he had attended in hallways, fetched

water and compresses, and eagerly waited for his own agonies to begin. Some of the boys who survived had been apprenticed to the Towers, which would have meant freedom, for him, from the incessant dreariness and sterility of his religious training.

But he had waited in vain, and it was long ago. Now, at the age of twenty, he knew that it could never happen. He would never be trained in a Tower, as he had nothing to work with. Besides, he was too old, and too much tainted with the unmistakable style of a *cristoforo*. He had heard the jests of travelers from Hali and Thendara, when they thought they were alone, about how they could smell a *cristoforo* a mile away. "They even walk differently," one flame-haired youth had snorted, "as if they're afraid their tails will fall off!" He'd wanted to smash the insolent face against the sturdy table where he sat, because he'd known that what the Comyn pup said was true.

A creaking door dispelled the fog of his reverie. He had just enough time to cover the letter with his hand before Brother Thomas, his onetime tutor, entered. He made no apology, as the room belonged to all.

"Ah, here you are, Brother Andra. I had thought first to find you in the chapel with the others. But then, knowing how you like to pray alone, my next thought was to seek you here. And here, by the grace of deduction, you are found!"

The young man smiled wanly at the familiar bit of shared blasphemy. "What is it, Thomas? Why do you disturb my prayers?"

"What," the older man chided. "No 'Brother Thomas' this morning? What ails the brother's manners, that he keeps his friends at bay? Am I just old Thomas, then, an object like the mat before your door? I should be too worn to be of use, if I have ever been!" Laughing, he plopped himself onto the rough wooden bench which served as bed, shelf, and, at the moment, garbage heap. "Your cell is looking ascetic as ever, my untidy friend."

"It hardly matters, Thomas. Don't you know about this?" He held out the letter, which was read in a few moments. All humor left the old monk's face, and his eyes began to fill.

"No," he said softly, slightly hoarse. "No, brother, they didn't tell me. May the Holy Bearer of Burdens reward such wisdom as it deserves!"

He was stunned to see his old teacher sob, and put his hands to his face. "Come, Thomas," he said, as lightly as he could, laying a hand on the robed shoulder. "Is it really such a dreadful thing? Don't you see the honor they are paying me, to say that I'm not worthy to remain with them?"

"You forget yourself," Brother Thomas warned, suddenly stern and scolding. "This place has been my life, these men my very guides to salvation! You insult me when you insult this place!" He had seen this in his friend several times before: a hurt he couldn't bear turning at once to anger, retreating behind the conventional phrases of his life of dogma.

"Forgive me, *Brother* Thomas," he said, not unkindly. "You know I never could keep it straight. We were both taught that the church is the balm for anger, and never its source. 'Look within for he who wrongs you,' as the Fathers say.

"Now then, why don't you help me tidy this cell up one last time? I haven't much to pack."

The little donkey brayed its disapproval as they clambered over the rough trail together. He might have chosen an easier route, he knew, but there would be traffic on the main road between Thendara and Nevarsin, and every brother or aspirant on the way would have tortured him anew with curiosity. He was known to many, and could not have made up a lie which would convincingly account for such a journey before trading season. Besides, he wanted only to be left alone.

It was rare to have such a fine day before midsummer, especially at the lofty altitudes of the city of the *cristoforos*. Though the snow was piled deeply all about the threadlike trail, he spied the occasional splash of pale green growth on trees and shrubs, attesting to the uncanny knack of Darkover's flora for taking advantage of the slightest break in the chill. They gave him courage, somehow, as he picked his way toward he knew not what, leading the burdened animal over treacherous sheets of ice. The bright sun had thawed out open patches under the crust; he poked ahead with his foot carefully, fearing a breakthrough which would end their lives in a pit of sheer, white oblivion.

In spite of the danger and the difficulty, his thoughts drifted back to what he'd left behind. It was easy to recall, because they were so constant, lessons and services whose utter nonsense made him tremble, even now, with laughter and disdain. Father Altamir intoning on the "God-given blessing of *laran*," and chiding the others to use their talents only for the greater good, never for gain, nor to raise themselves above their fellows. "If even half the Comyn practiced that," he had written in his diary, "we'd have wholesale unemployment in the Guards. And Comyn Council would fall into sheer boredom, as there is nothing the vaunted lords and ladies cherish so much as a good battle with *laran* between domain rivals. All forbidden by the Compact, of course." He could also hear the all-too-righteous Father Almyr, reminding them in his gentle voice that "All you know is illusion. The greatest powers on Darkover, moving mountains with the mind, are merely dreams to the eternal, and have no consequence within themselves. It is only by resisting illusion that you can know God, the face behind the dream, where no man's thought can go."

Yes, he *had* laughed when he first heard that, for he knew that the high *cristoforos* relied on *laran* to keep them in the Council's good graces, and that the church's very existence depended on Comyn decree. Now, however, he seemed to hear the words afresh, as though with a different part of himself, and the stones barking his shins reminded him abruptly that he may not have understood all the gray-haired Father meant. Had he perhaps spent his energies too well in finding fault? Going against, had he missed something to move toward?

No, he thought sternly. *The old man's head was soft. If there's any power in the universe greater than laran, or more far-reaching than the world-hopping Terran starships, it must be sound asleep, for I've not noticed it. And if old Almyr was so much in touch with it, why did he die the way he did, ranting and twisted with pain? Any power that does that to one of its faithful belongs out among the Dry Towns. They deserve one another!"*

They had gone only another hundred yards or so when the donkey slipped, and went down with a sickening crunch. It slid to the left, and he felt the lead rope stiffen as the little beast kicked and jerked, trying to stand. Then the snow mound it was leaning on gave way, and the creature toppled down the rock-strewn cliff. He was jerked violently forward, falling on his face, and barely managed to let go of the rope before he was dragged after the unfortunate animal. Its cries echoed about him, though he knew it must be dead already.

His face burned as he pulled it up from the bank of hardened snow. He put his hand to his right cheek, and felt the running streaks of blood. His side ached, and his neck hurt terribly as he hauled himself to a sitting position. Taking stock, he felt lucky that no bones were broken. As he tried to stand, however, his left ankle betrayed him, giving way and dropping him like wheat before the scythe. "Must have twisted it trying to keep her up," he thought. "Now it's just me and this godforsaken trail. I must have something to support me, or I'll simply starve to death before I'm found." He looked about him for trees or large shrubs, but there were only the snow, the rocks, and his growing pain.

Night greeted him with a mirthless grin. He had managed to drag himself only a half mile, and was sore and bleeding in two dozen places. There were still no trees, nor wood of any kind. "Just my luck," he said aloud, "to have this happen on an old rockslide. *Why* didn't I take a walking stick back there, among the trees? There were plenty of fallen limbs; I knew about this rougher part!" The answer was obvious, though he tried not to admit it: he had needed to prove, at least to himself, that he was made of firmer cloth than the old monks had thought.

" 'The man who needs to prove himself believes not in manhood'; I know, Father Almyr. I've heard it a thousand times!" As the darkness settled in, he felt the temperature drop. In spite of mounting fever and the fear that he was growing delirious, he knew that he would need to tap the inner flame if he was to survive the night. Painfully rolling himself out of his cloak and breeches, and pulling the boots from his feet (the left an agony), he lay down quietly, his back against a bed of snow, and calmed his twitching muscles and flayed nerve endings. With Father Luxor in mind, he felt again the soundless voice, and he let his strong heart and lungs monitor and nourish the fingers, toes, and pinkish skin, while he and the good father went elsewhere, to listen.

As always, he heard the joyous welcome in the silence. His breathing dropped away beside the pulse of the flames, which rose from deep within the core of his being. He heard their promise of freedom from pain, and believed in them, beyond all possibility of doubt. He gave himself to the flames, as so often in the past, and was dimly aware of the rush of warmth to his prostrate flesh, even as his sense of himself as a separate being began to melt away. It was no longer "him" and the flame "against" the numbing cold. His light, the flame's radiance, and the brilliance of the cold had become a single luminance, flooding his awareness with bliss. The oblivious night moved on quietly about him.

Many hours later, he returned to normal consciousness. Checking automatically in the pre-dawn glow, he found that he had been wholly successful. There was no trace of frostbite, or even numbness, in his fingers and toes, and he felt wonderfully rested and revived. However, he still could not stand, and the ankle was horribly swollen, and painful to the touch. "Blessed Bearer of Burdens," he exclaimed, "I've allowed it to swell! By protecting my body from the cold, I've ended all hope that I might be able to hobble out of here. I can't possibly drag myself all the way to Thendara." The situation seemed quite ironic to him: the ankle might have healed just enough, given the cold and a couple of days' rest, had he not been so eager to employ his greatest talent, to "save" himself. "There's always a price," he muttered through a self-reproaching grimace.

Still, he thought, *it could be worse. There's an intersection of trails about ten miles ahead; some of the main road travelers will surely take that route. If I can get close enough to hail them, they'll help me out of this.* It galled him to think that he'd be brought back to Nevarsin, but he had to grant that humiliation was preferable to a wasting death. He dressed himself as quickly as he could and, setting his jaw, began, again, to pull himself painfully over the jagged stones.

It was worse than he'd anticipated; without food, his

strength was a fleeting thing. He perceived, by full daylight, that he was crossing a high saddle between two treeless ridges. Beyond the second, he knew, lay a steep slope littered with broken talus. His last time over he had bounded from boulder to boulder like a mountain sheep, full of the easy strength of his young body. Beyond the slope was a short, switchbacked descent. Beyond that, he might be able to find a branch of sufficient size among the shrubs. If he could make it that far.

" 'Strength is what remains when the muscles give out.' Yes, brothers. Just give me time to find it!"

Nightfall found him at the top of the talus slope, which was thickly frosted with snow. He didn't dare try to clamber down in darkness; besides, his "strength" was more than spent. He could not think, and only stared numbly at the dark, oozing shadows on his legs. His stomach twisted violently, and tried to empty itself of its emptiness. Leaning back heavily, he simply blacked out. It was an abandonment of consciousness, as one abandons a sinking craft, rather than a willed "going to sleep."

That night brought him very close to death. He knew, when he awoke, that death had made a call, briefly inspected the premises, and had left reluctantly, with a promise to renew the acquaintance. He had not been able to shield himself against the merciless cold; his limbs were blocks of ice, and his ears were numb. He could feel his heart laboring to move the turgid blood into dying tissues, which wanted only to be left alone. He fought with panic, and cried out. Then he gave in to spasms of tears.

Much later, when a modicum of warmth had returned, he tried to plan his descent of the cluttered slope. Each task seemed more impossible than the last. On his knees, how could he hope to make his way past even the first of the walls of tumbled stone? There were smooth faces here and there, surfaces of giant mounds of stone. But he needed support to guide his way, or he might well fall again, probably never to rise.

He looked around. Incredibly, a large tree branch lay wedged between two rocks, less than ten yards away. He couldn't believe it; there were still no trees or shrubs in sight. It could only have been left by some other traveler, or else it was a gift from some place unimagined.

Dragging his aching legs, he found the branch to be more than twice the length he needed, which only deepened the mystery of how it had gotten there. Its thickest end was trapped unshakably between the two masses of stone. Grasping it in both hands, he managed to pull himself up onto one foot, though the rush of blood to his ankle and from his head nearly blacked him out again. When his vision cleared, though there were dancing flecks of light, he hauled with all his weight on the thin end of the branch. When he heard it splintering, he tried to pull once more with his arms. He was pitched abruptly to the shelf below, and his brittle prize landed next to him.

Shaping the handle occupied him for the rest of the morning, as he feebly pulled off the broken shards and strips which might cause him to drop the staff at some crucial time. The length was adequate, though it was a bit too heavy for him now. He would need both hands' grip to keep control, at least at times.

He melted some snow in a small depression in a boulder, as he'd done the day before, and let the sun heat it as long as he could stand to wait. It was the stuff of life, and encouraged him to try the descent that afternoon. He was growing steadily weaker without food, he knew, and might not last another night if he could not tap the inner flames. His hands and feet gave him great pain, as they had thawed out enough to become blood-starved flesh again. But the fingers were still working; it *had* to be today.

After resting, he pulled himself up with the staff, and noticed again the delicate lacework of worm channels cut beneath the bark. It was his wand, he fancied, his potent wizard's tool, rune-laden with charms which would help him conquer any foe. "Even death," he murmured. "Even the necromancer. Attend me, then, powers of light!" He smiled feebly at the picture he knew he made, a monk clad in brown *cristoforo* robes, invoking pagan forces while limping out onto the rocky shelf.

He spent more time on his back and chest than standing, as he poked and slid his way down with immense caution. It was less than a snail's pace, as he stopped frequently to muster what little strength remained for the next assault. The ankle throbbed horribly, and his bruises were too numerous to allow him a moment's solace from pain. Still he inched onward, going around major obstacles, and sometimes under and between the boulders, through crawl spaces packed with snow.

The magic staff was somewhat bent, he noted; he was careful not to pit his weight opposite its bow. This made the going more difficult, but he could not go on without the staff's support. "Even magic crosses me up," he thought grimly. From nowhere, the memory struck him of a little cross he'd seen in an obscure recess in the chapel. None of the monks had any idea what it signified, though some believed it to be as old as Darkover itself. He thought he remembered someone saying that it had once been some sort of marker for graves. "Well then," he said aloud, "we'll cross up the grave, my crooked staff and I!" He felt delirious and faint, and knew that his thoughts were nonsense. But they took his mind from the pain, at least briefly.

The sun flickered behind the farthest ridge. He was only a bit more than halfway down, but he had to keep moving. Staggering, he propped himself heavily on the C-shaped staff, and started down again. The bottom of the slope was just visible; he thought he saw a wisp of trail, curving toward a line of green.

And then, without warning, the staff gave way. It split up its length from the depth of its bow, and sent him careening to his right, toward sheer rock. He thought of his ankle; as he tried to roll off of it, his head struck something hard. The fall hurt him no more.

He was conscious, but not awake. He could see nothing at first. Amazingly, he realized, his body's pain was gone. But then, where was his body, for that matter?

Tiny points of light began to float before him, though they were distant, faint, and formless. He tried to approach one, but it moved away, toward another. Together, the two became a tiny face, recognizable, but vague. The face of someone he had known, but could not now place. It smiled beautifully, and then winked away. Then more lights returned, closer, and a different face emerged. No—now there were many faces, all brothers, and they seemed to float on the facets of a brilliant jewel. He knew it was a matrix, huge and powerful beyond all legend. The faces of the brothers were like pale white lights on its facets. Their mouths moved in unison, and they were urging, pleading, chanting a single word. He could not grasp it, though he felt he should have known at once. It was a familiar word, this thing they wanted, but he could not find its sense. He felt a touch from something within the giant stone, and he was drawn slowly past the moving mouths on ghostly faces, into the core of the stone itself.

Immediately he sensed an energy, a vast intelligence, radiating warmth without heat. There were many blue lights now—no, one cluster of blue, sparking, pulsating, taking form before him. He had heard tales of the blue lights within the gems, of how they had driven mad some who were not trained to use them. He began to feel afraid, though he suspected he had died. In truth, he did not know what was happening.

He tuned into the blue lights, and was amazed to see them taking on a definite shape. Father Luxor, his hair and eyes flaming blue, smiled reassuringly at him. Could this be *laran*, then? Was he being contacted by the Father, somehow, while his body lay elsewhere?

Luxor's image shook its head emphatically. He felt a strange shifting, as the blue eyes looked deeply into his. He was losing control of his thoughts, he feared, as unfamiliar images began to invade his awareness. But Father Luxor was still there, radiating trust and certainty. He let the images come, under the Father's guidance.

Dense forest, lovely beyond belief. Blossoming, embracing, cooling, sustaining—a forest clothing paradise. A village. Ghostly, elongated beings, basking in a life of utter harmony. Simple dwellings, few tools, yet a closeness and sharing which made his heart ache. And a kind of altar, in the center of the village, upon which rested a huge earthen bowl, dyed a brilliant blue. The tall, beautiful people (*chieri*, he realized) gathered about the altar, and waited in silence. Then the bowl began to blaze, and the bluish light was akin to that of his original vision. Yes—he understood. The *chieri* bowed before the cluster of blue lights, but their attitude was loving, rather than fearful. The lights were the makers of Darkover, he thought along with the *chieri*. They were Darkover's heart, he perceived, and they had fashioned the planet for the forest folk!

Then he saw the *chieri* constructing a stone, a matrix so gigantic it dwarfed all their simple buildings, filling the village, growing steadily larger. No—now he saw that it was underground, a great gem hewn and forged from deep within the planet. The blue lights came down from the altar, entered the vast mine chamber, and took up their home within the giant matrix, while their people rejoiced that they had pleased their god. From that throne, the blue lights gave out ever greater gifts to their people. Almost endless life was theirs, and the wondrous focusing of mind through the giant stone, by which the thoughts of individuals could be made known to all. Though they lived in separate bodies, they began to share a single soul, as they grew ever closer to their god ideal.

Next he saw an ugly thing: a space vessel, torn open in a crash, spewing out a harsh yellow light. Inside the glare, fearsome creatures moved about, sending out disturbing thoughts, violent and confused. Beneath the calm village, the blue lights dimmed. As the creatures left the ship and set up shelters, they were observed doing harm to one another, yet occasionally loving, even through hearts twisted in pain. He felt, with the *chieri*, a terrible pity. These poor creatures needed help, and the *chieri* made contact with them. But one of the creatures (a man, he saw) lusted after a *chieri*, and destroyed its mate with a blaster, a look of triumph in his eyes. At this, the giant matrix shuddered, and then burst apart, sending millions of pieces spinning deep into the caverns and the earth. The *chieri* scattered in horror and bewilderment. The Earthmen began to build and spread, like ants.

He was drowning in a sorrow which would never cease. It was the end of all things, the end of love and meaning. Any further existence would be that of shadows, wraiths who could never touch, but only grope and blunder. He saw, in sudden insight, that he was one of these, as were all the people of Darkover, descended from the angry creatures in the ruinous, infecting ship!

Then he was aware of Luxor again, and the good Father eased his pain. With a gentle shaking of his blue-crowned head, he sent a sort of interlude to the grieving soul. Within this grayness, a *chieri* and an earthwoman made gentle love, and a new being was born, a six-fingered human, tall and slender like its "father," but more human than not. It grew, chose to be a woman, and wore around its neck a piece of the great matrix which had destroyed itself in agony. And, within the tiny gem, he saw the blue lights move. They were much paler than before, but had not been wholly extinguished.

The familiar starstones then appeared in abundance, and he saw great and horrible deeds done through them. Mountains were razed, castles leveled, aching bodies healed, and many more bodies consumed in matrix-summoned flames. Then he was shown that many of the stones' lights had lost all connection with their fellow gods. Giving in completely to the anguish of humans, they sought only to be used, and became the mighty pawns of the power hungry. These lights were so pale, their blue life struggled to be seen. Their empty transparence gave pain to the eyes of even their long-term masters.

Then Luxor showed him an image in which he, Andra, was moving! He felt great pride in the young man—but it was not *his* feeling. Father Luxor, all the lights which were still united, were showing him the Andra they wished him to be. The figure looked like him, but seemed somehow remade. He stood so assuredly, and smiled with such grace, it almost seemed someone else, wearing his old skin. The figure approached a Comyn lord, perhaps the Elhalyn king himself, and bowed deeply, making a humble blessing. Then he stood very tall, and reached both hands out to the mighty lord, whose frown indicated that the audience would be brief. But then the large starstone, encased in leather and hanging about the royal neck, began to glow with a radiance that quickly turned the chamber a cool, comforting blue. The great lord seemed to change in countenance, and he held the stone out, for all to see, as his face reflected good will, gratitude, and an aching sympathy with those around him. Somehow, the Andra in the image had begun this awesome change! He felt it spreading to the court, and then to the streets below, as the normally closemouthed and suspicious city dwellers reached out to one another, their starstones beaming with their pure delight. This wave of belongingness was meant to spread throughout the planet; he could feel its promise as a living, growing thing.

But they were asking *him* to start the changing—Andra, the iconoclast. *Why me?* he thought in disbelief. *Of all Darkover, why should you want it to be me?*

Luxor smiled once again, even more beatifically, and yet another image filled his awareness. He saw a Tower, a darkened room, and a young girl with her Keeper. An even larger matrix lay on a table between them, and it pulsed with inner life. As the Keeper turned her awareness from the novice to the stone, in the final stages of the keying process, he saw that neither of them could see. Even as the young girl's heart beat faster, pressed by the awesome power of having her own matrix at last, he saw the color of the lights within the stone pale, as before. It was as though the act of being keyed, essential to the training of those with *laran*, somehow moved the stones even farther from their original source and nature. And he saw the pride and terror in the young girl's heart, feelings she was already accustomed to conceal from others, as well as from herself.

Then there was a last shift, and he saw himself again. But this was history; it touched a nerve of too familiar pain. He saw the interview in which, some five years before, the assembled fathers had told him he would never have *laran*. Their faces were somber, giving him their deepest sympathy. But he saw now, as he could not see then, that they were secretly glad for his lack of power. Strangely, it was as though they had feared him! Only Father Luxor's sorrow seemed genuine. And then he saw, at the darkest moment of his life, when his head had been bent in abject misery, that Father Luxor's stone, hidden in its casing, had brightened in its depths. It was glad for his failure! Could it be that he had somehow been *spared* from the Towers, his destiny lying outside of their high walls.

Luxor's image confronted him now with a questioning look, offering him a choice. It was clear: he could refuse, and go with all those others who had failed to live, and yielded to that of death within themselves. Or he could try, with his one gift, to overcome that coldness in his heart by which he'd set himself apart from others, that very coldness, he now saw, which was the death of humankind. It was not *his* failing, but that of his entire race!

He did not want to choose; it seemed too obvious. A dying man converts, when offered eternal life. But this would be his last truly cynical thought, for, even as it came, the thought recoiled from the light before him, which grew steadily into a blazing, bluish sun. He heard the chanting of the brother lights again, and this time their word was clear to his ears. They were saying "Fire!" Begging and commanding, they were sweetly yearning for him to . . . to what? The old inner flame was a part of his body, which he had lost. What would be the sense? But the chorus was insistent, and the brilliant blue sun was offering him a new kind of flame. He was commanded with love, and he agreed to try.

Concentrating, trusting completely in the lights, in their welcoming and warmth, and their indifference to death, he felt his doubts dissolve, and he embraced the flame. His separateness faded out, and, being one, they all rained down in bluish silver light upon an empty body, lying twisted in the snow. Its heart picked up their pulsing chant, and pumped new life into the battered shell. The breathing lungs took up the fiery dance.

He blinked his eyes, and winced. The sun was very bright. But he had died, he thought. Or had it been a dream? He moved his legs, which seemed to work. His ankle still protested painfully.

Then he was struck, full force, by what had come to pass. He remembered the vision, or whatever it was, in each detail. Father Luxor's face—like a sun itself! And the blue warmth, more loving than he had thought possible in this cold world.

He tried to rise, and felt a surge of unexpected strength. His head was throbbing, and his forehead was caked with blood. He found the broken staff, its magic spent, and used it to prop himself to a sitting position.

And then, beyond all hope, he heard a human voice! He called out hoarsely, and the footsteps came to him at once. He saw the dull brown robe and the concerned face, and reached out his arms in joy to this wonderful human being.

The monks who knew him remarked on how much he had changed. Even from his sick bed, where he'd remained for days, he seemed to bless with welcome every monk who entered. At first, they were only those who nursed his wounds; others were asked not to disturb his rest. But the news of his demeanor quickly reached his friends: Brother Thomas was the first to be allowed to call.

"Well, my boy!" He stuck his head around the door. "They tell me that you might live, after all!" His joviality was a little forced; he'd always had a low tolerance for the pain of others.

Instead, he found the youth sitting up and smiling, the scant breakfast leavings on a tray on his lap. He looked so happy, and welcomed him so earnestly,

Thomas half expected him to leap from the bed in greeting. He said as much, but the lad shook his head in mock sadness.

"No," he moaned, "they say that both my legs are spent. If I'm to walk again, they say, I must try not to move. Ah, they mean well, I know, but how's a man who's flying supposed to care about walking?"

"Why, what do you mean, brother? Perhaps they bandaged your head too tightly, eh? The only flying you did was down the mountainside!"

The young man's eyes grew wide, and he smiled generously. "Good Thomas," he said warmly, "always so light of heart. It's true my body must lie here for a while. But my spirit has been freed, and I soar, regardless. What happened to me, you see, is what must happen to us all, except that I was lucky. I was given a chance to come back, and to share the light. It is so *wondrous*, Thomas! The whole world is alive, and I feel that nothing dark or cringing can withstand this joy."

Brother Thomas felt tremendously buoyed by his young friend's presence. This was not the tortured cynic he had left three days before, the frustrated brother who seemed to resent all those with peace or power he had not attained. Why, even he had felt the sting of Andra's bitterness, when he had challenged the older man's right to carry his tiny shard of a starstone. Unthinkingly, his hand went to the leather bag he carried on his belt, and he felt the reassuring shape of the small gem within.

"Yes, Thomas," the lad said sadly. "I remember what I said before about you and your matrix. I apologize, my friend."

Thomas looked up sharply, meeting the clear gaze. "What's this," the old monk asked, "have you developed *laran*, Brother Andra?"

"No, Thomas. Not *laran*. It's something else; call it simple understanding. You know, I'm recalling more clearly now what was said before. I chided you for carrying a stone you hardly ever use, and called it a piece of Comyn garbage. But, Thomas, why *have* you used it so little? Do you know?"

"Why, no, not really. I just rarely have the need, living this simple life here in the church." Many of the monks had matrices, some much larger than his, and some of the elders used them often, joining with the Tower relays. Thomas thought a moment more, then swallowed hard. "There's one thing, though. I've never told a soul. Sometimes, when I look deep into my little stone, I see the lights moving, and they make me feel afraid. They seem to *want* me to use them, whether for ill or good. It's as though they need my fear, to act through me. No—that's all mixed up. The matrix is my servant, surely." He flushed slightly, and turned his face to the side.

"No, Brother. You don't have it all mixed up. Because you do not desire power, you have frustrated your matrix, which must be one far removed from its ancient source. It needs your fear, Thomas, because it has forgotten everything else. If you can teach your matrix, with the goodness in your heart, you can do wonders together. You can change the world!"

Brother Thomas didn't follow very much of this. He decided that the young man's head was still a bit addled and, making excuses, he moved toward the door. "You'd better rest now, Brother Andra. It's wonderful to see you so renewed, and happy!"

"Yes, isn't it, Thomas? And this is just the start, I know. The walls are down, and there are no limits to what might happen! Bless you, Brother Thomas, for caring when I could not care, not even for myself."

The old man backed out, and quietly closed the heavy sickroom door. As he started down the hallway, he felt a lightness in his step. He was tempted to trot along, he felt so fine! His fingers found the leather bag again, and he discovered that he was eager for the evening rest period. He wanted desperately to touch the little stone, with this heart filled anew with hope and gladness.

The next day, Father Altamir himself came to inquire after Brother Andra's health. The abbot strode in with great dignity, and took the chair under the window, several yards away from the bandaged invalid.

"Well, Brother Andra," he began stiffly, "they tell me you've had something of an experience! We must raise our heart in thanks to the Holy Bearer, that your injuries are not even more severe. Whatever possessed you to take that most treacherous of routes?"

"To tell the truth, Father, I sought to hide my shame. I took the route which no one else would take, so that I would not be seen leaving the city in disgrace. But that is all behind me, now. I . . ."

"Why, Brother Andra, surely you know that we meant you no disgrace? It only seemed you'd be so much happier elsewhere, outside the strict confinement of our way of life. You showed us, did you not, that it is not *your* way?"

Andra paused, and realized what was happening. Nothing had changed, as far as the abbot was concerned. Soon he would be giving him directions for staying on the main road to Thendara! "Father," he said firmly, "may we discuss something else? I am not the same person who left here full of bitterness. I have been changed, and I must tell you how it came to pass."

"What, Brother, don't tell me you've had some sort of vision? Did the Blessed Cassilda send you back to us, full of penitence and humility?"

He was stung and surprised by the cutting edge of the Father's words. Clearly, he was not prepared to forgive the young troublemaker. In spite of this, he told the abbot, in detail, what he had experienced.

Father Altamir's face was impassive, and he made

no attempt to interrupt or comment. When Andra had finished, the older man folded his hands deliberately, pressing his thumbs together, and was silent for a few more moments. Then he leaned forward abruptly in his chair.

"So, you interpret this dream following your head injury as having some sort of religious significance?"

He was being quizzed as though he'd come to the Father for counseling. But it didn't matter. "It's not a question of interpretation, Father. The meaning was, and is, perfectly clear."

"Perhaps it is, my boy. To you, at least. You say these lights commanded you to seize other men's starstones, so that they could no longer do evil with their *laran*?"

He was still being humored, though the Father was trying to hide it. He felt an immense compassion for the blindness which the abbot could not escape. His position as superior made him so weak! "Dear Father," he said quietly, "you know the way things are. To touch another's stone would cause him agony, or even death. No—it is their hearts which must be 'seized.' But not by me; it's by the truth and love which dwell there already!"

The Father hesitated. Something stirred uncomfortably within him. Could there be anything to this wild tale? The lad seemed so at peace with himself, so changed. But he reminded himself of his duty to protect the church against heretics and frauds, and pushed the vague feeling of uncertainty firmly beneath his concern. "You seem to forget, Brother Andra, that we have a Compact, faithfully followed for centuries now, which forbids the use of *laran* weapons. And the person who would use his stone to control another mind is the lowest form of criminal, outcast among the outcast. Your vision is a little late, I would say!"

"Surely, Father Altamir, you don't mean that you

see no problems with the use of matrices on Darkover? No abuses of *laran* to further private, or Council ends?"

"Of course, Brother, there are minor problems. Perfection does not exist in this world, save perhaps in the middle of the *terribly* young. The way to correct such errors is to avoid them oneself—but, then, you have no stone, so the problem doesn't really exist for you, does it?"

The level stare was frankly contemptuous; Andra felt his disdain almost as a physical blow. "Father," he said very calmly, "you, yourself, are among the proudest of men. Much wrong is done with the stones to defend such pride. It is not a grief to me that I've been spared the temptation."

Father Altamir stood abruptly, knocking back his chair. "You young whelp!" he cried. "How dare you imply that I've ever abused my *laran*, or done wrong with my stone? You are as arrogant as ever, still trying to tear down your betters. This 'vision' of yours is just another ploy by which you seek to undermine proper authority! You will leave this place as soon as you are well enough to travel, and you will *not* be welcome to return, ever!" He stormed out, slamming the door with a deafening report.

Andra was stunned by the tempest he had set into motion, and stared thoughtfully at the oaken barricade. "Well," he said aloud, "this may not be quite as easy as I'd thought!"

The Sum of the Parts

Dorothy Heydt

I first knew Dorothy Heydt as a musician; the owner of one of the loveliest soprano voices I have ever heard. Like myself, she seems to have discovered that a vocal career and the raising of two young children simply do not compute—at least not simultaneously.

Dorothy Heydt's first published story was "Through Fire and Frost" in SWORD OF CHAOS (DAW 1982), and she has also appeared in three of the four SWORD AND SORCERESS volumes (DAW 1984, 1985, 1986, 1987).

She lives in Berkeley, and she appeared on a panel about computers and writing at the last local convention, taking the "pro" position while Ray Nelson and I took the "con" one.

It was the year of the World-Wreckers.

After the crash, Marguerida found herself curled up like a bedraggled mudrabbit in the tail of the plane. The cushions that lined the passenger compartment had fallen into the tail ahead of her and broken her fall. She took stock of herself: no bones broken, no serious bruises, her nervous system intact on all its levels—but tired, and depleted of energy, almost dangerously so. Briefly she recalled the doings of the past two hours—the mob at the door; someone's hands pushing her into the plane; the flight over the dead slopes of her own mountains, into lands unknown to her.

Ah, if they could only have given her more time to practice! Alba Tower had had the plane—acquired through what dubious means, she had not inquired—for a year before the matrix drive had been perfected and installed. If only they could have brought in Terran fuel for the Terran drive, she might have been a pilot by now, and not be so weary from battling the air currents.

Well, she must sort it out later. *All the smiths in Zandru's forges can't mend a broken egg*—which this plane closely resembled. The door hung crazily from one hinge, high above her head—standing as tall as she might, she could just hook one hand over the doorframe. Once she caught her breath, she could climb out—*but not in these clothes.*

She was still wearing the formal dress of a Keeper, the loose-bodied stiff robe with its long skirts and the sleeves that came down over her fingertips. She could not scramble about in it; nor could she remain here; it was late afternoon and would soon grow dark.

Her veil had fallen away some time back and now lay half-buried among the cushions. Pulling it free, she uncovered a corner of a storage locker, its lid sprung, something dull gray visible underneath. This proved to be a garment of some kind, once the property of the unknown Terran who had owned the plane. It was shirt and trews all together in a single piece, absolutely plain drab gray without even a line of embroidery, consummately ugly like most of the Terrans' works. But it ought to be admirable clothing to climb in. She cast off her robe and stepped into the ugly thing, discovering by accident as she tugged it on that the metallic tab at the crotch was the business end of some kind of fastener that closed the thing up to her throat. Piling the cushions against the wall gave her a few extra inches' height, and she gripped the doorframe and pulled herself up and out.

The plane had landed in a tree, its nose wedged between two limbs, its frame twisted, one wing-surface crumpled like a grass blade beneath its body's weight. From where she perched, half inside and half outside, there was nothing between herself and death but seven thousand feet of air. But just above her head stretched a branch that looked sturdy enough, as branches went. . . . She swallowed hard. *I am no worthy Keeper if I cannot rule myself.* She pulled herself up onto the branch, and somehow (she was never sure quite how) scrambled like a chervine out of the tree, up the bank and onto flat ground.

She got to her feet, brushed off her hands, and looked round. She had traveled farther than she'd thought; this timber was still healthy. The blasted pine that had nearly skewered her as she took off had been only the tallest in a forestful of naked trunks, their needles striped away by the unnamed blight that had raged since last summer. But these mountains were still green, and showing such indications of spring as could be expected at this altitude: new shoots poking out of last year's dead bracken, sticky buds, and bright young needle clusters on the trees.

She was standing on a ledge a dozen feet wide, on one side an incalculable drop into the lowlands, but on the other side a quite reasonable four-handed climb onto the mountain saddle she had seen as she fell.

For a moment she concentrated on the memory. A great gulf of air below her, the lowlands beneath it hazy blue with distance. A sheer wall of granite above the timberline, blood-colored in the late sunlight, and a fall past the mountain's flank into a dark-wooden saddle between two peaks. And a momentary glimpse of a white shape against the green.

Yes,. a second plane, much like her own, but un-damaged perhaps? Another fugitive from the confu-sion and bloodshed that had spread over Darkover in the past chaotic year? There might be fire, food; per-haps a way of traveling on; at the very least, these people might know where they *were!* She scrambled up the slope onto the flat ground.

It was dark under the trees, even with the red sun-light falling almost horizontally between the trunks. It was by *laran* more than sight, and by scent more than either of them, that she found the plane at last. It was much like the one she had flown, but larger, with room perhaps for five or six instead of one or two. Its pilot had made a landing more orderly than her own, and had splintered only one wing, instead of the whole craft, against a clump of trees.

She looked inside and saw no one. The plane's fittings had been tossed about, and its front window cracked, but not shattered. To get inside she would have had to climb over a tangle of wire sprouting from the guts of some Terran machine lying just inside the door, so she let it be.

Here was no fire, no sign of life; at first she thought the craft abandoned before she saw the shape that lay a dozen feet from the door. A dead man? No, to her trained *laran* the signs of life still showed, dim and faint like the last glows of a dying fire. He was—she passed her hand above his body, not quite touching—he was unconscious, half-starved, and feverish; his lungs were badly congested, and there was a long festering wound along his left arm, trying to work its way in-ward. Nothing she could not handle—Avarra grant the man did not die before she could get to work.

Perhaps he had been knocked senseless by the fall, and never awakened? No, there were signs of an at-tempt to make camp: the man was lying on a strip of carpet taken from the plane's floor: some protection from cold and damp, but not much.

She could not spare time for speculation just yet. Swiftly she gathered dry moss from the southern sides of the nearest tree, a few dry twigs that hung from a tangle of needles overhead, and cleared a space of ground to receive them. She knelt down and took her matrix stone from its leather bag; she was weary still, but on balance she would be likelier to raise fire by *laran* than be contriving a fire-drill out of dry wood and a strand of her own hair. On the third try she was able to kindle a spark, and it caught the dry moss and flared up like a flower. Hastily she fed it dry twigs, and tended it till it grew into full life and could be left to digest its dead bark and fallen branches with little supervision. Then she turned her attention back to the man.

He was a man in middle life, she judged; past his first youth, but no graybeard. His close-trimmed hair and beard were as black as her Cousin Rafael's. He was wearing a plain one-piece garment almost identical to her own, and there was a bracelet on his wrist marked with characters she could not read, had never even seen before. Like his plane, the man was from another world, a Terran probably; she would ask him someday, if she could contrive to keep him alive.

His bit of carpet tore under his weight when she tried to pull it toward the fire. She looked at her hands, white and smooth-skinned except where the scars of old burns marred them. But that part of her training was past her; she could touch the man if she would; she forced down her aversion, took him by the shoulders, and dragged him nearer the fire. He was not so very heavy, and she could feel the bones under the Terran garment and the thin flesh beneath. Wasn't there anything to eat in his plane? She made a torch out of a branch from the fire and went exploring.

She found the food without recognizing it at first, for it was all wrapped in strange coverings with more of the alien writing on them; they crackled when she unwrapped them. Inside were hard blocks, like wood, but faint odors rose from them: this was dried meat, not so far removed from what a Darkovan would pack for a journey, and this was bread (she supposed; it was even drier and more tasteless than any journey-bread she had tasted), and this was something sweet and luscious, a taste not unlike *jaco*. Licking her fingers, she looked around for something to use as a pot. She'd make a soup or a stew, and hope she could get some of it down the man's throat.

There was a stream nearby, and a clump of web-waders growing beside it with leaves big enough to boil water in. She put blocks of the sweet stuff to dissolve in the water as it warmed, and in another leaf put blocks of dried meat to soften; tomorrow she'd make a stew. The leaves burned down from the top to the water level, but no farther. She'd found a spoon among the miscellaneous trash in the plane—its inside was a state of disorder that couldn't be explained by the relatively minor damage to its outside—and as soon as the liquid was warm she began spooning it into the man's mouth. The first few spoonfuls ran out again, soaking his beard, and then he began to swallow. She got almost a cupful of the stuff into him before the last of the sunlight faded from the sky. The fire was blazing well now, and both of them were growing warmer. She laid one hand on his forehead, and with the other took up her matrix.

There were poisons in his blood from his infected arm, she would have to deal with them presently; but the chief danger to his life was the thick clotted stuff in his lungs. She turned him onto his side, and with the finest filament of her attention reached out to touch his phrenic nerve and make him cough.

After an hour she let him rest, for they were both growing weary. The upper lobes of his lungs were clear, and she had opened enough of the tiny alveoli to let him breathe adequately. He had spoken a few

times, in a language she didn't know, but had never
really come up as far as consciousness. She propped
him against a cushion from the pilot's seat, and he
sighed, shifted his position a little, and fell into something like normal sleep. It was a pity there was nothing
with which to cover him, but the bulk of his plane
behind him reflected much of the fire's heat back
toward him. She banked the fire, and drank the last of
the sweet stuff herself, then lay down behind the sleeping man. Her last conscious thought was that there
were not many of those food-blocks left.

She woke with the dawn, quite hollow with hunger.
A Keeper was trained to pay little heed to pain or
pleasure, and she had ignored the cold, but she must
not allow her body to become weak. She fed the fire
and made a soupy stew out of the softened meat
blocks, some breadcrumbs, and one of the sweet bars
for flavoring. She had not cooked anything since she
had gone at the age of nine to the old house that
sheltered Alba Tower; on the whole, the stuff turned
out rather well, savory with the stuff that was not
quite *jaco* and rich with the juices of the well-stewed
meat.

The man still slept, his life signs stronger now with
the food and warmth. She fed him some broth from
the stew, and turned her attention to the wound on his
arm. It was covered with a crusty scab and the flesh
surrounding it was puffy and red. Poisons from the
infection were seeping into the rest of his body; that
and the cold must have made him too sick to eat.
Well, food was the best medicine, but she was going to
need more. She brushed the earth and moss from her
clothing, and set another leaf to heating water, and
went back into the forest.

She would rather have had soft cloths, and the concentrated distillates of Alba Tower's storerooms, but
what she got was more of the soft moss she had used

as tinder, and the first hardy shoots of thornleaf that had thrust themselves up through the litter of the forest floor, dry needles and last year's bracken, into the meager sunlight of early spring. She carried them back to the plane and put them into the hot water, and she saturated some of the wads of moss and laid them on the wound. It would take a while for the virtues in the thornleaf to steep into the water, but she could begin by softening that crusty scab. Then she took another damp pad of moss and washed the man's face. The film of dirt had been streaked by a few tears, but only a few, and under the dirt his skin was fair and smooth, not weatherbeaten like a mountain man's. Was there no weather where the Terran lived? Her teachers had told her almost nothing about the place; it represented much they had wanted her to avoid.

The man's dark lashes lifted, revealing eyes of a startling brilliant blue. Before she could speak, he had lifted his good arm, taken her hand, and raised it to his lips. She leaped to her feet and put the fire between them, so quickly that a careless observer might have thought she had teleported.

"I'm sorry," the man said in the spaceport dialect. His voice was deep and resonant, the accent strange but not too hard to understand. "Please come back; I won't hurt you." His arm fell to his side. "My god, I'm weak. I couldn't hurt you if I tried."

Slowly she circled the fire and knelt beside him again. "I know. I'm sorry, too. But I am the Keeper of Alba Tower, and you must not touch me."

"My apologies, *vai domna*," he said in *casta*. "I mean, *vai leronis*. I didn't know." His grammar was flawed, but his voice made subtle music out of the respectful inflection.

"There's no offense," she said. "I left my robe and veil in my plane when it crashed; this gray thing was better suited for climbing mountainsides and walking in forests."

"Your plane? You don't live around here?"

"Oh, no. I came from—here, lie back!"For the man had struggled up onto his right elbow, spilling the pads of moss from his injured arm. "At least, sit up, it will help you to get your lungs clear, but don't move your arm." She settled him against the cushion again. "Now I'll soak these again, and put them on your arm—yes, they're hot," as the man drew in a sharp breath, "—they're supposed to be hot, to draw the poison out of your wound. Now sit still and don't spill them again, and I'll get you some food."

She took a little more of the hot water to wash off the single spoon, and filled another leaf with stew. The man's brilliant eyes widened after the first spoonful. "My god," he said again, without specifying which one. No doubt it was unlike what he was used to eating. Was all Terran food compressed into hard bricks? Had they no cooks in their travels between the worlds? But he made no objection to the stew, and went on swallowing till it was gone. Then he closed his eyes again and said, "Thank you, *vai leronis.* You lend me grace. Indeed, I think you've saved my life."

"I've tried my best," she said. "You *are* a Terran?"

"Oh, yes." He opened his eyes again, blue as the sky on the very hottest day of summer. "Donald Stewart, formerly navigator on the TMS *Domina Anglorum*, and very much at your service, Or I would be if I could get up."

"My name is Marguerida Elhalyn, and I'm the Keeper of Alba Tower," she said. "That's on the Kadarin, not far from Carthon. I'm not sure where we are now; I headed east, but I don't know how far I've come."

"I could show you on a satellite photo, but there are no detailed maps of this region," Donald Stewart said. Cautiously he flexed his shoulders, wincing as the cramped muscles stretched, and the hot pads fell off his arm again. "Sorry. We're better than halfway to the Dry Towns. How do you come to be this far from your Tower?"

"All the land around Alba has been very hard hit by the plague," she said. "The forests are dying, the fields are barren even of weeds, there have been forest fires, famine, murders. The people turned for us for help, and we had none to give them. Then, today . . ." She fell silent, and gave her attention to replacing the hot pads along his arm.

The man said nothing. His silence was comforting, almost; he would not press her, but his silence encouraged speech. "Today some hothead got up and told them that the Comyn had set the plague to punish the people because they would no longer obey them. Maybe he believed it, I couldn't say. But they attacked the house. My teachers just had time to put me on the plane and send me away."

"You have a plane?" the man exclaimed, sitting bolt upright and spilling the dressing from his arm yet again. "Where is it? Can you fly it?"

"It's down the slope and I can't fly it because it's broken; will you sit still!" Marguerida cried. She soaked the pads once more and applied them again. Then she went to collect more moss, because the abscess was within a few minutes of bursting, as she judged, and she would soon need to clean it up.

On the second day, even before he could walk more than a few paces, Donald Stewart insisted on having his plane's radio brought to him. This turned out to be the pile of wires and junk that Marguerida had seen lying, like an eviscerated worm, just inside the door of the plane. With only two craft on the mountain, neither of them usable, his sole option was to use the radio to call the Terrans at Thendara Spaceport for help. The radio, however, had been damaged in the crash and was not responding to treatment nearly as fast as its master. As for Marguerida, she dug a privy

pit, and cleared out the plane's cabin so they could
shelter in it at night; and then she made some string
out of twisted bark, and tied three round stones to its
ends, and went hunting.

"What about the radio in your plane?" the Terran
asked when she came back. "Is it still working?"

"I don't believe it has one," she said. "We send
messages through the relays—or we did. The relays
are empty now, the matrix technicians have all gone to
Thendara. I got a bushjumper—see? it's a relative of
the mudrabbit, but not so muddy. And spiceleaves to
wrap it, and some clay to bake it in."

"Good," he said. "Yes, all the technicians, and all
the Tower folk have gone to Thendara, at the summons of Lord Regis Hastur. Why aren't you with
them?"

"My teachers did not altogether approve of Lord
Regis, or of what he is doing," Marguerida said.

"Such as trying to persuade his people that Darkover
must part with tradition, adopt new ways, and make
alliance with the Terrans?"

"You have it," she said. "Especially the part about
the Terrans—no offense meant."

"None taken."

"Though mind you, it's not Lord Regis' fault that
we have fallen so far from the old ways." She had
skinned the bushjumper with her little belt knife, the
only sharp tool they had between them, and was wrapping it in leaves before encasing it in the clay. "It was
in my grandmother's day that Callista of Armida built
her forbidden Tower, and demonstrated that a Keeper
can be Keeper, and yet be no virgin. If she had let
well enough alone, we would have had fewer griefs in
these latter years—or so my teachers always said. That
is why they brought me and my companions to the site
of Alba Tower—the Tower itself fell a thousand years
ago; the house is made of its stones—to train us in the
old ways. They did their best to make sure Lord Regis

and the Comyn Council never heard of us, and I think they must have succeeded."

"I think so," the Terran agreed. "I was in the spaceport hospital last week having a tooth fixed; I talked to one of the doctors working with Lord Regis and his group. They seem to think they've got every telepath on Darkover up there in Comyn Castle, and they're sending off planet for more. What will you do when we're rescued? (Assuming I can get this bloody radio to work.) Will you go to Thendara with the rest, or back to Alba?"

"I don't know," she said, and set the clay bundle in the ashes. "I've tried to call my teachers and my Tower circle; I get no answer. I think it's very likely they are dead."

They were both silent. "I wish there were something I could do," he said at last. "If you weren't a Keeper, I could put my arm around you and let you cry on my shoulder. Or if I were a great hero instead of a middle-aged second-rate spaceman, I could sling you over my shoulder and climb down this mountain in an afternoon. As it is—" he looked at the radio—" I'm not a great deal of use."

"Have you found out what's wrong with it?"

"I've eliminated most of the things it could be," he said, "and I'm afraid it's the tuning crystal. And if it's that, I don't know what I'm going to do about it. Whoever stocked this plane should've included a replacement in the emergency supplies, but he didn't, and I wish he was here and had to fix it instead of me."

"Show me the crystal."

He slid it out of its niche in the radio's interior and held it on his palm for her to see: a little sparkling thing like salt, the size of a barley grain. "It's cracked, I'm afraid. It's supposed to resonate at its own natural frequency—like a bell—which is the same as all the other crystals like it, so that the radios are all tuned to each other."

"Yes, the technicians do the same kind of thing in the relays." Marguerida reached inside the neck of her ugly Terran garment for her matrix. "Yes, it's cracked," she said after a moment. "I can hear the note at which it ought to sound, but it's too high for my voice to sing. But it occurs to me—"

"Oh, no," he said, quickly withdrawing his hand. "I know my limitations, I hope. I don't want to get near that stone of yours."

"No, you don't. If you touched it, it would knock me senseless and quite possibly kill me. No, but I've seen veins of quartz here and there in the mountainside. If I can get a bit that sings the right note—"

"Do you know, that might work." He peered inside the radio once more. "What you'd get will probably be the wrong shape, but I can deform the contacts to fit. My god, you're clever. What did you do before you were a Keeper?"

"I was a child. I came to Alba for training at nine. Before that I lived with my mother, walked in the woods, rode horseback. My Uncle Pablo taught me woodcraft; every child has to learn how to survive on the land. Is it any different on Terra? If you don't have blizzards or banshees, there must still be something. Don't you have to teach the children how to stay alive?"

"I haven't any children," he said. "Yes, they have to be taught to look out for traffic, and heavy machinery, and strangers. I grew up on a fishing station— it's an artificial island in the middle of the sea—and the first thing I had to learn was not to fall off."

"And when you became a spaceman, you had to learn—let me think—not to open a window?"

He laughed. "They don't open. No, the first rule is never to be out of reach of a handhold. And the second is not to get on your shipmates' nerves. Cooped up in a small ship for months on end sometimes, the smallest irritation can magnify itself into an outrage.

There've been murders done, or at least attempted, over a sneeze or a lisp."

Marguerida looked around her. On one side lay the forest, tree after tree standing deep in cool green shadows till they faded out like fishes in the depths of a pool. On the other side the mountainside fell away steeply, the nearest peak fifty miles away, a worldful of clear air between. "Why do people go into space, if it's so oppressive?"

"Ah! have you ever seen the stars? When all the little moons are down, have you looked up and seen them bright against the darkness, shining like jewels, like water after thirst, like music? From the time I could walk, I wanted to go among them. Six years of math I slogged through, when I could've been playing soccer or chasing girls or sleeping. And when you finally get there, with the long evenwatch ahead of you and the navigator's viewport curving around your head and nothing to see but stars! That's worth everything."

"It must be," Marguerida said. The sun was falling into evening again, and tiny Mormallor was glowing pale white above the western peak, and above it the bright evening star (but the Terran said it was another planet). "I wish I could go out there," she said, and knew it was the truth. "but I never can."

"Your planet needs you," he said. "That does happen." He folded his hands under his chin, and stared at his radio as if he did not see it.

Now it was she who said nothing and waited. She put more wood on the fire, and blew gently on the ashes to quicken them, and waited while the time grew ripe. Let the fruit hang on the tree long enough, and it will fall into your hand. "My first planetfall was on Megaera—that's Theta Centauri Four," he said at last. "There's an old Terra settlement there, older than Darkover. The chemistry of the air is strange; it changes human biochemistry, and it turns out that only certain women can be sure of bearing children safely. The others, the rest of the population, can only have children with the aid of these special women. Rhu'ad, they're called. They're telepaths, too; in fact, Alina was a lot like you, but pale: her skin and hair were like a pearl. And from the time she was born, it was arranged that she would marry the Lord of Mount Kali—not for his rank, I'll give them that, but for his genes—and do maternity duty to her co-wives, and her sisters-in-law, and her cousins twice and thrice removed. Nobody ever bothered to ask if that was what she wanted." He set the radio down, very gently. "And that was ten years ago. She's probably got fifty or sixty children by now."

"And that is why you never married?"

"That and being stony broke. Though Alina might have taken me even so, except her planet needed her."

"I'm sorry," There seemed to be nothing else to say. She put another branch on the fire. "And it is the same for me, isn't it. You're right. When we get to Thendara, I shall go to Comyn Castle and offer my services, such as they are, to Lord Regis. And you'll go back into space?"

He shook his head. "I've made a bad name for myself with the Merchant Service, I'm afraid. The Captain and I agreed to disagree, and I was given the opportunity to jump before I was pushed. I've been on Darkover most of this year, living off Distressed Spaceman's Aid and odd jobs. I'm up to my ears in debt."

"So is all of Darkover." Marguerida said. "You ought to feel at home here."

"At home? No," he said. "But it's as fair a world as any planet could be. Anyway, last week somebody hired me to deliver a message—to a chieftain named Barakh, in the Dry Towns—and lent me this plane to carry it in. I hope it's salvageable. All it really needs is fuel and a new wing, which could be flown in and bolted on in an afternoon—"

"Red Barakh of Shainsa? Who, in Avarra's name, would be sending messages to him? What was the message?"

"A Thendara merchant named Tamiano, and I don't know what the message is; I can't read Darkovan script."

"Show me." And when he hesitated, "Show me!" she cried. "This means more than you know."

After a moment he rose and went to the plane, pulled a little scroll out of a compartment in the pilot's console. Marguerida scanned it quickly. "I thought so," she said. "This says, 'Tamiano to Barakh, greetings. I send you the aircraft you commissioned of me. I got it of a Terran who no longer needed it. As for the pilot, I no longer need him; do as you will, but remember that flies cannot enter a closed mouth.' I thought as much. Tamiano killed the owner of this plane, and Barakh would have killed you as soon as you brought it to him. Donald Stewart, have you no nose for trouble at all? I thought you said Terrans taught their children to beware of strangers."

"Oh, Christ," the Terran said, clutching his head with both hands. "Now it fits together. Tamiano asked me if I was willing to get my hands dirty—for a substantial fee. I said I'd do anything that was legal. And Tamiano smiled, and offered me this messenger job instead."

"So that you shouldn't be able to tell anyone Tamiano is hiring assassins," Marguerida said. "I wonder who is hiring *him*."

"And now the Terran Empire police will be after me for receiving stolen goods. Damn! My friends always did say I needed—" he broke off, and looked away.

"We'll ask Lord Regis to intercede," she said. "That is the least of our worries. The bushjumper is done, and I'll get you your crystal tomorrow."

* * *

"The Keeper did a-hunting go,
And under her cloak she carried a bow,
All for to shoot at a merry little doe,
Among the leaves so green, oh!"

The Terran was singing when Marguerida came out of the forest the next day, and standing on his two feet, and using both hands to straighten the cushions inside the plane. (He had mentioned that spacemen had to learn to be neat.)

"I don't have a bow," she said when he had translated the old Terran words, "and there are no chervines on this saddle; there's very little game of any kind. I did find some tubers, we'll stew them with what's left of the bushjumper, and I got you some crystals," She fumbled half-a-dozen bright fragments of quartz out of the pocket of the Terran coverall. "I think this one will sing the best, but you try it. If it's too flat, I can probably trim it down a bit. Try it in your radio, while I cook supper."

The chunks of tuber, stewed in thin bushjumper gravy and a few herbs, were beginning to smell like the food of the gods by the time the Terran's curses became audible. Marguerida set down her knife, and the bit of nutwood from which she was carving a second spoon. "Won't it work?"

"Oh, it works, as far as that goes. I'm getting a carrier wave. But I'm not reaching anybody with it, not on any of the frequencies it's supposed to reach. I'm afraid you were right, it's not quite the right size and it's singing either sharp or flat."

"Flat," Marguerida said. "I knew it was a bit large. Here, give it to me."

She took her matrix in her left hand, and the quartz crystal in her right, and held them up together. The blue shifting light of the matrix played over her face, and the Terran thought of old stories of mermaids. He could see no change in the crystal, but after a moment she handed it back and said, "Now try it."

He put the crystal back in its place while she finished the spoon, and he turned the radio's controls this way and that, chanting, "Mayday, Mayday."

"If it's not going to work, we had better eat," Marguerida began, but the radio squawked like a frightened fowl and began to talk very fast Terran in a voice that sounded like the bottom of a well. Donald Stewart answered it, and they disputed back and forth (at lest, it sounded like an argument) for a minute or two. At last he sat back and turned the radio off with the kind of exaggerated gentleness a man will use when he'd rather kick the damned thing (whatever thing it might be) down the mountainside.

"I gather the news is not good," Marguerida said. We'll eat first, and then you can tell me."

"What it comes down to," he said presently, "is that there's a good-sized revolution going on—not so much in Thendara, but in the countryside. Think of what happened to your people at Alba, and multiply it by a hundred or a thousand desperate mobs. There've even been assassination attempts inside the hospital—no, it's all right," he said quickly. "They caught them. Lord Regis and his people are all right. But the long and short of it is that none of the authorities can spare a plane to come and get us for a couple of tendays at least, maybe longer. Can we hold out that long?"

"I don't think so. I said game was sparse around here; I think most of the inhabitants of this forest are birds who migrate to warmer regions in winter, and haven't come back yet. There's not much plant food either, not at this time of year; I can probably find a few of last fall's nuts, but the birds seem to have eaten most of them. There are a few more bushjumpers, but I'd hate to wipe them all out; this forest is one of the few that hasn't had its natural balance ruined already. And most of your Terran food bricks are gone, too."

"Were there any on your plane?"

"I don't think so."

"Well, let me think." He stared into the fire for a few minutes. "Was there any fuel left in your plane?"

"I have no idea. We weren't using the Terran cerberum engine; my teachers reconstructed the old matrix drive. I was flying off my own energy, and I crashed because I'd gotten tired. It's hard, making your way from one air current to the next when you're not used to it."

"Of course it is. How may hours' flight time had you had?"

"Two or three, I suppose."

"No more than that? If you weren't a Keeper, I'd like to shake your hand. We could make a pilot of you yet. Now let me think." He folded his arms and brooded.

Marguerida also had time to think. How many of her unquestioned assumptions the Terran had knocked base-over-apex in the last two days, all without meaning to. All men were not coarse brutes, prevented only by the threat of destruction from profaning a Keeper's sanctity with their crude touch. All Terrans were not barbarians, unable to make the distinction between "All men are brothers" and "You are a pack of boy-lovers." Donald Stewart had shown her the greatest respect both in deed and in word—even his grammar was beginning to improve. And her teachers were not always right, and Regis Hastur was not always wrong.

"Is your matrix drive still working?" he asked finally.

"I should think so. It was attached to the pilot's console, where I was sitting, and a blow hard enough to crack its crystal would have killed me."

"Could it be modified to run a welding torch?"

"Not by me."

"You don't think there's *any* cerberum fuel left in your plane?"

"I told you, I don't know. We'll have to go there and look."

"So we will," he said. "First thing tomorrow morning. If there's even a tenth charge, I can rig a torch, and I *think* I can repair this wing. At the least, I might get us to Carthon."

"Very well," she said. "Have you ever climbed mountains before?"

"No."

"Is there any rope in your plane?"

"Don't think so."

"Very well," she said again, and got up. "I'd better find more bark while the light lasts. Will you put some more wood on the fire?"

Morning found them on the cliffside, the Terran belaying Marguerida's bark rope round a tree trunk while she scrambled down the steep face to the wreckage of her plane. "I ought to be doing this," he protested once more.

"Oh, be sensible for once," she said. "Would you know a matrix drive if you saw it, to say nothing of the ten contact points that have to be taken off in one piece? There, now, I'm in the tree and it's rock steady; it must have roots as deep as the mountain's own. Make the rope fast, will you? Then you can come to the edge and watch." She climbed over a branch, ducked under another, and slid cautiously down the trunk to the gaping hole where the plane's windshield had been. The matrix drive looked all right, *felt* all right: now to get at it without putting her foot through it.

"How are you getting on?" he asked a little later, his face dark against the morning sky.

"Just got it." She coiled the last fragile contact strip, wrapped the drive in her gown, and tied the whole bundle into her veil. Soon she might be needing them again, even if they were a bit stained and creased.

"What about the fuel cells? They're the black cylin-

ders in the aft compartment, and there should be a
readout panel on each one. Aren't Darkovan numerals the same as Terran? If you can just read the figures
off to me—"

"No numerals," she said. "No black cylinders. No
aft compartment. I think they must have taken all that
out to lighten the weight. Now what?"

"Come back up where I can see you."

"All right." She took the end of her knotted veil in
her teeth and climbed back into the tree. "Here, pull
this up—" she tied the bundle to the end of the rope—"
it's not all that fragile, but try not to hit it against
anything."

"Got it,"he said a moment later. "Now, I'd like you
to take a look at that wing—the right wing, the one
near you. Is it badly damaged?"

"It isn't damaged at all," she said. "It's the only
part of this plane that's in one piece. Wait: here's a
hole in the skin the size of my thumbprint."

"Trival," he said. She couldn't see his face clearly,
but his voice was gleeful. "Did I bring that wrench?
Yes, I did. Would you say this rope was strong enough
to haul up the whole plane?"

"No, and neither are we," she said.

"And we haven't the time to carve pulleys," he
said. "Hang on, I'm coming down." There was scrab-
bling sound, and a shower of pebbles from above, and
to Marguerida's dismay the Terran came down the
rope hand-over-hand and came to rest in the tree
beside her. He had taken off his boots, and the thin
stockings on his feet were divided, each toe in its own
separate mitten. "Look at that wing," he said, and
pointed to it with his wrench."A functional right wing
is the major thing my plane is lacking, or hadn't you
noticed?"

"Not really," she admitted. "Do you mean you can
cut that wing off and—"

"Cut it, hell," he said. "Unbolt fourteen bolts, that's

all. The wing'll be a little shorter than it's supposed to be—mine's a TC-3, and this is a TC-2—but the base plate's exactly the same."

"And you can fly with it?"

"As far as Carthon, I should think. Maybe as far as Thendara, if you and your matrix hold out. Look, will you sit over on that branch, and just steady the wingtip with a coil of your rope? I don't want it falling away as soon as it's free." He slithered down the plane's side, gripping with fingers and toes like a Trailman, till he reached the base of the wing. Marguerida secured the wingtip as she was bidden, and settled down to watch.

"Make that thirteen bolts," he said after a few minutes' work. "One of 'em got torn out by the base of this branch. That's all right; it'll be stable enough without." He said little else that morning, but sang almost constantly: old ballads, she supposed, with tunes that she recognized, though the Terran words were strange.

The sun was reaching into noon when he called out, "That's the lot!" and tucked his wrench away. "Is the wing secure? Let me up there and I'll take a look at it—"

But if the wing was free of the plane now, so the plane was free of the wing, and it began to slide. (Later, after it was over, she had time to realize that that right wing, caught over the branch, had been the only thing holding the plane in the tree.) "Lord of Light!" Marguerida cried, not knowing she did so, and slid down the trunk, reaching down with her right hand as she gripped the rope's end with her left. "Donald, grab hold!"

He swarmed up the plane's side with desperate speed as it slid away under him, like a man swimming upstream against the current, gaining only a little. He flung up his arm, and she grasped it. Fear gave them both strength, and she gave one mighty pull and somehow they were both standing on the same branch, each clinging desperately to the other and to the trunk of the tree. Far below them, the plane struck a ledge and exploded into splinters.

"O god, O Marguerida," Donald muttered into her collar. "I am such a bloody fool. I forgot about gravity. You do that, till it reaches out and grabs you. Gravity is the enemy—right after stupidity—and the universe never forgives a mistake."

"It let you off easy this time," she said. "Can you let go now? We have to get back up there. Will you go first, or shall I."

"I'll go," he muttered, and climbed up the rope again, gripping very cautiously and not looking down. Then he hauled up the wing, careful not to damage it, and lastly he let the rope down again for Marguerida. When she reached the top he took her hands and gripped them hard for a moment. "Oh, sorry," he said, and let go her hands as if they were fiery hot.

"No harm done," she said, and set to rigging branches and the rope into a travois for the wing.

Once they had brought the wing to the plane, reaction set in. Marguerida felt icy cold, and sat by the fire trying to warm her hands; but Donald was full of nervous energy and bustled round the plane, unbolting the damaged wing and trying to get the replacement into position. At last Marguerida had to get up and help him build a framework of branches to hold the wing in place. Somewhere in the process her thoughts, like a batch of jelly, finally cleared and set into shape.

"Two hours, maybe, till sunset," Marguerida said when Donald's plane had been hauled out of the trees and the new wing and the matrix drive were in place. "Do we go now, or wait till morning?"

"It's up to you," he said "I'm just the pilot; you're the Chief Engineer. Do you feel up to it? You've had a rough day."

"*I've* had?" she said, smiling. "As for me, I feel

splendid; I think I could fight a banshee with one eye blinded. Let's go."

A Keeper must set an example for her people, she thought. *And if Darkover must break with tradition and make alliances with Terra, why, so must I.*

She took her seat beside him. The matrix drive sat just in front of the altimeter, so that she could reach it with one hand while Donald used the flight controls. There was, as he'd said, room for two in the cockpit, so long as they were friendly. "I'll take you to Thendara if I possibly can," he said. "They need you; they may not know it yet, but they'll find out."

"What about you?"

"I'd better tell the Terran authorities about Tamiano," he said. "Maybe they'll let me keep the plane, but I doubt it. After that, I don't know."

"And I used to think Terrans were practical men. You'd better come to Comyn Castle with me. I'm not sure yet what you'll do there, but I think you're my responsibility. By right of discovery, or something."

"Am I?" They glanced at each other, suddenly almost shy. "If you say so." He released the plane's wheel brakes, and the craft rolled down the bank, picking up speed, and launched itself into the air. The matrix sang in Marguerida's mind, a perfect fifth above the singing of her own delight. The plane fell and rose again in an elegant curve. Donald smiled. "My friends always said I needed a keeper." The plane was drifting just a little to the right, and he gave the controls a nudge to bring it back on course. It soared like an eagle into the westering sun.

Devil's Advocate

Patricia Anne Buard

Patricia Anne Buard is another writer who surfaced as a winner in the Starstone *short story contests. She says of herself that she was born and raised in the Chicago area, and has worked in theater as a costume designer and for small ballet and modern dance companies; her husband is a scenic and lighting designer. She began reading science fiction as a young teenager on finding Heinlein and Asimov in the library (didn't everybody?) but was so busy in theatrical work that she did no writing until the Darkover contests came along. "I am now doing some non-Darkover fiction, but no sales there yet."*

Keep trying; this is a good start, a story of the cristoforos which attracted much praise in the amateur story contest, but reads very professionally (MZB)

Father Sebastian Cerreno of the Society of Jesus, special emissary from Rome in the cause of St. Valentine-of-the Snows, pulled his cloak tightly around him as the wind swept down from the high peaks, stirring up eddies of snow along the road. If denial of physical comfort and discipline of the body assisted the spirit to holiness as the ancient monastic orders taught, then this planet was surely the place to forge the character of a saint. And this culture was more than enough to try the patience of one.

He looked at the cloaked figure of his guide riding ahead of him: Mirella n'ha Gwennis, member of the Order of Renunciates. Wishing to travel quietly, he had refused the offer of a formal escort; a Renunciate, even though a woman, had seemed a suitable choice. He could hardly find fault with her behavior, but the discovery that some of the customs she renounced were the very ones his Church held dear had been distinctly disconcerting.

So too, had been his first encounter with a *cristoforo*, the Darkovan religious group the Church hoped to claim as Her own. Outwardly, Lord Danilo, Regent and Warden of Ardais, was everything a young nobleman should be; but the extent of his relationship to that unusual young man with the snow-white hair, Lord Regis Hastur, had been unmistakable. Father Cerreno wondered, as he often did, just how he knew these things. Nothing in the behavior of either man had suggested it; still he knew, without doubt, the nature of their bond. It was a bond the Church proscribed as unnatural and, therefore, sinful. If these *cristoforos*—Father Cerreno frowned and reprimanded himself for his lack of discipline. Conclusions came after long and careful inquiry, not before. He was to spend the winter at Nevarsin monastery making that inquiry; of the *cristoforo* faith and, most particularly, of the man known as St. Valentine-of-the-Snows, who was also, perhaps, Father Valentine of the Order of St. Christopher of Centaurus.

As they rounded a bend in the road, the Free Amazon dropped back to ride beside him. "There's Nevarsin, Father. You'll be there in time for supper. I imagine you'll be glad to see the last of that horse. It's a long journey for a Terran."

"It's not been so uncomfortable, Mestra. I used to ride as a boy. My people kept some of the old traditions and skills, such as horsemanship, alive." They had also kept alive the concepts of courtesy and honor which Father Cerreno knew would be an advantage on Darkover. It was one of the reasons he had been chosen for this mission.

He looked up at the monastery on the mountain; solid and secure, a defense and a refuge like so many others. Like them, too, it was the preserver of knowledge, prevailing against the destruction of time and the destruction of men. The Hasturs had given him permission to study the *cristoforo* history. Darkover was slowly, carefully joining the Empire. Father Cerreno wondered what they would think if they knew that his mission was to prove that Father Valentine was not worthy to be called a saint.

Father Cerreno put down the book he was reading and rubbed his hands together. The weeks at Nevarsin had accustomed the rest of his body to the cold, but his long, thin fingers still ached at times, especially when he was tired. He had been awakened several times, last night by dreams that faded so quickly that their content eluded him. He had had several such nights lately and knew from experience that the dreams would cease of their own accord after a time. It was a pattern that had recurred throughout much of his life, but he had never found the cause.

He glanced at his watch and then at the man seated at a table in the corner of the room. The hour was almost gone, but he supposed that he would not need to say anything to signal its end. Dom Rafael, like everyone else at Nevarsin, responded to unsounded bells and walked as surely in the dark as in daylight.

About twenty-five years of age and dressed in the clothing of the Domains, Rafael MacAlastair was a secular scholar, one of the few on Darkover who chose such a life. He had been assigned to act as Father

Cerreno's secretary, but had proved to be an able assistant as well.

Exactly upon the hour Rafael rose from his stool, took up a sheaf of papers and presented them to the priest. "My translation, Father." He waited hopefully while his superior checked his efforts.

"Excellent, Dom Rafael, but then I have come to expect that from you."

Rafael smiled shyly. "Thank you, Father."

Father Cerreno's face remained impassive. "There is no need to thank me, Dom Rafael, good work should be acknowledged." The priest paused, then said, "You seem to have a facility for languages, but I have wondered why you want to learn Latin. You will find little use for it on Darkover."

"I realize that Father," Rafael replied, "but when you told me it was the ancient language of the Church, I felt I should know it."

"The language of my church, Dom Rafael," the priest reminded him. "We are not yet certain that it is your church as well. You must learn to reserve your judgment until you have studied your subject thoroughly."

'Yes, Father." Rafael acknowledged the criticism. "I can't help hoping, though, that they are the same."

"Why is that, Dom Rafael?" Father Cerreno asked. "You know very little of my church or my faith. Perhaps you will not find either to be acceptable to you."

"I don't think that will be true, Father," Rafael said. He added quickly, "I know it seems I am judging too hastily again, but I do not think that the beliefs of someone I respect as much as I do you could be unacceptable to me."

Father Cerreno regarded the young man evenly, hiding the uneasiness he felt. Rafael's words had been innocent enough, yet the priest instinctively drew back from any expression of emotion. Finally he said, "The Church cannot be judged by the fact of any one man's

service. Whatever you may think of me is of no importance in that respect. If you wish to learn more of the
Church, I will be glad to teach you." Father Cerreno
reached for the book in front of him. "And now I
believe you have some work to do in the library, Dom
Rafael."

"Yes Father." Rafael hesitated at the door. "You
don't have to call me *Dom* Rafael all the time Father;
Rafael will do just fine."

Without looking up from his book, Sebastian Cerreno
replied evenly, "Every man is entitled to be addressed
with the courtesy his culture affords. I have always
followed that precept, Dom Rafael." He seemed not
to notice when Rafael quietly left the room, but went
steadily on with his reading.

As the harsh, Darkovan winter ran its course, Father Cerreno probed deeper and deeper into the oldest records of the monastery in his search for the truth
behind the legends of St. Valentine-of-the-Snows. Dom
Rafael was an invaluable assistant. The younger man
had a true scholar's mind, and his enthusiasm had
been channeled by the priest into the diligence necessary for his work: his obvious admiration of his superior tempered by Father Cerreno's courteous distance
into a respectful desire to learn.

Father Cerreno filled the notebooks he had brought
from Terra with long paragraphs of Latin; quotations
from the writings of the *cristoforos*. Rafael MacAlastair
filled similar notebooks with summaries of *cristoforo*
history written in Terran Standard. Father Cerreno
was certain, now, that Dom Rafael's notes would provide ample evidence that the *cristoforo* faith derived
from the faith of his own church, but his notes only
proved that, isolated for thousands of years, the
cristoforos had deviated from the main body of the
Church's teachings. They did not yet prove that Father
Valentine was unworthy. Many of the writings, includ-

ing some of the oldest that claimed to represent the words of the saint, certainly verged on the heretical, but he had not yet been able to establish that they were truly the work of Father Valentine. Even the fragments that tradition held were actually written by Valentine himself were of Darkovan origin and it was impossible to tell if they had been written by the saint or an early follower. He had not yet found Father Valentine.

As spring approached, Father Cerreno's dreams returned. Waking suddenly one night, a name came unbidden into his mind: Ramón, one of his fellow students at the seminary, now Father Ramón Valdez, serving his order on one of the Empire worlds. Had the dream been about Ramón? They hadn't seen each other in years. He didn't believe in omens, but it would do no harm to say a prayer for Ramón Valdez.

When he entered the chapel he found he was not the only suppliant; Rafael MacAlastair was just rising from his knees. Father Cerreno greeted him quietly. "I see you are wakeful tonight too, Dom Rafael."

"I often come here at this hour, Father. It is so peaceful."

"Do you need to seek peace, then, Dom Rafael?" Father Cerreno asked.

"Sometimes," Rafael smiled ruefully, "when I wonder what I should do with the life I have been given."

Father Cerreno hesitated for a moment, then said, "I have wondered why you have not chosen the religious life. You are a *cristoforo* and from what I have seen, I think you are here as much to pray as to study."

"I would like to become a monk, Father. Even more, I wish I could become a priest like you," Rafael lowered his eyes, "but I do not believe I am fit to be one." He had not intended it to be a question, but Father Cerreno was acutely aware of the hopefulness in Rafael's voice. He was aware, too, of the meaning behind the young man's words. Once again, he knew things about another person that he did not wish to know.

"You are the only judge of that, Dom Rafael." The coldness in Sebastian Cerreno's voice said plainly, *I cannot help you.*

"Yes, of course, Father. Forgive me, I keep you from your prayers." Rafael turned, moving down the aisle with lowered head.

Father Cerreno knelt in one of the stalls, folded his hands and began to pray for Father Valdez, but found it difficult to order his thoughts. *Ramón, why have we lost contact with each other?* Messages could have been sent—distances didn't matter. *Why didn't I make the effort? Ramón, you were my friend.* He bowed his head. He knew the answer; he had turned away his friend long ago, as he had turned away Rafael MacAlastair this very night. It seemed to be the only way he knew.

Father Cerreno examined the book on the table before him. Crudely bound, worn and brittle, it was the oldest document the monastery possessed. His search for St. Valentine ended here. If this manuscript could not be proved to be the work of Valentine himself, then the man could not be found and his mission would be only a partial success. His report to Rome would be based on the interpretations and beliefs of the purported saint's followers; and, although much of it was damaging to the cause for sainthood, such secondhand material was suspect at best, always open to the charge that the man's followers had misunderstood or even changed the meaning of his teachings.

He had known of the existence of the book for some time. The monks at Nevarsin had not hindered his research, indeed, they had told him of the work and of

the tradition that ascribed it to St. Valentine; but
Father Cerreno had followed his usual practice of working backward in cases like this, fitting each piece of
the puzzle into place until he arrived, not at the end,
but at the beginning. This, he hoped, was that beginning. He had permission to take a small fragment of
one of the pages to Terra for dating purposes, but he
hoped that something in the material itself would indicate the authorship. He felt that his hope was not
unfounded; the monks had told him they could no
longer read the language well enough to make any
sense of it. In fact, there was a tradition that no one
ever had been able to do so, although similarities to
the older forms of *casta* had been found in it.

Father Cerreno got up and went to the window,
opening the shutter. The air had lost its bitter cold and
the roads were passable now; he would be leaving
Darkover soon. It was a world that both attracted and
disturbed him. The severity of the monastery pleased
him; he should have found peace in such a place, yet
he had felt the need to retreat, to barricade himself
from the life around him. Would he never find a place
where he could devote himself to his God and his
work without that terrible awareness, that unwanted
knowledge of people that constantly threatened to in-
trude upon his innermost being? He offered a silent
prayer. *Oh, Lord, help me to accept the things I cannot
change.*

He closed the shutter and returned to his table. A
few more hours of study if he could read the language,
a few hours of copying if he could not, was all that
remained of his task. When he was finished, he would
pack his belongings and prepare for the journey to
Thendara. He would have to stop at Castle Ardais. He
couldn't refuse that invitation without a sufficient reason; the fact that Lord Danilo disturbed him by not
adhering strictly to his *cristoforo* faith was not a reason

that could be openly given, and Father Cerreno would not offend against his conscience by lie.

He took up the book and gently opened its fragile pages. The faded script was still legible. More than legible, it was understandable to Sebastian Cerreno. He realized he held in his hands the private diary of Father Valentine; his thoughts, his words, his deeds, written for his own purposes alone, since he had never taught anyone else the language; Latin, the ancient language of the universal Church, now used only by scholars and the clerical orders to retain their link with the past. Father Cerreno drew his notebooks toward him. He had found St. Valentine.

Later that evening Father Cerreno copied the last pages of Father Valentine's diary and closed his notebook. He packed the notebooks and other materials carefully, leaving the room as clean and empty as he had found it. He sat at the table, his fingers resting lightly on Valentine's manuscript. His mission had been successful, but he felt only a cold emptiness spreading throughout his body, holding him rigid in his chair, his eyes fixed on the wall across the room. Father Valentine's words filled his mind. Denial of his priesthood, rejection of ritual and the sacraments, doubt of the divine origin of the Son of God, and finally, sodomy and murder. This was Father Valentine.

There was a knock on the door, but Father Cerreno did not move, only called "Enter," in a flat voice.

Rafael MacAlastair crossed the room to stand beside the table. "Father, is something wrong?" he asked in a worried voice.

"Nothing is wrong, Dom Rafael," the priest replied distantly. "I have finished my work and will leave Nevarsin in the morning." He continued to stare at the wall.

Rafael felt a sharp sense of loss which he dared not express to the priest. Instead, he tried to bridge the distance between them in an unemotional way. "I, too, leave tomorrow, Father. I am going home for my brother's marriage. Perhaps we can ride together part of the way." When he received no reply, Rafael knew that the priest was deeply disturbed. Never before had Father Cerreno been discourteous and this abrupt dismissal was almost rude. The priest remained unmoving, his face impassive, but Rafael could feel his distress as clearly as if it were something he could hold in his hands. Unable to conceal the feelings that he had suppressed because of Father Cerreno's distant manner toward him, Rafael knelt beside the priest. "*Vai dom*, Father, something is wrong. Let me help you if I can." He reached out and laid his hand on the priest's arm.

Father Cerreno drew back, closing his mind and heart to the friendship he could not accept. "I have no need of help from anyone, Dom Rafael, least of all from you." He rose from the chair, Valentine's diary in his hands.

Rafael got to his feet, struggling to conceal the pain the priest's words had caused. He sought for some acceptable way to say farewell. Finding none, he tried to mask his emotions by speaking of the work they had shared for so many months. "May I know, Father, if you succeeded in finding St. Valentine?"

Sebastian Cerreno turned, seeking to close the last door in the wall that he had built between himself and Rafael. He held out the manuscript. "This is his diary. Read for yourself about your saint; it is written in Latin." He picked up the case containing his notes. "You were right, Dom Rafael, you are not fit to be a priest; neither was Valentine. You are alike in that, and for the same reason." Sebastian Cerreno forgot that there was more than one reason for his judgment against the saint. Valentine and Rafael had become one in his mind: he had to reject them both. He walked from the room, closing the door behind him.

* * *

Early the next day, Father Cerreno packed the rest of his belongings and made his formal farewells to the monks. He did not see Rafael MacAlastair, but a novice brought a written message. *I have returned Father Valentine's diary to the library. I beg your forgiveness if I intruded when I only wished to help. I never meant to offer anything that was unacceptable.* Father Cerreno thrust the note into his traveling bag and started for the courtyard. His guide and their horses were waiting, along with two other men who wore the badge of the MacAlastair house. As he mounted his horse, Father Cerreno saw Rafael come through the doorway on the other side of the yard. He turned his mount toward the gate and rode out of the monastery.

Father Cerreno sat in the hall of Castle Ardais waiting for his host who was still occupied with his duties as Warden of the Domain. He wore a riding habit and carried a slim steel dagger, its hilt chased with silver, on his belt. It had been in his family for generations. He usually didn't wear it, a weapon was not suitable for a priest, but it seemed appropriate on this world. The daily rides with Lord Danilo had brought a measure of peace, but the cold that had blanketed his mind since his last evening at the monastery remained. He sometimes feared he might snap into pieces as easily as these brittle icicles that had hung outside his window at Nevarsin.

He heard footsteps coming toward the hall and rose as two young men were ushered in by one of the Ardais retainers. They were introduced as Dom Ruyven Harryl and his cousin Dom Darren, whose families had holdings under the Ardais Domain. Father Cerreno was puzzled at the look that passed between them at the mention of his name.

Ruyven Harryl smiled at his cousin. "It seems we have come at the right time, Darren; won't Lord Ardais be surprised when we tell him his guest is a Terran spy."

In spite of the danger he could sense surrounding the two men, Father Cerreno replied calmly, "I have been studying the history of the *cristoforos* with the permission of Lord Hastur."

Darren stepped forward, his hands resting on his sword belt. "The Hasturs won't think so well of you *Terranan* when they learn what we have to tell them. Lord Ardais will like it even less when he finds out you have come here to destroy the *cristoforos* and their saint."

Father Cerreno stood very still while his mind grasped for a truthful answer. "Neither I nor my Church have any intention of destroying the *cristoforos*." The Church only wanted to be prepared for the time when the *cristoforos* themselves would ask if they were members of the same faith. If the Church could not accept the sainthood of Father Valentine, a way would be found to acknowledge them as brothers in the general community of Christians without the insult of formally rejecting their saint.

Darren persisted. "We have our friends in the Trade City; they tell us what you Terrans are up to, so don't try to deny it. Someone came through who knew you, priest. We know what your real purpose is."

Father Cerreno realized what had happened, but didn't know how he could ever explain it to these two hot-headed young men. "It is not true, Dom Darren, I believe . . ."

Ruyven cut him off. "Do you call us liars, priest?" His hand went to his sword. "On Darkover we don't take that as lightly as you *Terranan* do. I challenge you to prove your words." He drew his sword. "Well, priest?"

"As you can see, Dom Ruyven, I don't carry a sword."

Ruyven smiled and dropped lightly into a fighting stance. "Darren will loan you his, won't you cousin?" In reply, Darren drew his sword and pushed it across the floor to the priest's feet.

Father Cerreno did not move. His Castilian forebearers had been accomplished swordsmen, but the days when he had handled a weapon were long past. He would be no match for this man.

Ruyven moved forward. "Are you a coward like all *Terranan?*" He flicked the point of his sword across Cerreno's chest, cutting the cloth of the priest's habit.

"Hold!" The voice came from the doorway. Danilo strode rapidly across the room. "Zandru's hells, Ruyven, what goes on here? Father Cerreno is a guest in this house and has the protection of Lord Regis. Put up your sword."

"He called us liars. I challenged him to prove his words."

"The man is unarmed, Ruyven; we can settle this another way. Now put up your sword or you will have to answer to me."

Ruyven made no move to obey Danilo's command. Instead, he said hotly, "He's a Terran spy. Lord Regis wouldn't have given him his protection if he had known that he came here to prove that your St. Valentine isn't a saint at all." Ruyven took another step toward the priest, his sword moving in his hand.

Stepping between them, Danilo drew his sword and struck Ruyven's blade aside. Angered and unthinking, Ruyven returned the stroke. With a growing feeling of despair, Father Cerreno whispered, "No, Lord Danilo, don't fight for me." Danilo ignored the words and brought his sword down against Ruyven's, striking it from his hand and sending it skittering across the floor. Danilo returned his sword to its sheath. "You have disgraced yourself and your house, Dom Ruyven.

If you have any complaint against Father Cerreno, bring it before the Council. Now go."

Ruyven silently retrieved his weapon and left the hall, followed by his cousin. Danilo watched them go, then turned to Father Cerreno. "I am sorry that such a thing happened while you were a guest in this house, Father." Seeing the priest's pale face and the tear in his clothing, Danilo became concerned. "Are you injured, Father?"

"No, Lord Danilo." Father Cerreno replied. He moved to a bench beside the long table. Was that the truth, he wondered. He felt as if the brittleness inside him had finally broken. He raised his head and looked at Danilo. "You shouldn't have defended me; what he said is true."

"I know that," Danilo replied.

"Then why did you risk your life for me?" Father Cerreno felt that there was something very important here that he must understand.

"I was not only defending you, Father, I was also defending the word of Regis Hastur. I am his paxman, his sworn man, we have exchanged the oath of *bredin*. I am vowed to defend him and his word with my life if necessary."

Father Cerreno listened to the words of the *cristoforo* nobleman whom his Church considered to be in a state of sin. He had always accepted that teaching without question and yet—his hand went to the crucifix he wore around his neck. "Greater love than this . . ." He looked at Danilo. "I believe you say it in a slightly different way."

Danilo smiled. "Yes, Father, but I know what you mean."

Sebastian Cerreno looked away. He sat very still, one arm resting on the table, his fingertips tracing the edge. There was no coldness within him to place between himself and this young man's words, no coldness to place between himself and Ramón Valdez or

Rafael MacAlastair. Finally he said, "All my life I have built a wall around myself. I have no friend for whom I could lay down my life; I turned away anyone who would have been my friend. I thought it was the only way to come close to God. But I know now that I was afraid. I feared what I knew about other people, but I could never shut out the knowledge, so I shut out the people. I have always known too much about others; I see now that I have known very little about myself. I was afraid of what I would find." He turned and looked steadily at Danilo. "I could not accept in myself what you have accepted in yourself."

Danilo said quietly, "That is not always an easy thing to do, Father, I have reason to know." He paused, then continued, "If you know that about me, and if you know more than you wish to about other people, you are probably an empath; you instinctively read the emotions of the people around you. In fact, I am almost sure you have that *laran*; it's how I knew Ruyven Harryl spoke the truth about your purpose here. You felt so strongly about what he said, I couldn't help knowing."

Father Cerreno said slowly, "The *cristoforos* don't have the sacrament of penance in the way we do, Lord Danilo, but I would like to confess to you. I have sinned by omission. I did come here to study your history, but I also had a special mission. I was sent here as the Devil's Advocate in the cause of St. Valentine." Seeing Danilo's puzzled look, he said, "The Church moves with great caution when considering a candidate for canonization. It is a very great responsibility to proclaim a person worthy of veneration by the faithful. A thorough investigation is made of the candidate's life. The Church seeks to find not only the good, but the bad, if it exists. Someone is always charged with the task of presenting the case against the candidate. In this instance, I am that person. It doesn't matter what my personal feelings are, nor am I to present any judgment; I am only to present the evidence. Another person will be charged with the task of being the advocate in favor of Father Valentine. He will seek only the good."

Father Cerreno stopped speaking; there was so much more to explain, but he found he could not continue. Instead, he said, "I will have to learn how to love God; I thought I knew, but now I will have to start from the beginning."

"What will you do, Father?" Danilo asked.

The priest rose. "I, too, have vows to keep, Lord Danilo; of obedience and of chastity. The Church moves slowly; it will be years before any decision is made about Father Valentine. When the time comes, I think you and Regis Hastur will know how to deal with it." He hesitated a moment, then said, "You will see Rafael MacAlastair at his brother's marriage, won't you?"

"Yes, I will," Danilo replied.

Father Cerreno drew his dagger from its sheath. He would keep his vows of ordination, but he could no longer deny his love for his fellow man, no matter what form it took. Perhaps this was the first step toward a new understanding of the love of God. He held out the dagger. "Will you give Rafael this and tell him that I would be honored if he will accept it. He is my brother in Christ and also in my heart. I don't know if I will ever return to Darkover, but my brother Rafael will be with me wherever I go."

Danilo took the dagger and said, "I will deliver your message, Father. I think Rafael will accept this."

Father Cerreno walked slowly across the hall. At the door he turned and said, "Will you tell him, also, that I was wrong; I think he would make a very good priest."

Sebastian Cerreno strapped down his traveling bag and prepared for the liftoff that was but minutes away.

He fingered the knife he wore at his belt and reread Rafael's note. *Bredú, you, also, will be always in my heart; my friend and my brother in Christ. Wherever you go, may it be with God.* Father Cerreno folded the note and held it in his hand. The ship's engines thundered into life and Darkover fell away beneath them.

Kihar

Vera Nazarian

Vera Nazarian (of Glendale, California) is the youngest writer ever to sell to me; when she sent "Wound on the Moon," which I bought for SWORD AND SORCERESS II, she was not yet out of high school—a fact I did not discover until her contract arrived back countersigned by her parents.

Now she has turned her considerable talents to Darkover, with a story investigating a really unusual use of laran *and that untranslatable concept of* kihar— *which does not mean precisely* pride, *nor even* integrity, *but partakes of both. (MZB)*

It is said, *What is done under four moons need not be remembered or regretted.* What irony! Every now and then, as we rode, I looked up to see that celestial Hali necklace of four jewels, pale violet Liriel, sea-green Idriel, shimmering peacock Kyrrdis, and pale pearl Mormallor, and I thought, *I am mad. This cannot be happening. . . .* And then I touched the cool copper bracelet at my wrist, and looked at the man riding at my side, my husband.

Yes, I had been mad, to agree to this mockery, or he was mad. He did not love me, never pretended to, not even to lady Elviria, she who had birthed me.

They had spoken long, that night at Scathfell, he, aloof, gaunt, and coldly handsome with his pale gray eyes and shocking red hair, bright as the flames in the fireplace of the Great Hall of my home in the Hellers. I watched the flames often when I was little, fascinated by the element of fire. My dark hair, too, Dame Vilma used to say, had in it the same odd flame-red tints, which ran in my family through generations, bred alongside with that hateful power of the mind, *laran*.

My father was Korwin-Garris Aldaran, lord of Scathfell. All my life, for as long as I can remember, he had been dead. My mother said he had been a tall proud man, flame-haired and flame-tempered. She would only mention that he was killed in a minor war, but how or why, I never knew. It was the times, clan warring against clan, bloody rivalry.

Lady Elviria was proud also. Never truly beautiful, she was stately and dark, with pale ivory hands and haunting eyes like the blessed Cassilda. She could be cold or tender to us indiscriminately. I and my older sister Irmelin adored her, and were afraid of her at the same time.

"You must be proud, always," the lady Aldaran would say to us, "For in the days of Carolin Hastur, your kin was exalted. Your great-great-aunt was hawkmistress to the king Himself, and traveled as His close companion."

By Aldones, that doesn't make me *great,* I thought bitterly, but never voiced it.

My sister Irmelin was different from me. Serious, slender and beautiful, like the golden-flower, she had been tested by a *leronis*, when still a child, and found talented beyond expectations, having the Aldaran Gift of precognition, in full. She was three years my elder, and was now being trained at a Tower, while I, now that I'd turned fifteen, agreed dutifully to be married, and was being shipped off as my husband's movable property.

Really, I had no excuse to be bitter at all. My father had left no male heir, not even *nedestro*, and there was no other man Gifted enough among kin to take the Heirship of Aldaran. It was not the first time in our family's history that the Heirship had been given to a woman, although it was not usual. Thus, Irmelin was Heir to both Scathfell and Aldaran.

And I, too tall for my age, plump and fleshy, yet not womanly at all, with my loud laughing voice and hands quick at anything but woman's handiwork, had no right to complain. Rather I should praise Evanda that the husband my mother out of her love procured for me was not old and impotent, nor cruel, but young and handsome, and of a Great House. I, with my looks and manners, did not deserve *Dom* Cerdric Lanart-Elhalyn. In fact, I probably deserved no man of noble blood, nor deserved to bear my own noble name. For all practical purposes, I was worthless.

For I, Calvana Aldaran, second daughter of Lord Aldaran, had no *laran* whatsoever.

The same *leronis* that had tested Irmelin had confirmed it. Nevertheless, together with Irmelin, she had given me a starstone to be hung around my neck, an empty consolation, more for lady Elviria's sake than for myself.

And after a while, I did not care. It was almost a relief. A freedom was opened to me, and I roamed the hills, played with the hunting birds and the horses, sketching their likenesses upon the gray stones with coals from the hearth, carved with a knife figurines from the good wood given me by old Manwell, my father's stablehand. I fought with the boys in the yard of Scathfell Keep, bloodied noses, and kicked shins. "Fat pig!" they teased, and when I kicked again, "Zandru's fat pig!"

And when I was thirteen winters, a harper-craftsman

came by our Hall, peddling, and lady Elviria bought
from him several harps. Music had been absent in our
family ever since Lord Korwin, my father, died, but I
remembered his men speaking of his harping and singing, back *then*. He had a sorcerous touch upon the
harpstrings, they said.

I was given a small *rryl*, and was dutifully instructed
in the playing and singing arts. It was almost as though
my mother wanted to carve a bridge away from the
sad past, and returning music to our lives was the
outward gesture. At that point I had once stopped to
wonder why she had never remarried. But then, everything else was forgotten as my hands touched the
rryl strings, and I heard the first pure diamond-bright
chord. And thus, I learned and sang.

It was true that after a while, those who heard my
playing and the timbre of my voice, noticed to their
surprise that I was much better at it than they expected. My mother was told, and ever since then she
began to pay special attention, if not to me, then at
least to this aspect of myself.

At last, I had revealed a talent.

Only, what did all this matter now? I was of no use
to anyone, not even with all my fine singing, and yet
they had treated me kindly. My mother had been
fostered, when little, with Mirhana Elhalyn, and they
had sworn a friendship-oath together. And now,
Elviria's foster-sister offered her son Cerdric to me in
marriage.

It had all been arranged without my knowing. My
mother did not doubt my final consent, and thus, a
month and fortnight ago, *Dom* Cerdric came to
Scathfell, and a tenday later, without being handfasted,
we were married *di catenas*, and left immediately,
crossing the Hellers, on our way to the Lanart estate
in the Kilghard Hills. It all had a strangely rushed air
to it, as though my mother were afraid to wait another
day. I did not doubt she *was* afraid, and I was only

surprised that upon seeing me, *Dom* Cerdric did not at once turn on his heel and fly back to his lowland holding, never to return.

He does not know me well enough, yet . . . I thought. I knew that he had *laran*, well-developed, mother told me, which meant he could read me like a book, anytime he wanted to. *Well, the more fool was he that he still wanted me. Or was he? What were his motives, his real purpose? Why did he even agree to marry me?* Although he was not an Heir but a second son, there were still better prospects open for him. Indeed, anything else, including a wild banshee, was a better prospect.

One thing I am not is stupid. I knew there was something I did not yet understand here, something. I am sure that at least once in those days spent with him on the road, I read something other than cool solemn politeness in the steady gaze of his gray eyes.

As a non-telepath, I had learned to pick up these outward physical signs more acutely than if I had *laran*. It was all I could do to guide me, in those days of silence, the trip much longer than necessary, in my opinion, with endless stops along the way which I, being mountain-bred, found intolerably wasteful. What did these people do when they traveled in a hurry, I wondered?

And another thing. He was my husband, but he had not yet taken me like a husband should, not once. I had known all about *that,* seeing animals mate in the spring; I was no ignorant simple. Yet the closest I and my husband came to the lovers' way was a touch of his cool lips upon my hand, and one equally cool kiss on the cheek, immediately after our marriage ceremony—a mockery which I hated ever since.

And to all this I agreed, silently, dutifully. It was what was expected of me, of course, the only thing to do. Yet it was not what *I* expected of *myself,* for I knew myself like no other could, not even they with *laran*, who might try to know me.

Calva, Zandru's hellion, fat pig that I am, why did I agree? I am mad indeed! I thought. Yet was I not even more mad to think that I should have behaved any differently? What did I want anyway? What did I expect? I had gotten, after all, more than I had ever had right to hope for, being in my position. I was truly blessed by the Lord of Light!

Yet again, I could not help now to look up at the mocking four moons, and think, *What have I done? Whose failing is it anyway? Or, maybe, there is nothing wrong with anything, and it is only I, madder than a* kyorebni?

I was jolted out of my half-delirious thoughts as we neared, in the heavy violet twilight of the evening, the Lanart estate. There was a cold wind here in the Kilghard Hills, reminiscent of home. I savored it, the crispness. The grandeur of the Hellers was missing, however; it always will be in my mind.

At the gates we were met by several of *Dom* Cerdric's—or rather I should say—my husband's men. The courtyard was empty, except for the sound of horses and stag ponies' hooves on the cobblestones. They had carried not only us and the guards, but also all of my earthly belongings.

My husband, previously silent at my side, was greeted by animated rough voices, speaking unaccustomedly coarsely to my ears. He dismounted and spoke in reply, and for the first time I had seen him change. Life came to his voice, his eyes, and he talked excitedly in rough camaraderie, giving directions. Laughter, like a warm hearth, was all around. He was, I realized, well-loved. . . .

I was helped to dismount, and taken inside the great building. *Tomorrow I shall meet many which are now my new kin,* I thought, and dreaded it. And yet at the same time, all Gods stand me witness, I was excited,

breathless at the prospect! I had seen *Dom* Cerdric's
eyes shine bright as the moons, warm as the summer
Ghostwind, and I did not need to read his thoughts to
see that here he had known happiness, always, and
was coming back to it.

If only this happiness would touch me also.

*Bearer of Burdens, why is it that a man must do his
duty? And why must the duty always be so contrary to
his true self?*

Cerdric Lanart-Elhalyn lay sleepless, alone in his
bedchamber. The room was cold, stark, with no fire lit
to warm him, but under his thin coverlet he heeded it
not, heeded not the cold. In Nevarsin he had been
used to it, had learned to know his body to the point
of creating inner warmth. This and other things he had
learned from the monks, for he himself, since a while
ago, had found an inner calling, was *cristoforo*, and
would have pursued a life of quiet celibacy and con-
templation, if not for *this*.

He now had a wife. It was to be his life burden, that
Cerdric would do that what those he loved best wanted.
Domna Mirhana, his mother, was dying. It was a slow,
wasting malady, and every moment was filled with dull
pain. She bore it all, in her proud stoic way, and
continued strong and graceful. She was the family's
warm fireside, and he loved her more than anything in
his life, more even, it turned out, than his calling.
Mirhana Elhalyn's strongest wish had been to see him
marry and stay in the family alongside his brothers.

She also was, he thought, the only person he knew
who placed the least amount of importance on *laran*
and its development.

"We, of Hastur-kin," her soft voice would say, "are
maddened by this power, maddened to the point of
making breeding programs. And to what point? We
value *laran* over ourselves, over our children, who fall
victim to the choice. Our love—is dying out, in the

process of the choice-making. In the end, we will be a red-haired race of super-human mindless *tools* of power—like the living starstones!"

His older brother Dayvin would only grin at Mirhana, and say lovingly, "Mother, that is a ridiculous exaggeration!"

"Beside, surely we would never *get* to that point, to be—mere tools, starstones on two feet!" laughed his sister Lyanella, as she would raise her sweet face from her always perfect handiwork.

And little Rafael would break into a peal of laughter and run around the room, crying, "Look, look, I am a living matrix!" until *Domna* Mirhana would tell him to hush.

There had been joy, back then, when Jerald Lanart had been still alive, and his mother was not yet ill. *Dom* Jerald, he knew, was not his real father, despite what was officially known. Cerdric had the Alton Gift. This suggested that he might have had higher origins than he supposed, and a right to bear three names instead of two. However, he had no wish to pry, despite the occasional strange memory-thoughts he could get from his mother, or *Dom* Jerald. It had all been so long ago. . . .

Strange, then, that his mother, so perfectly just in all matters, suddenly wanted him to abandon his track of self-realization,. What he did had nothing to do with the *laran* of which she did not approve, but it was only *himself*, that he wanted to know better. Besides, he knew, she could not in all truth condemn all *laran* completely, for she herself had that elusive sense of the Elhalyns, of the different possible futures, and although she rarely spoke of it, he could see it in her. Was it this *laran* knowledge that made her insist suddenly and so oddly that he abandon his personal way to remain at her side and marry?

For it was *Domna* Mirhana that had informed him that she had found a wife for him, of Great House blood. She told him that Calvana Aldaran, daughter of her foster-sister and childhood *breda* lady Elviria, and the late Lord Korwin Aldaran, had turned fifteen this late spring, and was willing to marry.

Firm in many matters except saying "no" to his mother, Cerdric had at first protested in surprise. Mirhana knew him! Why did she then insist upon this marriage alliance? It was as if she herself was promoting that breeding program which she so hated, and of this he accused her.

And then, to his horror, he had found out something else. It was not so much that he learned that his bride was much too plump to be beautiful, or that she was not overly skilled in wifely tasks, but she had no *laran*! Mirhana could not conceal this one thing from him, as he read her thoughts. Grim, he thought of the indescribable heavy sorrow of spending all his life with one who was completely head-blind—for he was sure of that now, from what little he picked up, despite Mirhana's careful guard. And then, worst of all, he remembered that he had to love this woman, and give her children, enduring a bodily union which lacked more than half of that wholeness possible to those of his kind . . . for he had known a woman with *laran* before, known how it could be. . . .

He swore by all Zandru's Hells, then, that he no longer understood his mother. And he refused, refused to have anything to do with that accursed Aldaran bride who was dumber than any good horse he rode. But his refusal lasted only until he saw what was happening to his mother, how she began to wilt. And then he could no longer hold back.

Dayvin was Lord of Lanart now. He had married last spring, and brought home Orina Ridenow as his wife. Already, she was heavy with child. And Lyanella was to be handfasted, later this year. And now, Cerdric himself returned from the Hellers with a wife whom he could not stand, all because he did not want to bear for the rest of his life the extra burden of having shortened his mother's life.

Am I a true cristoforo *or a mere coward, a slave, to something, to some deep fears of myself?*

And Calvana Aldaran, he found out soon enough, was herself cold and proud like her godforsaken Hellers. From the first, she had not once smiled at him, or said a kind word. White-skinned, full-fleshed and dark, she was in truth not unpleasant to look at, with her sharp blue eyes which danced with energy when he pretended he was not looking. However, a dark cloud of hostility met him every time he attempted to touch her with his thoughts, the hostility mixed with bitterness and strong suppressed anger. She hated him violently, it appeared, or if not him, then hated everything, and projected it strongly and thoughtlessly as any telepath mindful of the comfort of others would never do. *But she was not a telepath!* he remembered, again and again, and a heavy sickening pain returned to torment him.

And thus that first night of their arrival at the Lanart estate, Cerdric slept with heavy thoughts, nightmare-ridden, alone, uncomforted, and in a cold bed.

He woke up late the next morning, birds singing and warm sunlight bathing the chamber. Slowly, he dressed, dragging out every moment, winter inside him.

He was purposely the last one to come down to breakfast. However, it was not as he'd hoped—the whole family was gathered there, waiting for him. They were all here, he realized, because officially, a new member was to be welcomed. He need not have bothered to delude himself that he might avoid *anything*.

It was a warm day, and they were served not in the large Hall, but in a smaller room where great windows could be opened to let in the fresh air and the sun. *Domna* Mirhana's frail form was seen drowned in a great chair beside the window, sunlight tinting her ash hair bright russet, the very shade that once it had been. Her faraway gaze was upon the open violet skies and the hills beyond.

Lord Dayvin sat at the head of the table, fair and heavy-set, with *Domna* Orina, a pretty redhead, dressed in a loose gown to hide her visible pregnancy, at his side. Between Orina and lovely-in-white Lyanella, sat his wife. She wore a simple, plain brown gown, not very becoming to her shade of hair, and her eyes were lowered.

Seeing him, Dayvin started to grin, then his smile cooled somewhat at the sight of Cerdric's heavy face. "Cerdric! Where have you been? The tea is getting cold."

"Good morning," he replied, "I am sorry." His eyes touched all but *her.*

From her chair came Mirhana's soft voice. "Come, son, at last. So you are here."

Quickly he went and embraced her, then exchanged greetings with all and took his place at the table, noting the odd arrangement—they had not placed his wife at his side.

And then he saw Rafe, his youngest brother. The boy was stuffing his cheeks with buttered bread and honey, and shyly glancing at the young girl, his new kinswoman. Once, his eyes met Cerdric's, and he smiled. How quiet everyone was!

"So," again came Mirhana's voice, "Cerdric, tell us of the journey. Calvana already told us some of it. From what I've heard, she thinks you've wasted quite some time on the way."

At lease she is honest, he thought. And then, with a glance at Calvana, he said, "My lady should have mentioned it to me then, I was only being careful for her sake."

For the first time, Calvana spoke. "*Vai dom,* I did not know the right thing to say." She raised her eyes, and he saw honesty indeed, and with it, awkwardness.

Also, he noticed, there was less anger in the thoughts coming from her.

Be kind . . . to her. Cerdric felt a thought-touch of his mother.

"Well, then," Mirhana continued, "You should have said the wrong thing, my dear. I see the two of you haven't spoken much at all during your trip. Anything, even an argument, would have been preferable to silence."

Calvana watched her in silence. "My lady? Are you saying I should have *quarreled* with your son?"

Soft laughter. "Quarrel, *chiya*? Why, you two have been in a quarrel, silently, since the start. Not a word from one of you to the other! You haven't even properly met!" Slowly, she rose forward in her chair. "I dare say, Elviria did not bother to make you friends, not a bit."

"Do not move so, mother, it might make you ill!" exclaimed Lyanella in sudden worry. She half-rose from her seat.

"Quiet, daughter, what will you have me do—die petrified? I sit still, and you fear for me, I move and you fear worse. What is one to do then?"

Rafe's eyes widened. "Oh, don't say that, mother!" He turned. "And you, 'Nella, leave mother alone! You fret like an untamed *verrin* hawk, day and night, scaring all of us. Cerdric, you wouldn't believe, while you were away, she—"

"What ails you, *Domna* Mirhana. . .?" suddenly came a tentative voice. Everyone turned to look at Calvana.

"Age, my daughter, I suppose. I have overstayed my time here. Mother Avarra only knows." Her smile was soft, kind. Calvana was suddenly reminded of Elviria in her loving moments. And she warmed to this woman, seeing in her *that* which she sought.

"My mother has been ill for some time." said Cerdric coldly. "It is the lungs."

"This milder weather is doing her good!" said Orina Ridenow, speaking for the first time. Her voice was brisk but gentle, and together with a look of love, Cerdric could feel the mental caress she sent to the older woman.

Orina would know, he thought, suddenly relieved in that point. *She has the empathy, and she had been Tower-trained also. Blessed Valentine, how good it is that everyone loves Mirhana!*

"Well, then," said Dayvin, changing the subject, "Is this family going to remain like this for the rest of the morning? I say the weather is perfect for riding, and cousin Calvana might want to try some of our good horses, and meanwhile get to know us better. Will you now, *mestra*?"

He had assumed, Cerdric noted, the tone of the head of the household.

Calvana's eyes flared with life. She suddenly smiled. "Indeed, Dom Dayvin, I would like that very much! Your fine horses are well known to us, and I would like to be better acquainted with all of you. Only—" she paused, "would everyone please stop calling me Calvana? I am Calva. Calvana was my grandmother's name, and every time I hear it, I warn you, I tend to look around for her!"

"Agreed, cousin, but only if you stop calling me '*Dom* Dayvin,' like you were my steward. I am Dayvin."

Orina laughed, then spoke in her whimsical way. "Do you know, Calva, I am going to hate you, I just know it! You've taken away my husband already!"

Calva stopped, suddenly bashful.

Damn, I did not mean to make her feel like that . . . Orina used mind-speech.

It is true, but she is still awkward, you must be more careful, flowed Mirhana's soft mind-touch.

Besides, think how horrible it must be for her to know that we can all communicate like this, talk about

her, and she would never know. Even little Rafe—he
can hear this. . . came from Lyanella.

Yes, we are all in rapport, even marginally, always
. . . thought Cerdric. Yet strangely unbending, as
though something held him stiff, he refused to con-
cede any warmth, not now.

"All right, go on, all of you," said Mirhana then, in
the normal way, "Enough, you are giving me a headache. Go ride in the hills, but return in time for dinner."

And then, breakfast was over. They rose, Dayvin
giving orders to saddle the horses, while Orina graciously declined to go with them, due to her obvious
condition.

They rode, breathless, at the foot of the hills, and
Cerdric was surprised to notice how well his wife sat in
the saddle despite her girth. In fact, he realized, she
was better at it than all of them.

Calva was quickly on kin terms with Dayvin and
Lyanella, but there was also something childish about
her that made her at times seem oddly most fitting as
Rafe's companion—and truly, the boy was bewitched
by her laughter, by everything she said.

She spoke much and quickly. And she was brilliant.
Whether she talked with Dayvin about the breeding of
horses, with Lyanella of embroidery—which she immediately admitted to dislike greatly—or explained to
little Rafael how to carve a manikin out of wood, she
appeared to know everything on the subject. And
also, she managed to make everyone laugh at least
once over her clever turn of phrase.

The only person she ignored was Cerdric.

It was almost as if Calva had set out to charm all,
and thus to show them that she did not care what he
thought of her, did not need *him.* The few words she
did speak to him were not rude, but so blank that they
managed to insult merely by their absentmindedness.

And Cerdric knew that in all these ways she had
succeeded. Not only was he angered, but he could

read the beginnings of affection in everyone's thoughts, and once Orina even paused, stumbling upon his own telepathic displeasure, and in surprise questioned: *Is something wrong? Why aren't you pleased with her?*

To that he had nothing to say, and only resolved to tighten his barriers so that no other private thought might leak through to the others.

What is the matter with me, Bearer of Burdens, what? I know I must love, but I can't. I cannot feel love. And how can I, when she—

But he knew not what he meant, how he wanted to end that thought. Later that day, at dinner, he was glum and silent, so that even Domna Mirhana commented that he was making her lose appetite just at the sight of such a long dog-face.

For once, hearing his mother's rough-gentle manner of joking which he had always loved, Cerdric did not care.

"Tell me, *chiya*, how do you like it here?" Domna Mirhana asked me after a tenday had passed since our arrival. I did not quite know how to tell her the whole truth. Fact was, I both loved and hated this place which was now my new home. This, I knew, she could find out with her *laran* easily, and that was what frightened me. How was I to explain that I had already come to love these people, these kinsmen, in that short time that I've known them, come to love their warm openness and easy welcome, never knowing the like of such at home, while at the same time I dreaded the fact that they pitied me? I needed no *laran* to tell me that, for I could see it in their exceeding carefulness in treating me kindly. Almost, I wanted to hear sharp words, to tell me they knew I was human, simply accepted me as I was. And yet, that I was not to have.

And my husband? It was strange at first, but we had quickly fallen in a routine which no one questioned—we politely and coldly ignored each other. It was almost humorous, how things came to be, to the point that we almost forgot about the copper marriage bracelets on our wrists. In the household we were the only and the strangest of strangers.

Only, one thing made me wonder: why was it that no one had tried to bring us together? Did they not care that we had not even shared a bridal bed—all were perfectly aware of this. What then, had been the purpose of this union? I was sure that material wealth had the least to do with it, since both our families had been proud of our high standing and riches. And even less had *laran*! What then?

I could not bear the sight of Dom Cerdric. He, I soon learned, was *cristoforo*, and if not for me, would have made a monk at Nevarsin—that was the best explanation I could get for his almost dainty aversion of me, which I felt quite well. I have heard of their creed; one of their monks' beliefs had been *never to look with lewdness on women,* or something to that extent. I respected their religion of spiritual love, but did not fully understand it, nor wanted to. I was not of the *cristoforo* mold.

And that is why I was angered even farther, having to endure Cerdric's handsome gaunt face, and read the clear disgust in his eyes. I could almost sympathize with his aversion, for I saw that he had to force himself greatly, go against his nature. But then, the sight of me would make anyone sick, including myself. It was I that was making him hate instead of love, and also, it was his kin. That was the one thing I could truly grudge them, for they were the cause of all of this—this mockery.

The others, however, had in one way or another, accepted me. The boy Rafael—if I did not know better, I would say he worshiped me. I believe I entertained him well like an older sister. Once I had sat down to show him how to capture a likeness of beast or man upon paper—he was open-mouthed, and I ended up drawing everyone in the family. When the older family members saw it, especially Domna Orina, I was surrounded by exclamations of wonder and praise, and many questions. It seemed I had indeed duplicated their likeness too well. I assured them no one taught me how to do it, and then, Orina started asking me other questions.

I finally managed to make a joke of it. Later I talked again with Domna Mirhana.

These talks of ours were becoming quite regular, she in her great chair, I perched at her feet, like a child, on a footstool.

"How sharp-sighted you are, child." she would say, "You see things precisely as they are. A rare talent. It is almost as precious as *laran*."

At that word, I suppose, I winced. She looked at me steadily, saying, "Does it pain you greatly, my child, not to have *laran*?"

Silently, I nodded. Then, "More than anything, Domna. I feel—I *know* I am almost handicapped."

"And so you make up for it by excelling in everything else."

"I, excel?" I laughed, "But I can do nothing right! Women's handiwork wilts in my hands! My embroidery stitches are like the step of a drunk harlot! My knitting—"

"Oh, but that is only because you have no will, no true desire to pursue those tasks. Indeed, your *kihar* feed itself by rebellion, so you strive to be like a man."

"I, never! I—"

"Yes, you think yourself unattractive, so you charm with your tongue. You hate yourself for not having *laran*, and therefore you eat, and eat, and therefore, look at you!"

"Yes, I am a fat cow! A pig! I know that!"

"Then stop wallowing in self-pity, girl! Zandru knows,

you do not need that extra burden—in every sense of the word—upon you!"

She had moved forward, staring sharply at me, and the growing lump in my throat was choking.

"Aldones, help me . . ." I whispered. And then, tears came. I was within a flood of lonely pain, stifling all around. "I—I hate everything!" I stammered, then cried, "I hate you, and your son, and your mockery of hills! I want to go home . . . or die!"

And then, as I looked up, there were tears in the eyes of Domna Mirhana. *Gods! She knows! She knows exactly how I feel, everything,* I remembered. *And— and she is hurting also, hurting with me, with my own pain added to her own!*

I was a selfish bitch to have been so blind! *Domna Mirhana knows exactly what pain is, and she is dying. Gods!* I thought, suddenly, *What have I done!*

And then it came to me, I must ease her pain, I must make her happy! Her last days will not be spent in silence, no—for I knew then, as surely as if I had *laran* that she would be gone soon—no, I swore, I will do something, bring her joy, in whatever way I can.

With loud sobs I came to hug her frail form, and for a while, we wept together. "I am sorry . . . oh, I am sorry!" I cried between sobs. "Forgive my words, oh, I did not mean . . ."

"I know, you did not. I know, *chiya*. And I was too harsh with you. It is just that it is so hard to see you live in that kind of self-inflicted pain—"

"But you, too, *you* live in pain!" I exclaimed. "And why isn't anyone doing anything about it? Why do they walk around pretending that if they ignore this, you will improve, all by yourself?"

"I am beyond help, *chiya*. They have tried." And as if to add to her words, she coughed raspingly.

"I cannot believe that!" I persisted. Her kind eyes were on me, gentle.

"Domna," I suddenly said then, "How would you like to hear some music? Tonight, here?"

Her brows rose at the change of topic, then a smile came to her eyes. "I have not heard music for a long time . . ." she said musingly.

"I play the *rryl*." I said, "And sing. A little."

And then, she probably picked it up from my thoughts, and she shook her head. "Putting your accomplishments down again, are you? I will have none of that! So, you shall play and sing, for all of us, tonight."

Cerdric learned that Calvana was to entertain them that night, and not only was he displeased, but angry. "Just what mother needs," he mocked to Lyanella, "Noise to disturb her, in her condition. When *my lady* does something, she does it *thoroughly*." "Besides, I believe I will, unfortunately, be unable to stay for this treat. I have unfinished business to do—"

"Oh, Cerdric," Lyanella interrupted his bitterness. "Will you for once *try*, bend yourself to oblige *her*, once? Why can't you try to befriend her, try—"

"I am sure Domna Calvana does not need my friendship. I am sorry, *breda*."

His thoughts were guarded. Lyanella sensed it was futile to attempt knowing more, for he was the family's most powerful telepath, and his anger, she knew, could maim, or if necessary, kill.

Dayvin, however, came to her rescue. "Brother," he said, in the most convincing voice—and he could be quite formidable—"I insist, this time, that you not pile this one more insult upon others. The two of you have insulted one another too much, already. Do this, I say, for your mother's sake. You are *cristoforo*, then bring us unity. There is enough dissension in this family." And then he added: "Besides, as Lord of Lanart, I command it."

Cerdric's thought-touch was sardonic and bitter. *Brother, you leave me no choice. . . .*

After dinner, Calva was less talkative than usual, and then later went upstairs shyly to bring her *rryl*.

Mirhana was helped gingerly to her seat by Lyanella, while Rafael chattered excitedly to Dayvin that "cousin Calva was to sing for them!"

Indeed, everything cousin Calva does is great in his eyes, thought Cerdric. And then, with bitter irony, *Truly, she has usurped my place here. . . .*

He watched his wife's return with distaste, seating himself far away from the newly-lit fire, twilight on his face. In the firelight, Lyanella's face and red-blond hair glowed with a *chieri* delicacy; Orina was lovely, too, in her robust way. And his mother, he thought, his mother was loveliest of all, with her great expressive eyes in a noble hollowed face, made otherworldly by her disease.

Calva returned. Tonight, he noted with some surprise, she was dressed differently, more becomingly, and her dark hair held by a butterfly-clasp glowed like red coals. Once, she turned her profile to the fire, and her half-lit face was truly striking—something strong and haunting in her eyes, and a new seriousness replaced her usual bright liveliness.

Why, she is not ungainly at all . . . he suddenly realized, watching her move, for there was grace in her full figure, her height compensating for it. And when at some point she looked at him, his eyes met hers, for once, in full. He turned away, for the first time uncomfortable, not having the usual hostility to shield himself.

Her *rryl* was of fine quality wood, and she removed it gingerly from its casing, then tuned it. Abruptly, then, she was embarrassed before them all, like that first time.

"How lovely . . ." remarked Orina at the *rryl*.

Rafe's eyes shone. "What will you sing, Calva?"

Calvana turned to Domna Mirhana. "Lady, what shall I sing? What do you want to hear?"

"Oh, anything . . . *chiya.* Something old and . . . sad."

Gravely, she nodded. "Well, then. I will sing of the Hellers—of my home." Touching fingers to the strings, she began:

> Great ice-winds blow, the day is done,
> Sinks in ice-cliffs the bloody sun,
> Still, long the trail ahead of us,
> Again, we brave the treacherous pass . . .

It was not the simple words of the song, nor the wild and plaintive mountain melody that made them all pause, suddenly—it was the voice. It tore through them with an intensity of a sharp knife, actually physically painful. And then, it burned like fire. For a moment, Cerdric was not even sure what kind of voice it was, alto or soprano, beautiful or ugly. It just *was.* And then, he began to *feel.*

Sweeter than anything he had ever known, was the wind in the Hellers, cold, inevitable. And the wind was himself. He flew in a rush of madness, struck against the sparkling ice of the mountains, which at the same odd moment, was also himself. He was a majestic range of ice and rock, a wasteland, and within him drowned tiny specks of warm life, the humans, struggling—

> Alone I stood, the place so steep,
> And watched her fall into the deep.
> Her cry, once echoed, was done,
> And silent sank the bloody sun . . .

And with the red sun, he sank, burning and majestic. He fell to his death at the bottom of the cliff, and he stood, alone, and watched his beloved thrown to

her death, his heart breaking, while tears rolled, like
great diamonds, down his cheeks, and were frozen by
the icy wind. . . .

Cerdric jerked into awareness suddenly, feeling his
face wet with tears, while the inhuman voice continued, and he heard her sing in an odd stereophonic
manner, both physically and telepathically, a siren,
and then, once again he was wrenched from himself,
and drawn. . . .

The song ended. Dayvin and Lyanella were sob-
bing. Rafe's face was contorted with fear, and Orina's
was hidden in her hands, while her shoulders shook.
Mirhana alone seemed as stonelike as before. Only
when Cerdric glanced into her eyes, did he see trails of
tears running down her face.

Mother Avarra, what was that! came from Dayvin.
What did she do to us?

It is laran, *it must be!*

The same thought passed through everyone's mind.
Calva meanwhile watched them in surprise and fear.
"What? What have I done?" she stammered, "Why—"

"Sing again, child!" suddenly whispered Mirhana,
harshly. "Sing a happy song!"

And the girl, no longer knowing what was happening, could only obey. Quickly she struck the *rryl* strings,
a dance beat, and the voice came again.

Only this time, suddenly, Cerdric wanted to laugh.
It was about two misunderstanding lovers, and he was
in every nuance of the song, every ridiculous, silly,
joyful moment, and he wanted to scream at their
antics, scream with laughter. And so, he laughed—
openly, simply, unroariously—at himself.

When the song ended, quicker than the first, they
were all gasping for breath, sides aching with laughter,
joy dancing inside. And suddenly, everyone paused,
because they realized that Mirhana was half out of her
chair, bent over in a fit of giggling mirth. *Oh, my
children, this is joy! Yes, joy is back, is with us now!*

"Yes, I am all right, daughter," she reassured Lyanella, and they all knew that, truly, she was better than she had been in a long time.

"Come here, *chiya*, let me kiss you, my joy!" She said, turning to Calva, who all this time watched in minor amazement.

"But—nothing has ever happened like this before, when I sang . . ."

And then she saw Cerdric. He was watching her with glistening eyes, and his face blushed and paled repeatedly.

Suddenly, he said, "Thank you . . . domna. And forgive me." And then he quickly turned on his heel and left.

Domna Mirhana held Calvana close, and whispered, "And I, I thank you, too. Not only for myself, but for my own son."

And suddenly, through a warm cloud of love, coming from all of them, Calva knew why.

"You have *laran*, *chiya*." I was told. "You are not telepathic, but your *laran* manifests itself through your voice. You have Ridenow blood, don't you?" spoke Mirhana.

"I think so . . ." I answered.

"Well, it is the Ridenow Gift that you have then, oddly convoluted, a hybrid of sorts. Through your voice you make others feel exactly how you want them to feel, a kind of empathy. Ironic, that so far you have been using an extension of this Gift to make some adore you—like Rafael—and others—like my son Cerdric—dislike you, or look down upon you. That is exactly how you wanted Cerdric to see you, in order to feed your self-pity, and he did, spurred on further by his own *kihar*."

And then she grew silent. "That, *chiya*, is why I married off the two of you, to each other. *Kihar*. His, and unknowingly, yours. I have the Elhalyn *laran* of—

seeing different futures, possibilities. It rarely works well when I look upon those close to me, but once— once I *saw* Cedric. And what I saw were only two possibilities—either he was married to a plump girl with dark red hair, or he—or he was a human *monster*. For I saw him first with the *cristoforos*, and then he left them and turned perverted, cold and cruel, and proud. . . . and he caused misfortune, *horror*—"

She broke off. "No matter. In any case, I knew always, Cedric would make no true *cristoforo* monk. It is not in his nature—he is too proud. Again I repeat the word, *kihar*. An odd thing, that. Both good and bad, and every man and woman has it, for it is our inevitable sense of dignity, you *must* have *kihar*. Yet *kihar*, when not balanced by proper humility and sympathy toward others, can be the greatest scourge. It becomes a self-destructive force. It eats a man alive. . . .

"Only I knew that somehow, you would save him from being eaten alive, from becoming that horror."

"And did I. . .?" I asked tentatively.

"Time will tell all," said Mirhana.

"I apologized to him also," I said, "but he still hates me. . . ."

"Oh, no, daughter. Like you, he only hates himself."

And somehow, I believed her. However, it was much, much later that Cedric told me himself.

"Your voice . . ." he said, looking at me with gray eyes full of promise, "it awakened something. You made me truly *see* others and myself, and all things. And," he added, "yourself."

"And you are not sickened, husband?" I asked, so jokingly and meaningfully, that he burst into laughter.

"Oh, no, Calva. *Vai Domna*. How *can* I be, after I have *seen* you?"

"I don't know, but I certainly can be!" I exclaimed, continuing in the same joke manner.

"Stop it!" he suddenly said, sharply, and I could feel

a pain in his eyes. "Don't ever say that about yourself again, Domna, *ever*! Not even in mockery. . . ."

"And do you care?" I flared.

"Yes," he cried, "yes, I do!"

And looking at his eyes, pained for me, I had for the first time truly, sincerely, believed him, or anyone else, for that matter.

It was then, I think, that my own *kihar* broke and was forged anew.

Playfellow

by Elisabeth Waters

Elisabeth Waters, better known as Lisa, first appeared in Darkover fandom as the author of "The Keeper's Price," a short story which gave the title to the first Darkover anthology; like Diana Paxson, she may be said to dwell legitimately on Darkover. She has written several stories (which may someday surface as a novel) about the still-minor character Hilary Castamir, who appears briefly in THE FORBIDDEN TOWER and in THENDARA HOUSE. I've always liked Hilary—I, too, wrote a couple of stories about her, especially "The Lesson of the Inn" in SWORD OF CHAOS—and was delighted to read one of her early adventures.

Lisa is a computer programmer by trade, and has had stories published in THE KEEPER'S PRICE, SWORD OF CHAOS, GREYHAVEN, SWORD AND SORCERESS III, and FREE AMAZONS OF DARKOVER, as well as Andre Norton's anthology MAGIC IN ITHKAR. She lives at Greenwalls, has spent several years making Order out of the Chaos of the Darkover/MZB Enterprises business, and is about to abandon her work as a programmer to write full time. She has nearly finished her first novel—based on the character introduced in her story "A Woman's Priv-

*ilege" in SWORD AND SORCERESS III (DAW 1986).
I've read it and am sure you'll soon share the privilege
of reading it. It's good. (MZB)*

The trouble with working in a Tower, Damon Ridenow
thought ruefully, *is that some things are impossible to
keep secret, and our resident "ghost" definitely falls
into that category.*

Fortunately the circle had finished its night's work
before ten-year-old Hilary Castamir, their newest technician, had voiced her desire for some dried fruit. Not
that this was at all unreasonable; it was customary to
eat something sweet after the grueling matrix work—
but it was unusual for a bar of pressed dried fruit to
suddenly materialize on the table under the eyes of six
startled *leroni.* And Hilary clearly hadn't teleported it
there; she was so tired she was barely able to murmur
thanks, pick it up and chew on it.

Damon, who had been working as monitor for the
circle, quickly went to the cupboard to get fruit bars
for the rest of the circle. He handed the first one to
Leonie, Keeper of Arilinn Tower, as always being
careful not to touch her. He was dismayed to see that
her hand was trembling.

She shouldn't be this tired, he thought, using his
laran to check her condition more closely; as monitor,
he was responsible for the physical well-being of the
people in the circle. Her heart was beating more rapidly than normal, her breathing was quicker than it
should have been, and she was watching Hilary, who
sat innocently munching on her fruit bar, with real
dread. *She's afraid,* Damon realized in shock. *Leonie
is afraid of the ghost—or whatever it is.*

But Leonie was a proud, strong, self-controlled
woman. She dismissed the members of the circle to
their beds in a calm voice, and only Damon guessed
how much effort it cost her.

*   *   *

Damon went to bed deeply troubled. He loved Leonie, despite his attempts to convince himself that his feelings were merely the respect due the Lady of Arilinn. To him, Leonie was Arilinn; he could not imagine a Tower without her. He wanted nothing more than to see her well and happy. *And if that means getting rid of this ghost,* he thought, *so be it.*

Having come to this resolve, he slept, heedless of the sun rising past his window.

Damon woke in the late afternoon, confused by fleeting fragments of a dream in which he had been running away from Nevarsin Monastery—wearing only a light tunic and barefoot in the snow, of all silly things. The dream had been terrifyingly real, but his conscious mind promptly dismissed it for the nonsense it was. He had never even been to Nevarsin; his family was not *cristoforo*. He had been taught at home until it was time for him to do his stint as a cadet and then officer in the Comyn Guard. He had not been much of a soldier, but he had done his best with the role expected of a Comyn son. But nobody had been more relieved than he when he proved to have enough *laran* to enter service at Arilinn Tower at the age of seventeen. His years here had been happy ones; his fellow *leroni* were all the friends and family he needed, and he was a top matrix technician.

He dressed and went to the conservatory to enjoy what remained of the afternoon sun. As he approached, he heard a girl's voice softly singing an old ballad, and when he entered the room he saw Hilary sitting in the middle of the floor playing jackstones against herself. At least, he hoped so—there was no one else in the room, so the two uneven piles of stones must both belong to her.

"Hello, Hilary," he smiled at her. "Would you like another player?"

"Please," Hilary replied, looking up at him. "But I

hope you're at least a little bit out of practice; Gregori's been beating me all afternoon."

"Gregori?" Damon sat on the floor beside her. Strange, both piles of stones had been pushed together in one heap, but he hadn't seen Hilary touch them.

"Don't you know Gregori?" Hilary asked, puzzled. "He's been around ever since I came to Arilinn."

"Who or what is Gregori?" Damon demanded.

"Well," Hilary struggled for words, "he's just Gregori." She thought a moment, then added, "He finds things when people lose them."

"And produces dried fruit bars on demand?"

"Request." Hilary corrected him primly. "It's not polite to demand things."

"True enough," Damon conceded. *This is a crazy conversation.* "Where did he come from?"

"I don't know," Hilary said. "He's been here longer than I have." She gathered up the jackstones, tossed them deftly from palm to back of hand, and started her turn.

They played in silence for Hilary's turn and then Damon's turn, but when he handed the ball back to her after his turn, she said, "No, it's Gregori's turn," and held out the ball. to Damon's amazement, *something* took the ball from her fingers, tossed the jackstones, and set the ball to bouncing.

Hilary is right, Damon thought dazedly as he watched, trying to believe what he was seeing. *Whatever it is, it's a terrific jackstone player.*

"If you want to know where Gregori came from," Hilary said, returning to their conversation, "why don't you ask him?"

Why not? Damon thought. Aloud he said, "Gregori, where did you come from?" Feeling like a fool, he listened, but heard nothing but the bouncing of the ball. He looked questioningly at Hilary.

"Can't you hear him?" she asked. Damon shook his

head. "Oh," she frowned, "that's odd. I wonder why not. Anyway, he said 'Nevarsin.' "

Fortunately for what remained of Damon's peace of mind, they were interrupted before he had a chance to consider the implications of Gregori's origin combined with his dream. Floria, the circle's third technician, came in and said, "Damon, Leonie wants to see us."

Leonie, as it turned out, wished to discuss Hilary. "She's made great progress in the short time she's been with us, and I believe that we can make a Keeper of her."

Damon bit back an instinctive protest. Being a Keeper, as they all knew, was a hard life, and Hilary was just a child. Of course, Leonie had presumably been a child once, difficult as this now was to imagine.

Floria did protest. "It's really to soon to tell, and you can't begin training her seriously until her woman's cycles have started and become established."

"It is true that this is firmly decreed by custom," Leonie replied, "but we are in desperate need of Keepers in these days, and you well know, Floria, how many girls fail in the training." Damon knew, too; he had seen five of them in the time he'd been at Arilinn. "While I certainly am limited in the amount of training I can do while she is still a child, I believe that it is worthwhile to begin the training now. If nothing else, it will give her time to accustom herself mentally to being a Keeper; that may be enough to ensure that she succeeds."

"It may." Floria sounded thoughtful. "And she may mature sooner than we expect; she seems lately to be manifesting poltergeist activity—remember the fruit bar this morning?"

Leonie frowned. "I don't feel poltergeist activity is a sign of a future Keeper—and I don't think she produced the fruit bar, aside from asking for it."

"But what else could it be?" Floria asked.

"I don't know," Leonie replied, "and it worries me.

I don't want anything in this Tower that I don't understand; it's too dangerous with the work we do."

"For what it's worth," Damon volunteered, "she says it's somebody named Gregori, he's been here longer than she has, and he came from Nevarsin."

Both women looked at him incredulously. "Nevarsin?" Floria said. "Nevarsin doesn't train telepaths. Furthermore, if this Gregori is a person, where is he? He's obviously not on the physical plane, and I don't remember seeing anyone strange in the Overworld."

Leonie was more practical. "Well, if she can communicate with him, well and good. Damon, I want you to work with her, find out what this 'Gregori' is, and get rid of it. We need her too badly as a Keeper to have her playing around with—" she paused, uncertain, "—whatever this is. I'll excuse both you and Hilary from the Circle, after tonight's working, so you can devote your time and energy to this, but please deal with it as quickly as possible. You're both needed in the Circle."

Damon didn't worry about Gregori again until early the next morning; the work of the matrix circle didn't leave room to think about anything else. Hilary was monitor that night, so Gregori had no reason to teleport anything across the room to her, and Damon was quite sure that he was the only one seated so as to see that the tray of dried fruit met her halfway when she went to get it.

"Hilary?" He opened his mouth to tell her about their assignment, paused to chew a mouthful of his portion of dried fruit, and abruptly decided that dealing with Hilary and Gregori could wait until he'd had some sleep. "Leonie has excused us from tomorrow's Circle; there's some research she wants us to do instead. Will you please wake me at midafternoon, if I'm not up by then?"

"Surely, Damon," Hilary nodded sleepily. "I'll see you then."

Damon dragged himself off to bed, collapsed into it, and promptly fell into a nightmare.

He was a young boy, wearing a rough homespun tunic, sitting on a bed in some sort of dormitory. All around him were boys, some younger than he was and some a year or so older and starting to grow hair on their faces. Three of the largest were confronting him.

"You think you're so smart, bastard—well, you're not, you're nothing! Son of a woman too stupid to know who fathered her child—"

"If she looked anything like him, she was too ugly for anybody who lay with her to be willing to tell her his name! Look at that hair on him—he looks like he crawled out of Zandru's tenth hell!"

"Or maybe from under a rock," the third giggled.

Damon sat there and kept quiet; part of him knew that if he ignored them they'd get tired after a while and leave him alone. But suddenly the biggest boy looked at him differently; the game was changing its rules.

"Of course, if he were a girl, he might be passable, in a delicate sort of way."

His followers obviously didn't understand, but they tried to play along anyway. "I don't know," one of them said, "he looks more like an icicle than anything else."

"Icicles can melt," the first boy replied, "if they get hot enough." He reached out toward Damon.

Damon felt something, some energy, pass through him. He wasn't sure what it was; it wasn't *laran*, exactly, and it wasn't threshold sickness, though it felt somewhat like it. He felt his body rise to its feet and heard his voice say, "If you want heat—"

The tunic of the boy facing him went up in flames. Damon was conscious of a strong sense of satisfaction, of rightness. It was right that the bully should be running around the room screaming as the flames seared his flesh; this was what he had wanted, wasn't it? He'd been hot, and searching for an answering fire in Damon, hadn't he?

The other boys were screaming, too, and the novice master came running in and rolled the boy in a blanket to smother the flames. As they went out, the force holding Damon in place released him, and he sat down abruptly on the bed.

The prior arrived, alerted by all the noise. A dozen boys hastened to tell him that "it was all Gregori's fault, Bevin was just talking to him, honest, and he set him on fire, he's a devil—"

The prior shook them off without a word, and stalked over to the cot where Damon was still sitting, thoroughly confused. Was he Gregori, then?

The prior grabbed him by one shoulder, his bony grip painful on unhealed bruises that Damon hadn't noticed before. Still saying nothing, although his face was an eloquent indicator of his distaste, he dragged Damon/Gregori to the front gate of the monastery and flung him forth. "Go join your father in hell, boy; it's plain you don't belong among those who follow the Holy Bearer of Burdens." He slammed the gate shut.

Damon rose to his feet and stumbled down the road warmed by the late afternoon sun. *At least*, he thought, *I don't need to worry about direction; from Nevarsin all roads lead south.*

And another voice inside him said, *I don't want to go to hell; I'm going to Arilinn.* So Damon—or Gregori—headed toward Arilinn.

He walked, putting one foot in front of the other. He was soon out of Nevarsin and walking alone down the road. It was getting dark when he heard a troop of riders coming along behind him. He hid behind a tree, so they wouldn't see him. He didn't want anyone to see him; they'd only be angry at him, everyone got angry at him. . . .

It was getting dark quickly now, but Damon thought that the riders were women, all wearing crimson tunics like some sort of uniform. They passed too quickly for him to be sure though, and he went back to the road, once they were out of sight, and continued to walk south. It was cold, but three of the moons were out so there was light enough to walk.

He walked quickly so that the cold wouldn't get him; he walked until he was too tired for the cold to bother him; he walked until he was falling over with weariness. He crawled off into a hollow at the side of the road and slept. As he fell asleep some small bit of his mind told him he shouldn't sleep in the snow, but he was too tired to care.

When he woke things were gray and foggy; he couldn't see much of anything other than the road. But he could make out the road quite clearly, and he felt much better. His body didn't ache and wasn't cold and didn't seem to slow him down at all. He went on down the road, and on, and on, and on. . . .

The road seemed to last forever, and he'd lost track of how long he'd been following it, but finally he saw it—Arilinn Tower, gleaming in the sun, the most beautiful sight in all the world.

And Hilary was calling him. "Damon? Damon, wake up! Damon, you told me to wake you up at midafternoon."

He pried grainy eyelids open and looked up at her. The view from his window was shadowed, which meant the sun had moved to the other side of the tower. *It must be quite late in the afternoon,* he thought, struggling to orient himself.

"Hilary?" She was looking at him, obviously concerned. "Go down to the kitchen and get me some *jaco*, will you?" She nodded quickly and left. Damon dragged himself out of bed and managed to get some clothes on before she returned, bearing a tray with a pitcher of steaming liquid and a mug. Damon took it gratefully, collapsed in one chair with it, and waved her to another.

She curled up, kittenlike, wrapping her skirts around her feet. "What's happening, Damon? What does Leonie want us to do?"

"She's worried about Gregori, Hilary. Being new to the Tower, you may not realize it, but it is not the custom for a Tower to have a resident poltergeist."

Hilary sat for a moment with her head a bit to one side, obviously listening. "He says he's not going back to Nevarsin. They don't like him there." She frowned and continued on her own, "Why doesn't Leonie like him?"

"Leonie doesn't dislike him; she's merely concerned that he's interfering with your training. She wants to train you as a Keeper."

Hilary's eyes opened wide. "Me? A Keeper?" Her voice was reverent, as if they were offering to make her Queen in Thendara. Well, Keeper of Arilinn was just as high a rank.

"And she's concerned for him, too," Damon went on, suddenly remembering something. "Hilary, ask him who the women were on the road, the ones in the red tunics."

Hilary listened, looking blank. "What's the Sisterhood of the Sword?" She shook her head. "No, I don't know; I've never heard of them." She listened for several minutes, then turned to Damon. "They seem to be something like the Renunciates."

"Hilary," Damon said gently, "Gregori, the Sisterhood of the Sword hasn't been in existence for over two hundred years."

"But Gregori's not that old!" Hilary protested.

"Gregori's dead," Damon said softly. "He died the first night on the road from Nevarsin. Remember, Gregori? You lay down in the hollow beside the road and fell asleep, and when you woke up you were dead, but you were so determined to get to Arilinn that you didn't notice. You didn't have the experience to realize that you'd left your body behind you and come on without it."

"Is that why nobody can see him?" Hilary asked in a small voice.

"Yes, that's why," Damon replied.

"What do we do now?" Hilary asked, and added, "Gregori wants to know."

"If you'll monitor for me, Hilary, I'll go out of body, meet him, and lead him to where he belongs now."

"Is it a bad place?" she asked anxiously.

"No," Damon reassured them. "Not at all."

"Can I come, too?" Hilary asked.

Damon shook his head. "I need you to monitor me; Leonie would be very cross with us both if I went out without a monitor. And where Gregori is going is too dangerous a place for the living; you don't have enough training yet to return safely."

"When I'm a Keeper, I'll be able to," she said. It was a statement, not a question.

"Yes, then. But not now."

"All right." Hilary rose and dragged her chair over to the bed, while Damon lay down and arranged his body so that it would function during his absence. As he slipped free, he could hear Hilary thinking, *But I'm going to miss Gregori.*

He saw Gregori almost immediately, a small fragile boy with pale white hair dressed in a finer version of the rough tunic he had worn at Nevarsin.

"You say I've been dead for more than two centuries," he said. 'Why do I have to leave now? I don't want to leave Hilary; she'll miss me."

"Yes, she will miss you," Damon agreed readily. "And I'll miss you, and even Leonie will miss you. You should be missed; nobody ought to die unnoticed and unmourned. But your work here is done, and your place is elsewhere now." He pointed to a glow in the distance. "We go that way." He started slowly toward the light, and after a brief pause, Gregori followed him.

They walked, or perhaps floated, for a time, then Gregori spoke. "Will you take care of Hilary for me?"

"Hilary's growing up, Gregori; she can take care of herself. But I shall certainly be her friend."

"Is she still allowed to have friends if she's a Keeper?"

"If she allows herself to, yes," Damon said, thinking of Leonie, who didn't seem to think she was allowed to have anyone.

"I hope she will," Gregori said. "She's nice. I liked her." He didn't seem to notice he'd used the past tense. "It's getting warmer," he added in surprise. "I've been cold for so long." He looked around him. "It's so beautiful—can you hear the singing?"

Damon could, very faintly, and he knew it was time for him to turn back. Already he was beginning to feel he could stay here forever, soaking in the warmth and the light, listening to the singing until he learned enough to join in . . . he shook himself. "Can you find your way from here, Gregori?"

"Oh, yes," Gregori said absently. "Give my love to Hilary. Fare well, Damon."

"Fare thee well, Gregori."

"I shall." Gregori passed him, heading farther into the light. Damon caught himself starting to follow him, wanting to follow him. He shook his head violently.

He was back in his own body, with his head aching as if it were being split apart, feeling as if he'd fallen all the way back.

Hilary was bending over him. "You look awful!" she whispered. Damon was very glad she was having that much consideration for his headache.

"It's hard to get back from there." He whispered, too. "Gregori sends you his love. He's found where he belongs, and he's happy."

"I'm glad," Hilary said. "But I will miss him." Her

gray eyes filled with tears. "Now I won't have anyone to play with."

"You should miss him," Damon agreed. "Nobody should die unmissed— No wonder he didn't realize he was dead."

"Do you suppose Leonie will miss him?"

"I'm sure of it," Damon said. *No need to say that she'll be happy to miss him.*

Hilary brightened. "If I'm a Keeper, I won't have time to play with Gregori anyway. But I'm still going to miss him."

"Me, too," Damon said, surprised to realize that he truly would.

Different Path

by Penny Buchanan

In the guidelines which I send out every year making suggestions for the current anthology, I suggest a few stories to which I am not receptive. For this anthology I suggested a moratorium on Free Amazon stories, especially since we had just done an anthology devoted to Free Amazons, and it seemed to me that our male readers might be feeling neglected. I suggested that Free Amazons were OK as characters, but that stories dealing particularly with the problems of being a Free Amazon were not especially wanted.

However, when Penny Buchanan appeared in my yearly Short Story Writing intensive class, it was my pleasure to tell her that the story she'd sent had been selected.

Free Amazon stories still outnumber all the other subjects put together; and not all of them are written by women. I assume from this that they are popular with all readers, not only women; and this one struck me as an interesting adventure, dealing as it did with two favorite characters, Camilla and Rafaella.

Penny Buchanan, asked for biographical details, gave me a list of the kind of jobs usually suitable only for a Free Amazon; she's worked, among other startling things, as an arc welder; she also told me stories of a psychic cat; unfortunately, the slip of paper on which I filed this information has disappeared into the black hole on the desk—or did Penny's psychic cat teleport it into our local time warp? Whatever may have happened to it, I'm sure you'll enjoy this adventure as I did.(MZB)

I think the time warp had it; I found it on top of the table she was working at, right smack dab in the middle—even though it was face down. In addition to being a welder, Penny was also a Marine and a truck driver, and she holds a B.S. in Archaeology.(EW)

Head cocked to one side, Reba listened. Farther down the trail she could hear the clash of sword on sword. Squinting up at the lowering red sun, she sighed. "It's too damn late in the day to play hero." Nevertheless, she tightened her grip on the pack chervine's rein and kicked her horse into a fast trot. Coming around a bend, Reba saw a man on foot fighting off two men. The man's copper hair blazed bright against the dark granite boulder at his back. The other two were a scruffy pair of thieves. Throwing back her cloak, Reba drew her blade and engaged one of the bandits. With the sudden evening of the odds, the pair took off through the woods, cursing, but glad to have their skins in one piece.

The man slumped back against the rock to catch his breath. Reba eyed him. "That's a nasty slash on your thigh." Going to her saddle bags, she pulled out a small jar of salve and a roll of bandage. Dropping them in his lap, she said, "Wrap it up and I'll see if I can find your mount."

After a brief search she found the horse and, while leading it back, she noticed the fine leatherwork and ornaments of the bridle and saddle. *So "Red-Head" is a man of means. Comyn, no doubt.*

"Here she is, Red-Head, and none the worse for your adventure. Some free advice—travel in these parts is easier if you don't display your wealth." Reba turned to gather her reins and mount up.

"Wait a minute!" he called. "Who are you? I would like to know who to thank for the timely aid." He saw a young woman, tall, well-formed, dressed in a set of well-worn trail leathers, high boots, and a heavy fur-trimmed, hooded cloak. The pushed-back hood revealed a face that was handsome in its strength, firm about the mouth and chin, with just a hint of a wry smile tugging at the corners. Deep green eyes, though sober now, looked as though they could blaze or twinkle at their owner's whim. Dark curly hair with red highlights worn shoulder length, completed the picture.

"Reba is how I am called, but I'm sure you could have managed those two on your own. Neither of them was particularly good with a blade. I thought only to relieve the monotony of the trail with a little exercise. You owe me nothing, Red-Head. There's a Shelter down the trail, you'd best head for it soon. I can smell snow in the air, we'll have it come nightfall. Cold stiffens wounds."

Moving with the athletic ease and litheness of a forest predator, Reba gathered her reins and remounted.

"Wait!" the man called. Reba merely raised her hand in salute and headed down the trail at an easy pace. The man limped to his horse and stroked her nose. "Talkative woman, isn't she?" The horse just snorted and gave him a nudge.

Reba reached the Trail Shelter well before dark. Leading her animals to the barn in the back, she saw that several travelers had arrived before her. The thought of company raised mixed feelings. Having grown up in an isolated area with only her father for company, she had never been at ease around large groups of people. Apart from a few traders they dealt with in Edeleiss two or three times a year, nearly everyone was a stranger to her. She had no memory of her mother, and her father seldom spoke of the times

before they had moved to the foothills of the Hellers.
They had made their living by hunting and trapping
for pelts and hides. The few crops they grew, the
chervines and woolies they raised, supplied most of
their needs. As long as she could remember, Reba had
worked alongside her father—as the son he'd never
had. Her father had taught her skills that most women
on Darkover never learn—woodscraft and swordwork;
he had insisted that she be able to read, write, and
figure numbers.

Reba rested her head against the flank of her horse
and drew a deep shuddering breath—how she missed
him. His death, half a season back, had left an aching
void. She missed his laughter and warmth, the quiet
evenings they spent together. His gentle wisdom and
strength had shielded her more than she had ever
realized. On her own, she was struggling now to main-
tain their small trade in furs, more and more uncertain
if this was an undertaking that she could manage.
Reba had seen how the townswomen of Edelweiss
lived and was sure that she could not accept their lot.
They were good women to be sure, but dominated by
their menfolk, and Reba would not, or could not,
accept that possibility.

This was the last trip into Edelweiss before everything in the Hellers dug in to ride out the winter
storms. Reba reckoned that a winter of solitude would
give her plenty of time to decide what course her life
would follow in the future. For now, it was enough to
manage this first trip on her own. She had made the
journey many times before with her father and knew
the trail well enough to travel it even in the worst of
conditions. Being at this familiar stopping place without him made Reba feel more alone than she had ever
felt in all her eighteen years. She shook herself. "Come
on girl, long faces won't feed the animals or get a hot
meal in your belly."

Burying herself in the task of putting her animals to

bed for the night and checking her gear for tomorrow's early departure, Reba was able to put her grief at a distance. With her work done, she turned and made her way back to the Shelter. Snow was starting to fall gently in big, fat, lazy flakes, and she could feel the temperature starting to drop. *Wonder if Red-Head has enough sense to get in out of the weather,* she thought as she opened the door and stepped through with her saddle bags slung over her shoulder.

Closing the door behind her, Reba paused and looked around the large room. The Shelter was built of massive hewn logs and the large granite fireplaces at either end filled the room with a warmth and a golden glow. Two men were warming themselves and joking with a third who was fixing their evening meal at one end of the room. One of the men called to her, "Come, join us girl! We'll keep you warm and safe tonight. What's a toothsome wench like yourself doing running about without male companionship?"

"Aye, we can remedy that situation for you!" a second added.

Reba flicked the cloak back over her shoulders and let them see the sword and dagger at her belt. "Thank you for your offers, but no. I am quite capable of seeing to my own warmth and safety."

"That's a big blade for a little girl to carry," noted the first who had spoken.

"Well, if you feel you can do it, why don't you try relieving this 'little girl' of its weight?" A reckless grin flitted across Reba's face.

One of the others spoke up, "Don't be an ass. If she's carrying a blade, it's very likely she can use it. Besides we are all bound by Shelter truce. Would you become outlaw for a mere woman?" The others growled, but turned back to their fire.

At the other fireplace were two women who had been observing the exchange attentively. The older of the two motioned and called to Reba, "Come join us, sister, there is enough for all." The younger already had turned back to finishing the meal preparations. Reba cocked an eyebrow at the woman and recognized the two women as being of the Renunciate Guild. She walked toward the fireplace and the women.

As she approached, the older woman stood and watched her. "Sister, the blade you wear goes beyond that which the Charter allows us to carry."

Reba stopped, resting her hand on the hilt of her blade. "I would join you, but not as a sister," she said. "I am not of the Guild and I am not bound by your Charter."

"Come," said the younger woman. "All women are sisters, whether sworn to the Guild or not. Sit down and share supper with us."

The older woman said, "I am Camilla and this is Rafaella." Camilla was tall and lean almost to the point of gauntness, with short reddish hair gone mostly to gray. Despite her apparent age, the way she moved spoke of wiry strength and agility. Rafaella was shorter, with dark hair and eyes, slightness of build, and a lively manner. She passed a bowl of stew to Reba.

"Call me Rafi; Rafaella is only for when the Guild Elders are scolding me for some imagined misdeed."

"There is nothing imaginary about your misdeeds, Rafi," Camilla chided, "no matter how the Guild Mother might will it so. If you stayed out of mischief, we would forget your full name entirely."

"I am Reba. Let me add some bread, cheese, and dried fruit to the meal if we are sharing it."

"They will be a welcome addition, as I've seen a bit too much stew of late," said Rafi.

Camilla drawled, "I could make some bean soup tomorrow if that would suit you."

Rafi laughed, "That's all right, Camilla. Your talents lie mainly with the sword, not with the cookpot!" She told Reba, "There is no other I would rather have at my back in a fight, but it is truly an act of madness to turn Camilla loose in a kitchen."

Reba began to relax; the stew had warmed and filled her inside. The fire was melting away the tensions of a day spent on the trail. She watched the easy companionship of the two women and felt a slight twinge of envy. She could not help but wonder if she would ever find a similar sense of belonging for herself.

Camilla spoke up, "May I ask where you're headed so late in the season?"

"I am packing a load of hides and pelts down to Edelweiss and picking up winter supplies to take back home," Reba answered.

"That's a hard trip to take alone at this time of the season," said Camilla. "There's been some talk of bandits at work on the trail of late."

"Aye," Reba agreed. "I ran into a couple this afternoon, an hour or so up the trail from here. I assisted one who had been unfortunate enough to catch their attention. They left, but not happily."

"And the one you helped?" Camilla asked.

"He was a young Comyn; he had only a slight wound. I rounded up his horse, gave him salve and bandages; and went on my way." Seeing Camilla's raised eyebrow, Reba added, "I have no use for Comyn, especially foolish ones."

Rafi changed the subject, asking, "Have you no kin to assist you with this journey?"

Reba paused before saying, "No, my father died half a season back. I am on my own. We had always made the trip together. This year, I am running later than I would have chosen, but with only myself to hunt, trap, and cure pelts, it took longer to get the load together. I am the only one left to keep the business going."

"Camilla and I escorted a caravan to Caer Donn, we are returning to Thendara for the winter. We are of the Guild House there," said Rafi.

Suddenly there was a clatter at the door. Everyone turned to see the cause as a snow-covered figure entered, stamping and blowing like a chervine in season. The process of unbundling revealed Reba's red-headed acquaintance. Spying Reba at the end of the room, he headed her way. "Hey! Reba! Why did you take off so fast, girl?"

Reba turned. "Why not? What reason had I to stay? I thought the aid rendered was sufficient." Reba's tone was getting cool.

Camilla and Rafi were watching the exchange with interest. The red-headed man turned to them. "Excuse my lapse of courtesy, I am Donal of Serrais. Your companion aided me this afternoon on the trail, and then with some haste took off."

Reba cut in abruptly, "I am not of their Guild, my faults are my own. What manner of aid should I have rendered, that you so bemoan the lack?"

Heatedly Donal answered, "Had you not been in such a rush, I could have remounted my horse with your aid and not hobbled all the way to the Shelter. It was not well done to leave a hurt man on the trail."

"Listen, Comyn lordling, it was not by my leave that you chose to trot down the trail with a rich rig, as if you were trotting the trails of your own domain. We owe each other nothing."

Donal answered, "There are basic courtesies of one traveler to another."

Green eyes blazing, and face set, Reba answered with mocking tones, "You are hardly at death's door, screeching in here like a banshee done out of its supper. Who do you think you are, Comyn, that you can put demands on me, judge the suitability of my actions, or order my doings as though I were a server in your Domain? I walk my own path, and I walk it alone." Turning her back on him, Reba stalked back to the fireplace and stood warming her hands.

Donal followed behind her and put his hand on her

shoulder. "Girl, I can see Comyn blood in you and would like to know your parentage."

Reba turned, white-faced, and knocked his hand away. "Keep your hands to yourself, Comyn! What blood flows in my veins is my affair. It is enough that I count none of your kind as kin!" Donal stood stunned at the hardness of her tone. Reba donned her cloak and stalked out the door.

Camilla spoke up, "Donal, let me see that wound. Many years of mercenary service have given me some skill in tending battle wounds." Gently she peeled back the bandage on his thigh. "Ahh, it is as I thought—your walk has aggravated it and opened it more. A few stitches will see it right."

Having taken care of Donal, Camilla donned her cloak. "I'm going to see what can be done for Reba. I think there is an angry child hidden in a grown woman's form, maybe needing help, but too proud to ask for it." So saying, Camilla headed out the door.

Approaching the barn, Camilla could see a light within. Entering quietly, she found Reba sitting slumped on a bale of winter feed, elbows on knees and head down.

"What troubles you, child?" Camilla asked softly. Startled, Reba jerked upright. Camilla could see her cheeks were damp. "What has happened that calls for these tears, *chiya*?"

Reba stiffened. "I am not a little girl, I am a woman grown!" she retorted.

With a sigh, Camilla sat down on the bale next to Reba. "There is a bit of the child in all of us, Reba. No matter how many seasons come and go. Why does Donal trouble you so? I, too, can see the Comyn bloodline in you—is this where your troubles lie? Are you a runaway from some Comyn house? Your sword skill—only the Renunciates and a very few Comyn women ever learn such. The common women never learn it. I noticed a book in the top of your open saddle bag. Reading is an equally rare skill. So child, if you are a runaway, you'd best come up with a better disguise."

Reba sighed. "I am not a runaway. It is as I told you earlier. My father and I worked at trapping pelts. My father was of Comyn blood—but he disliked everything to do with the Comyn. I don't know what house he came from; he only said once that he was a minor son of a minor house. I don't know anything about my mother's people. Father avoided Comyn folk altogether. He said he left his family because he hated Comyn politics. I think he had a quarrel with his older brother who was to have inherited the Domain. He believed that the arrival of the Terrans would make the Comyn change for the better, but they still cling to the old ways. Father always said that to deny change was to deny the future, and tomorrow will always come, whether we want it or not."

"And you? What do you want for the future, Reba?" asked Camilla.

Reba shook her head. "I don't know. Maybe I want only to go my own way without hindrance."

"Reba, there are only four paths for a woman on our world. The path a woman born to the Comyn must follow is that of duty to her house and political expediency. She is a pawn in the game of Comyn politics, and a brood mare. A few Comyn women have made a broader place for themselves, but it is rare. Then, there are the common women who are governed by the whims of the menfolk of their families. Their sole purpose is to keep house and children for a man. There are a few who are skilled at a craft; they may make some choices for themselves. They are still governed by a man's desires and find that their own wishes come a poor second. Thirdly, there are the Guild women, such as myself. We make our own choices, yet we still have some restrictions imposed by the Charter. However, we are oathbound to the Guild and are governed by that. Lastly, if a woman has *laran*, she may go to the Towers and live by the duties and traditions there. No woman goes her own way on this world. These are your choices, these four paths."

Reba shook her head. "No, this is not my future. You would have me choose one set of chains from the four. Is any one of the sets lighter than the others, less restrictive? I was not raised for any of these paths, I cannot live any of those lives without losing a part of myself. I am all that I have! I will not throw any of myself away. My father raised me to be what I am. He had a purpose in what he did. I don't know what he meant for me in the future, but I will not deny what he gave me—independence! Freedom from the old ways!"

Camilla stood. "Come *chiya*. We cannot solve all the troubles of the world, or even your own in one night. It is late and we all look for an early start tomorrow. Dull heads from no sleep are a hazard on the trail." She gave Reba a quick hug. "Perhaps there is a different path for you. Where it goes, who can say? Sometimes the open eyes of the child see more than one with many seasons behind her."

Reba gave a tentative smile. "Thank you for caring to listen to this 'child.' "

Together, they returned to the Shelter. Everyone had already bedded down for the night and the darkness was lit only by the glow of the banked embers. Rafi had laid out their bedrolls before she turned in. Reba climbed into her blankets and closed her eyes. She drifted into sleep on the gentle swells of soft snores from the others. Her mind was still bothered, but the trouble had softened somewhat and receded into a far corner to be studied at a later time.

The night had not yet given way to morning when Reba awoke. Her internal clock told her there were a couple hours left before the red sun would rise and start lighting the sky. She had half a mind to wait until the others got up and ride with them. The company would be a change and she knew that sooner or later she must accept being around others. Swaddled in the warmth of her blankets, Reba thought about the people she had met last night. Camilla stood foremost in her thoughts. Already she felt a bond with the older woman, appreciating her warmth and kindness. Rafi made a good companion with her quick laugh and easy ways; she could easily travel with these two for a while, until she came to know her own mind. It would be easy to drift a bit while she decided her future.

Thinking of Donal made her uncomfortable. The man represented a group of which she had been taught to be wary. It was true that she was intrigued by the young man, but could she trust him to leave her past unquestioned? She suspected he wasn't done delving for answers and she knew she was not ready to discuss her parentage with a Comyn. Comyn were known for looking out for their own. Suppose he felt it his duty to bring her before Comyn Council so that her Comyn kin might be found! That thought gave her a jolt of dismay. Reba decided that she had best move on before Donal had a chance to satisfy his curiosity.

Quietly she rose and packed up her gear. Saddlebags over her shoulder, Reba slipped out into the chilly darkness. The snow had stopped falling and everything was covered under a fresh white blanket. Entering the barn, she was greeted by her animals. "Well, at least you'll get your breakfast before we leave." Reba gave them a measure of oats to work on while she saddled her horse and got the pack chervine loaded. Everything was finally loaded and she was ready to go.

"Well boys, we've got a full day of trail ahead of us. If we push it a bit, maybe we'll reach Edelweiss late tonight."

Reba grinned at the thought of a warm, soft bed. So saying, she gave each a pat on the nose and a fistful of dried fruit. Leading the animals from the barn, she paused and looked at the Shelter. It was still dark and silent; she'd have at least a two-hour lead on the others. Reba swung up into her saddle and quietly led her pack chervine down the trail. She was sorry to leave Camilla and Rafi, but she needed to be moving on.

The going would be a little slow until the sun came up and burned the frost off the trail, but that was all right. There was something about the early morning peace that felt healing to her soul and Reba would savor it while she could. It was her favorite time of day, when everything had a freshness to it. She loved to see the sun come up, watch the trees gradually take shape out of the darkness, and see the character of the sky change with the rising sun.

The sky was just beginning to lighten when Camilla and Rafi rose. "Ah, Reba has already left. It's a shame, I was looking forward to her company on the trail today," Rafi said.

Camilla looked up from her packing. "The young Comyn, Donal, makes her nervous, I think."

Looking around the shelter, Rafi noted, "Well, he's got an early start, too. But with that leg of his, I doubt he'll be able to catch up to her. While you and Reba were outside last night, Donal and I talked. He is attracted to her; thinks she needs looking after."

Camilla chuckled. "Hmm, I don't think he'll get far with Reba. She's wary of Comyn. Why don't you get breakfast while I ready our horses."

Rafi laughed, "Better me than you. I'll be glad when we get home. It's been a long trip."

Reba paused on the trail. "Well this is as good a place as any to stop for breakfast." The sky was turning a bright pinkish orange. Reba dismounted and tethered the animals. Breakfast would be a few hand-fuls of the dried fruit, but a hot cup of tea would drive off the morning chill. While the tea water was warming, Reba walked a way back up the trail. It was strange, but once or twice she thought she had caught the sounds of someone else on the trail behind her. She stood quietly and listened for awhile, but could hear nothing. She smiled. "Whoever it is must have stopped for breakfast, too." Going back to her fire, she warmed her hands about a cup of tea, and watched the morning start to unfold. Refreshed and warmed by the tea, Reba proceeded on down the trail.

Every so often she would pause and listen, but the noises of her own animals and the awakening birds were masking what she sought to hear. She was just entering a narrow stretch of trail, when the rumble started. She stopped, twisted about, but could see nothing. Quickly she dismounted. There was an overhang of rock on the mountain side of the trail. She led the animals under it and braced herself against their sides. The rumble was louder and she could hear the crashing of brush and trees. Within moments, rocks and small boulders were bounding down the mountainside.

The animals started to shy. "Easy now, easy, we're safe," she told them, talking quietly and rubbing their noses. Most of the rocks hit the overhang and bounced on over the trail and down the mountain. A few of the smaller cobble-sized ones hit boulders on the other side of the trail, careening off in all directions. These were the ones that worried Reba.

This rockfall is out of season, and damn particular about the size of rock; nothing too large or too small for a man to handle, she thought.

Just then a large cobble ricocheted under the ledge, striking her sharply in the shoulder. She heard a sickening crunch and her own scream sounded distant as the black and red waves of pain started to pound her down.

She struggled to keep a grip on her reeling senses;

fire was shooting through her shoulder and alternating waves of nausea and dizziness had her stumbling and falling to her knees. The rockfall had stopped and vaguely Reba knew this was important. She fumbled out her sword and tried to focus on the trail in front of the overhang. She could hear scuffling footsteps coming down the slope and low voices.

Two figures appeared before the overhang. She couldn't see them very well, but she could hear and sense them.

"Well, well, well. It's the interfering bitch from yesterday that's wandered into our little surprise. We couldn't ask for a better catch could we?"

"Yes, we have some unfinished business with you. Where's the Comyn, bitch? He lose his nerve for mountain trails or did you get tired of playing nursemaid?"

Reba shuddered. Staying on her feet was taking all she had; there was nothing left for swordplay. She fought to make her eyes focus on the bandits approaching her. Raising her sword, she brought the flat of it down on the animals' rumps. They bolted out from beneath the overhang, scattering the two bandits.

"Damn you! There goes our loot!"

"Never mind, we'll round them up later, after we take care of this one."

Reba put her back to the rock wall, fighting to shove aside the fog enveloping her mind.

"Hold it there!" came a voice from behind the two bandits. "You'll have to take care of me first, wood rats!" The bandits spun around. Donal was on his mare watching them. Kicking her to a fast trot, he came down the trail.

"Both birds in the hand is even better," said the first bandit, grinning evilly. "Saves us the trouble of setting an ambush for you."

The fight was short but sharp. Donal's mare finally blocked one of the bandits against a trailside boulder while Donal spitted him through the throat. The other, realizing he was no match for a man on horseback, scuttled under the overhang to make Donal dismount and come after him. He had forgotten that Reba was there. As he moved backward, keeping his eyes on Donal, Reba's swordpoint came through his chest. It was to be the last sight his amazed eyes saw as his life faded.

Donal dismounted gingerly. "Reba, are you all right?" He limped under the overhang to see her sitting slumped back against the wall, bloody sword held loosely; he could see the darkness staining her leather tunic on the right side and shoulder. He started toward her, until a snarl brought him up short. The sword was no longer held loosely. "Please, Reba, you have got to let me help you. It's me, Donal. The bandits are dead!"

"I know who you are. I do not want any Comyn aid," she mumbled. "Don't come any closer."

"Reba! You are hurt badly. You need help," he pleaded.

"I don't need anything from a Comyn. I know what you want. I'll never tell you anything and you'll never take me to the Council."

"Reba, you are raving—let me help."

"Come closer Comyn, and I'll spit you like a rabbit-horn."

Turning back to his mare in desperation, Donal remounted and galloped back up the trail, going for all he was worth, cursing bandits and stubborn women alike under his breath.

Camilla and Rafi were riding easily down the trail, enjoying the morning and each other's company. Rafi was in the middle of telling a ribald story she had heard in Caer Donn when Camilla held up her hand. "Listen!" In the sudden quiet, they could hear someone riding hard up the trail. "We'd best get to the side before someone rides us down in their haste. Whoever is riding that hard has got more guts than sense."

As they rounded a bend, they could see a rider galloping up the trail toward them, bent low on his horse's neck.

"That rider will be luckier than he deserves if he gets through the day without breaking a leg," Camilla observed.

"You mean the horse will be lucky."

"Yes, that too."

Faintly they could hear their names being shouted. Rafi leaned forward, straining to see. "I think it's Donal!" She looked at Camilla. "Shall we make it three fools on the trail?"

They kicked their mounts into a gallop and rode to meet him. Somehow, everyone managed to come to a stop without collision. A torrent of words poured out of Donal.

"Slow down, Donal," said Camilla. "You're babbling."

Donal stopped to catch his breath. "Quick, you must come. Reba has been hurt! She won't let me help her. Hurry! We must get back to her!"

Camilla growled, "Who hurt her?"

"Bandits set an ambush, a rockslide. Reba rode into it. I think a rock must have hit her. I got one of them and Reba killed the other. She wouldn't let me look at the wound or help her. She's raving, threatened to skewer me if I came near!"

They all headed down the trail as fast as the horses could go. An hour's ride saw them back at the overhang.

Camilla swung down out of her saddle and grabbed one of her saddlebags. "Why don't you see if you can find her animals and dispose of those two carcasses? I'll see what I can do for Reba."

Entering the overhang, Camilla could see Reba slumped over, but still clutching the sword. Hearing someone approach, she tried to sit up. "Stay back, I'll skewer you."

"Reba, it is Camilla. I've come to help you."

"Camilla? What are you doing here? You were sleeping when I left."

"Reba, let me help you. You need to have that shoulder looked at. Here, *chiya*, let me help you sit up." She started cutting away the leather tunic, as gently as she could. "Goddess! What a mess!"

Rafi came under the overhang, and peered into Reba's glassy eyes. "I think I'd better brew up some herb tea. This child is going to need it."

"Please, while you're at it, put a pot of water on to boil. I need to clean this wound. I can't see how bad the damage is for all the blood. Here, help me lay her on her side. Put the pack behind her so she can't roll on me. Thanks Rafi."

Carefully, together, they cleaned the wound. Then Camilla sat back on her heels. "Rafi, it is bad. Bad as any I've seen on the trail. The shoulder is pretty well smashed. I can set it well enough to move her. But she's got to get to a healer soon or the shoulder will be worthless. Will you hold her while I do my work? Reba, Rafi is going to hold you while I set and bandage your shoulder. Don't fight her. She is helping you. This is going to hurt. Pass out if you can. It will be easier for you."

Camilla set to work. Reba bit back the first scream, but the second one got away from her as Camilla's strong fingers probed her shoulder. Gratefully, she surrendered to the fog rolling over her mind.

Sometime later, the sound of Camilla's voice sounding from very far away filtered through the fuzziness in her head. "*Chiya*, you must try to sip a little of this."

Reba shook her head. "Can't."

"Come child, it will ease the pain and fever. Reba, we must ride and get you to a healer. This tea will make the trip easier for you.

She struggled to sit up. "I don't think I can sit a horse."

"Don't worry, I am going to put you up in front of me on my saddle and you can ride easy."

"My animals, where are they?"

"Rafi has them safe, *chiya*, relax. We will care for you."

Reba sipped the tea. A gentle glow stole over her. Her shoulder seemed more cumbersome than painful. The gentle jog of Camilla's horse rocked her away into a gentle sleep. The wiry strength of Camilla's arms around her gave Reba a sense of security. There were occasional stops to change horses, or drink a little broth, or the ever-present tea. It could have been days or even weeks before they stopped at the big gray stone house. Reba had no sense of time. She had a vague sense of others crowding about, but Camilla was still there; she could still feel the arms.

Camilla laid her down on a wonderfully soft bed. She could hear a soft babble of voices in the background. "You're in luck; Ferrika's in for a visit, she'll be able to patch that shoulder . . . Camilla, go to bed, before you fall down . . . There's a hot meal in the kitchen. Better hurry if you don't want Rafi to gobble it all! . . . Who is this Donal, out on the front steps? . . . He keeps demanding to talk to Camilla . . . Amazing, two days! Must have ridden nonstop . . ." The babble retreated into the distance as Reba let the soft waves of sleep overtake her.

Camilla wearily came into the kitchen of Thendara House. Rafi was attacking a bowl of hot porridge and honey. There was a basket of fresh baked rolls still warm from the ovens. Camilla took a roll and slumped onto the bench. "How's Reba?"

"She's sleeping like a baby," Camilla assured her. "Ferrika has been sent for and Marisela will assist her. Between the two of them, Reba's shoulder should be well mended."

"It is time you and I got some sleep. I sent Donal

home with the promise that he would get word when the healers were done."

Tentatively, Reba came out of her sleep. The shoulder gave only a mild throb when she shifted it. Opening her eyes, she saw Camilla in a chair nearby, mending a torn tunic.

"Ahh, you are awake," she smiled. "The kitchen has some warm broth for you, I'll go get it."

Camilla returned quickly with the broth, and held the cup for Reba to sip.

"Where are we?" Reba asked, looking around the room.

"We brought you to the Guild House in Thendara. There was no healer in Edelweiss, so we rode straight on through."

A stricken look was on Reba's face. "How will I ever get home before the snows shut down the Hellers?"

"*Chiya*, you won't. If we had not gotten you to a healer quickly, you would have had a useless shoulder for the rest of your life—if the infection and fever did not kill you first. Get some rest, we'll talk some more when you are feeling stronger."

When Reba awoke again, the room was empty. Gingerly she sat on the edge of the bed, waiting for the room to stop dancing. Her shoulder showed only red scars already fading to pink; *laran* had assisted the healing. The thought sent a shudder through her. *Laran* was a Comyn skill. Her gear lay on a table in the corner of the room. Slowly she got dressed, feeling like a thief, looking to slip away unnoticed.

Reba was aware of the debt she owed these people and the burden weighed her down. She would repay the debt, but in her own way. Thendara made her nervous. Too many Comyn; too many chances for her to lose the direction of her life; too many people here who would take the choices out of her hands.

Reba slipped out into the hallway and quietly headed downstairs, only to come face to face with Camilla.

They both froze, looking at each other. Camilla leaned against the wall, arms folded. "Well, where were you looking to go? *Chiya*, you are not a prisoner that you need to sneak out." Patience was heavy in Camilla's voice.

Reba flushed and inspected the floor at her feet. "Truly, Camilla, I did not think that. But I was just feeling—"

"Trapped, maybe? You have trusted me to this point. Could you not have trusted me a little more?"

To her shame, Reba could feel the tears rolling down her cheeks and her shoulders starting to shudder with the sobs rising up from her chest. Camilla's arms came around her in a hug. "Let it go, Reba. The heart must have its chance to heal, too."

Reba quit fighting and let her tears take over. Weak, but feeling purged, she leaned against Camilla's shoulder.

"Come, there's some nice hot tea in the kitchen." As they sat with their cups, Reba thought about her future. This house was pleasant—but it was not her place; somehow she must carve out a niche for herself somewhere. Camilla broke the silence, "I have been thinking about the talk we had in the barn. There is one way you might be able to live your own life without too much bother."

Reba raised an inquiring eyebrow. "What way is that?"

Camilla answered, "If you have a valuable skill that others need; people tend to overlook the oddness of a useful person."

Reba's face lit up. "You're right, that may be the best way for me to go."

Just then Rafi came in. "Camilla, Reba, Donal is asking for you. He's out on the front steps." Reba and Camilla went outside to find Donal pacing the steps.

"Reba! How are you? Is the shoulder going to be all right?"

"Yes, the shoulder is fine, a little tender yet, but healed. I want to thank you for the help you gave. I know I wasn't very gracious at the time."

"Reba, I would like you to come to Comyn Castle with me. There are people there who can help you. You are of Comyn blood. It is your right."

"Donal, you are right. I do have Comyn blood, but my father cut all ties to the Comyn and his family. I do not know if or when I might rebuild those ties. Right now, I want only to find my own future, and I am no longer afraid to look for it."

"But what are you going to do?"

"I think, I will take a walk in the Trade City and see what sort of people these Terrans are. They may hold a key to my future—my father thought they brought a new future for our world. He may have been right."

Camilla laughed. "It may well be that your independence lies in that direction, but dinner will be ready in a couple of hours, so don't go too far down the path of tomorrow."

"I'll be back on time. Don't worry."

Donal watched Reba's back go down the street. He turned to Camilla. "Give her a few more years and she will be a woman without match. I think I would like to be around for that."

Camilla laughed. "Who knows where Reba will be in a couple of years?"

The Shadow

by Marion Zimmer Bradley

Since I write the Darkover novels as much for my own pleasure as to make a living, it's not at all surprising that I often write "out-takes" from these novels—episodes detailing further adventures of my favorite characters to answer some question in my own mind. Sometimes these episodes grow into books on their own; THENDARA HOUSE and THE FORBIDDEN TOWER both grew from these private writings about unanswered questions. Sometimes they don't. The short story "Blood Will Tell," answering "How did Lew Alton meet Dio Ridenow?" was eventually incorporated into Chapter Two of SHARRA'S EXILE.

I have often been asked how Regis' relationship with Danilo, and Danilo's with Dyan Ardais, grew from the basically unresolved state at the end of THE HERITAGE OF HASTUR to the much more accepting situation in SHARRA'S EXILE. I had no way to answer that except to throw my characters into a story; this is it.

This story was criticized, when first I allowed it to be printed in a Darkover fanzine, on the grounds that Regis' approach to Danilo was ill-timed, so soon after Dom Felix's death. I don't think so; Darkovans by and large are free from Terran superstitions about death.

*And I can't think, myself, of anything more suitable—
more loving and life-affirming—than this. (MZB)*

Danilo Syrtis signed the estate books and handed them
back to the steward.

"Tell the people in the Hall to give you some dinner
before you start back," he said, "and my thanks for
coming out in this godforgotten weather!"

"It was no more than my duty, *vai dom*," the man
said. Danilo watched him leave and wondered if he
should go to his own dinner now, or send for some
bread and cheese here in the little study he used for
estate business. He did not feel like making polite
conversation with the steward about business or the
weather, and he supposed the man, too, was eager to
get back on the road and be home with his wife and
children before dark set in. There was more snow
coming tonight; he could see the shadow of it in the
great clouds that hovered over Ardais.

*Snow coming, and it was cold in the room. And by
nightfall I shall be on the road . . .* and Danilo started,
wondering if he had fallen asleep for a moment. There
was no such luck coming his way, that he should be on
the road, away from here, by nightfall. Danilo rubbed
his hands together. His feet were warmed by a little
brazier of charcoal under the desk, but his fingers
ached and he could see the breath between his mouth
and the books which lay on the desk before him. He
had never grown used to the cold in the Hellers.

I wish I were in the lowlands, he thought. *Regis,
Regis, my brother and* bredu, *I do my duty here at
Ardais as you in Thendara; but though I am Regent
here at Ardais, I would rather be in Thendara at your
side, no more than your sworn man and paxman. I
shall not see my home again, perhaps not for years,
and there is no help for it. I am sworn.*

He put out his hand to the bell, but before he could

ring it, the door opened and one of the upper servants came into the study.

"Your pardon, *vai dom*. The Master would like to see you, at once if convenient; if you are still occupied with the steward, he asks you to name a time when you can attend him."

"I'll go at once," said Danilo, puzzled. "Where will I find him?"

"In the music room, Lord Danilo."

Where else? That was where Dyan spent much of his time; *like a great spider in the center of his web, and we are all in his shadow.*

Dyan, Lord Ardais, was Danilo's uncle; Danilo's mother had been the illegitimate daughter of Dyan's father, who had had many bastards. Dyan's only son had been killed in a rockslide at Nevarsin monastary; when Danilo proved to have the *laran* of the Ardais Domain, the catalyst-telepath Gift believed extinct, the childless Dyan had adopted Danilo as his Heir.

He had been at Ardais now more than a year, and Dyan Ardais had proved both generous and exacting. He had had Danilo given everything he needed for his station as the Ardais Heir from suitable clothing to suitable horses and hawks; had sent him to a Tower for preliminary training in the use of his *laran*—more training than Dyan himself had had—and had had him properly educated in all the arts suitable for a nobleman; calligraphy, arithmetic, music and drawing, fencing, dancing and swordplay. He had himself taught Danilo music, and something of mapmaking and of the healing arts and medicine.

He had also been generous to Danilo's father, sending breeding stock, farmhands and other servants, and a capable steward to manage Syrtis and to make life comfortable for the elderly Dom Felix in his declining years. "Your place is at Ardais," Dyan had said, "preparing yourself for the Wardenship of Ardais. For even if I should some day have another son—and that

is not altogether impossible, though unlikely—it is even
more unlikely that I should live to see that son a man
grown. You might need to be Regent for him for
many years. But your own patrimony must not be
neglected," he stated, and had made certain that the
estate of Syrtis lacked for nothing which could be
provided.

As he approached the door of the music room, a
slender young man, fair-haired and with a sort of
feline grace, brushed past Danilo without a word. But
he gave Danilo a sharp look of malice.

*Now what, I wonder, has happened now to displease
him? Is the Master harsh with his minion?*

Danilo disliked Julian, who was Dyan's house *laranzu*;
but Dyan's favorites were no business of his. Nor was
Dyan's love life any affair of his. If nothing else,
Danilo realized, he should be grateful to Julian; the
presence of the young *laranzu* had emphasized, to all
the housefolk, that there was an enormous distance
between the way Dyan treated his foster-son and ward,
and the way he treated his minion. He himself had
nothing to complain of. Before Dyan had known who
Danilo was, or that he had the Ardais Gift, when
Danilo was simply one of the poorest and most power-
less cadets in the Cadet Corps, Dyan had tried to
seduce him, and when Danilo had refused, in distaste, Dyan had gone on pursuing and persecuting
him. Danilo was a *cristoforo* and in their faith it was
shameful to be a lover of men. But never once, in the
year since Dyan had adopted him as Heir, had Dyan
addressed a word or gesture to him not completely
suitable between foster-son and guardian. Yet the
shadow of what had once been between them lay
heavy over Danilo; he had, he believed, forgiven Dyan,
yet the shadow was dark between them, and he never
came into Dyan's presence without a certain sense of
constraint.

As far as he knew, he had done nothing to displease

his guardian. But it was unprecedented that Dyan should send for him at this hour. Normally they met only for the evening meal and spent a formal hour afterward in the music room; sometimes Dyan played for him on one of the several instruments he had mastered, or had his minstrels and entertainers in; sometimes, to Danilo's distress, he insisted that Danilo play for him; he had required that his foster-son learn something of music, saying no man's education could be complete without it.

Dyan was standing near the fireplace, tall and lean in the somber black clothing he affected. Despite the fire, it was cold enough to see his breath. He heard Danilo come in and turned to face him.

"Good day, foster-son. Have you had your noon meal?"

"No, sir; I was about to have it when I received your message and came at once."

"Shall I send for something for you? Or, there is fruit and wine on the table; please help yourself."

"Thank you, sir. I am not really hungry." Danilo noticed that Dyan's mouth was set; he looked grim. He felt a little inward clamping, tight inside him; he was still a little afraid of Dyan. He could not imagine what he could have done to bring that look of displeasure to his guardian's face. Mentally, he ran over the events of the last tenday. The estate accounts, with which he had been trusted for the last four moons, were all in order, unless the men had all conspired to lie to him. As far as he knew, his tutors would all give good reports of him; he was not really a brilliant scholar, but they could not fault him for industry and obedience. Then he saw Dyan's eyes shift a little in his direction and was suddenly angry.

He is trying to make me afraid again. I should have remembered; my fear gives him pleasure, he likes to see me squirm. He drew himself up and said, "May I ask why you have sent for me at this hour without warning, sir? Have I done something to make you angry?"

Dyan seemed to shake himself and come out of a daydream. "No, no," he said quickly, "but I have had ill news, and it has distressed me for your sake. I will not keep you in suspense, and I will not play at words with you. I have had a messenger from Syrtis. Your father is dead."

Danilo gasped with the shock, though he knew the bluntness was merciful; Dyan had not left him to worry and wonder while he broke the news in easy stages.

"But he was perfectly well and strong when I left Syrtis after my birthday visit . . ."

"No man of his age is ever 'perfectly well and strong,'" Dyan said. "I do not know the medical details; but it sounded to me as if he had a sudden stroke. The messenger said that he had finished his breakfast and thanked the cook, saying he planned to go riding, and suddenly fell on the floor. He was dead when they picked him up. It was to be expected at his time of life; you were born, I understand, at an age when most men have grandchildren on their knees. He had ill-luck, I know, with his elder son."

Danilo nodded, numbly. His older brother had been killed in battle before Danilo was born; he had been paxman to Regis Hastur's father. "I am glad he did not suffer," he said, and felt tears rising in his throat. *My poor father; he wanted me to have a nobleman's education, he never stood in my way. I hoped a day would come when I would know him better, when I could come back to him as a man, free of all the troubles of youth, and know him also as the man he was, not only as my father. And now I never will.* His throat closed; he could not hold back his sobs. After a moment he felt Dyan's hand on his shoulder; very gently, but through the touch he felt something like tenderness; inwardly he cringed with revulsion.

He thinks, because I am grieving, he can touch me

and I will not draw away from the touch . . . he never stops trying, does he?

Abruptly the touch was withdrawn. Dyan's voice was distant, controlled.

"I wish I could comfort you; but it is not my comfort you wish for. Before I sent for you, I made inquiries through my household *laranzu.*" Now Danilo understood the look of malice Julian had given him.

"I learned through the Towers that Regis Hastur was in Thendara, and is riding today for Syrtis; he has said to his grandfather that as your sworn friend he owes a kinsman's duty to your father, and he would await you there. You may go as soon as the necessities are packed, unless you would rather wait until the weather clears . . . only the mad and the desperate travel in the Hellers in winter, but I did not think you would want to wait."

"I am not afraid of weather," Danilo said. He still felt numb. He had wanted to see his home, and Regis; but not like this.

"I took the liberty of asking my own valet to pack your clothing for the ride and for the funeral. But have some food before you ride, my son."

Startled at his tone—Dyan was indeed showing extraordinary gentleness—Danilo raised his eyes to his guardian's face. Dyan said gently, "Your friend will be waiting for you when you reach Syrtis, foster-son; you need not face the funeral alone, I made sure of that. I would myself come to do him honor but . . ." Dyan took Danilo's two hands formally in his own; he was perfectly barriered, but Danilo sensed a threat of some emotion he could not quite identify; regret? sorrow? Dyan said quietly, "Your father was one of the few men living who dared to incur my displeasure in honor's name; I have great respect for his memory. Stay as long as you wish, my boy, to set his affairs in order. And convey my compliments to Regis Hastur." He released Danilo's hands and stepped back, formally dismissing him. Danilo bowed, his emotions too mixed to say anything. Regis Hastur, already awaiting him at Syrtis? He went slowly to his room, where he found Dyan's body-servant packing his saddle-bags; Dyan had sent a purse of money, too, for the expenses of the journey and to make gifts to his father's servants. He had told off three men to escort him, and as Danilo went down to the hall, he found a hot meal, which could be eaten quickly, already on the table and smoking. Danilo was too weary and troubled to swallow anything, but he noticed distantly that the *coridom*, or hall-steward, brought a basket of food and packed it with the saddlebags on the pack-animal; inns were almost nonexistent and travel-stops few and far between.

II

The snowflakes were falling into the open grave, mingling with the lumps of dirt there as the men and women of Dom Felix's household, one after another, stepped to the side of the pit and let a handful of dirt fall on the coffin.

". . . and the Master said to me, 'your daughter, she's a good clever girl, it's too bad for her to stay here milking dairy-animals and scrubbing pots all her life.' And even though we were short of kitchen help, he sent her with a letter to the Lady Caitlin at Castle Hastur, and the Lady took her into her own household as a sewing-woman and later she became the lady's housekeeper and married the steward, and he always asks . . . asked me about her," the old cook finished, her voice shaking, and crumbled the lump of dirt between her hands, letting it fall with the snowflakes into the grave. "Let that memory lighten grief."

Each of the housefolk had told some small anecdote, some kindness done, some pleasant memory of the dead man. Now the steward Dyan had sent last year was standing at the graveside, but Danilo hardly heard what he said. Regis was behind him; but they had had no more than the briefest chance to greet one another. And now Regis stepped to the graveside; and as he looked up, his eyes met Danilo's for the first time since they had greeted one another that morning. Between Dyan's efficient steward and Dom Felix's own men, there had after all been very little to do. Danilo had been beginning to think that he might as well have stayed at Ardais for all there was left for him to do here.

"When first I saw Dom Felix," Regis said, the snowflakes falling on the elegant blue Hastur cloak and on his coppery hair—he had, Danilo thought dully, gone to considerable trouble to present himself as prince and Heir to Hastur before these men—"he snarled at me as if I had been a naughty small boy come to rob his orchards. He thought I had come to trouble his son's peace, and he was willing to send me away angry and incur the ill-will of Comyn, to protect his son. Let that memory lighten grief."

But that, Danilo thought numbly, was almost exactly what Dyan had said; would no doubt, have said if he had come here; that his father would face angering powerful men for his son's sake. He thought, *I should have been a better son to him.* He took the crumbling ball of earth Regis had put into his hand. He was remembering how Regis had sought him out here at Syrtis. *We sat over there,* he thought, *in the orchard, on that crumbling log.* At the time he had been no more than a small-holder's son, without even a decent shirt to his name; no one knew he had the Ardais Gift. Yet Regis had said, *I like your father, Dani.* Regis had come here when Dyan had contrived to have him expelled in disgrace from the Cadet Corps. And Dom Felix had been rude to him. Danilo said, blind with pain and unable to pick and choose at his words, "My father cared nothing for the court, or for riches and power for himself. His older son had been taken from him—" *Taken from him twice; once when my brother Rafael chose to follow a Hastur as his sworn man, and then when he followed that Hastur to death. And I struck him a blow on that old bruise. Yet . . .* "Yet he willingly let me go from him when most fathers would have kept me at his own side, to serve him in the obscurity he preferred. He let me go first into the cadets, and then to Ardais. Never once did he seek to keep me at home for his own comfort. Let that memory . . ." his voice broke and he could hardly finish, "lighten . . . grief. . . ."

His fingers tightened convulsively, crumbling the lump of dirt. He felt Regis' hand over his own, and suddenly he felt numb. It would soon be over, and all these people would go away, and he could go inside and drink hot soup . . . or hot wine which might be more to the point . . . and get warm, and sleep. The funeral feast was over, the burying was over, and now he could rest.

Brother Estefan, a *cristoforo* monk who had come from the village, was saying a few kindly words at the graveside. ". . . and as the Bearer of Burdens bore the Worldchild across the swollen river of Life, so our departed brother here strove all his life to help his fellow-men bear their burdens as best he could; Dom Felix was not a rich man, and much of his life he lived in great poverty, yet many in the country round here can speak of having been fed in his kitchens when the winter was hard, or that he sent his men to bring firewood to cold houses when that was all he had to give. Once I came late after visiting some sick folk on his estate; his cook and steward had gone to bed, so he welcomed me in with his own hands and brought me to warm at his fire; and since he said his cook had left him too much supper, he simply poured half of his soup into my bowl and cut a chunk from his own loaf, and because there was no one to make up a room for me, he set down some saddleblankets by the fire to

make up a bed for me. Let that memory lighten grief;
and may the Lord of all the Worlds welcome him to
the Blessed Realms, having held there in store for him
all the kindnesses which when he dwelt among us he
shared with his fellow men." He made the Holy Sign
over the grave and signaled the workmen to start
filling it in. "So we on earth may cease to grieve and
allow our brother to journey to the Blessed Realms
untroubled by the thought of our mourning. Farewell."

"He has laid down his burdens; farewell," chorused
the watchers beside the grave, and turned away. *So,*
Danilo thought, *there he will lie, in an unmarked grave
here on his own lands, resting beside my great-great
grandfathers before him, and my sons and grandsons
after him. Or does he truly feast this night in the Blessed
Realm, in the presence of his God, with my mother on
one hand and my elder brother on the other? I do not
know.*

Only Brother Estefan returned to the house with
them. Danilo went to fetch some of the money Dyan
had sent with him to make gifts to Dom Felix's men,
and came back into the hallway; the priest had refused
to enter the main Hall saying he knew Danilo needed
to rest after the long journey and the funeral feast and
burying. Danilo knew he was eager to get back to the
Longhouse in the village.

"The snow will be heavy tonight; what a good thing
it did not begin to come down so hard until the burying was over," Brother Estefan said.

"Yes, yes, a good thing," Danilo said, thinking,
*Surely he is not going to stand here and make small-
talk with me about the weather!*

"You will remain here at Syrtis now, my lord,
in your rightful place, and not return to Ardais? All
through the Domains and beyond, it is known that
Lord Ardais is a wicked man, fearing no gods, licen-
tious and wicked . . ."

"He has behaved honorably to me," Danilo said,

"and he is the brother of my own mother; I am sworn as his Heir. It is my duty to my mother's blood, and to Comyn."

The priest's mouth tightened and he made a small expressive sound as Danilo said, *Comyn.* "Your father was never really at ease about you in that place. And it is rumored that Lord Regis is one of the same debauched stamp; he is neither married nor handfasted, and he is eighteen already. Why has he come here?"

"I am his sworn man and paxman," Danilo began, but behind him in the shadowed hallway Regis Hastur said, "Good Brother." Danilo had not noticed before that Regis' voice had deepened and strengthened to an almost organlike bass.

"Good Brother, if anyone you know has complained to you of my conduct toward him, I am prepared to make an accounting of my behavior, to him or to you. If not, I have not appointed you as keeper of my conscience, nor is that office vacant. May I send a servant to guide your donkey through the storm? No? Are you sure? Well, good night, then, and the Gods ride with you." And as the door closed behind the priest, he muttered, ". . . or anyone else who is willing to endure your company!"

Danilo felt almost hysterical laughter rising in his throat, but he turned away into the main Hall. Regis caught at his sleeve; at the touch memory blazed between them, but then Danilo drew away, and Regis, shocked less by the withdrawal than by the refused rapport, said vehemently, "Naotalba twist my feet . . . I am a fool Dani! I know you do not want it gossiped, especially among those who are all too ready to seek scandal of Comyn!" He laughed, embarrassed. "I am to blame, that I thought myself above suspicion, perhaps; I had only feared to expose you to rude jesting, not to Brother Estefan's long-faced concern about the state of your soul and your sins!"

"I don't care what they say," Danilo blurted, "but I can't bear that they should say such things about you . . ."

"My own honor is my best safeguard," Regis said quietly, "but then I am not exposed to their talk; there are not many who will dare speak slander of a Hastur. I, at least, am not ashamed of the truth. Of all evils I hate lying the most . . ." They were still standing in the doorway, and the old cook, who was still setting out a simple supper in the Hall—porridge sliced cold and fried with bacon, a baked pudding which smelled of dried fruits, bowls of steaming soup—raised eyes still blotched and red to summon them. She said with the freedom of an old servant—when Danilo was very small she had fried him dough-cakes and mended the torn knees of his first riding breeks—"You should ha' asked the Brother to dine with us, Dom Dani . . . Master Danilo," she corrected herself quickly.

"True," Regis said in a lazy voice. "We could have done with his company, I suppose, for an hour more, if we must, and it is a pity to send the poor man out into the snow with nothing in his belly. What would they say to you at Nevarsin, Dani?"

"He will dine better in the Longhouse, nanny," said Danilo to the old woman, "and he would probably not wish to dine in the house of a sinner; I made it clear I was none of his flock."

"And I am just as glad to be spared his company," said Regis. "I had all I could stomach of pieties when we dwelt together in Nevarsin, Danilo; I had enough for a lifetime and more, of their solemn nonsense. Oh, I suppose some of them are good men and holy; but I cannot believe what they believe, and there is an end to it. I do not wish to be rude about your father's religion, but it is not mine, and I feel no particular obligation to your priest. Well . . ." his face sobered, "we have had no time to talk. I was eager to see you again, *bredu*, but not like this." There was a stone jug of wine on the table, too; he poured a cup and handed it to Danilo. "Drink first, my brother, then eat. You are exhausted, and no wonder, and I saw that you could eat but little at the funeral feast."

Danilo drank off the wine, feeling it warming him all the way down. Then he put a spoon in his soup; but he felt Regis' eyes on him, puzzled.

Damn that priest, he thought; *now it is all between us again. I had not wanted to think of that. It is enough that I swell in Dyan's house and am forced to turn my eyes away from that accursed Julian, flaunting Dyan's favor, and the knowledge that Dyan's household thought, for a time, that I was there in that position, Dyan's favorite, his minion or catamite . . . I am sworn to Regis. But what lies between us is more honorable than that.*

His mind returned for a moment to a small travel-hut in the Hellers, where he and Regis had acknowledged the bond between them, had been, through their *laran,* more open to one another than lovers. Surely no more was wanted nor expected of him. *I cherish Regis, and I love him with all my heart. But he would never ask more than that of me. Perhaps, if we had come to one another as young boys . . . but that was spoilt forever when Dyan sought from me what it could never have been in my nature to give.* And tonight in the hallway Regis had been apologetic about exposing him even to the accusation.

He reached up for the bowl of fruit-spread for his fresh porridge, and met Regis' eyes. Regis smiled at him and said, "What are you thinking, my brother?"

Danilo said impulsively, "Of that night in the travel-shelter . . ."

"I have not forgotten," Regis said, reached across the table and squeezed Danilo's hand in his own. And at the touch, for a moment, they were there together, wholly open to one another, and a moment when Regis had drawn back, saying softly, "No. You don't want to stir *that* up, do you, Dani?"

*And they had both withdrawn . . . it was acknowl-
edged between them, but they had both drawn back.
The shadow of Dyan lies heavy on us both . . . neither
of us wished, then, to admit what we wished for. It was
enough that we knew. . . .*

But the elderly cook was standing before them again.

"I made up the first guest-room for Lord Regis last
night, sir," she said to Danilo, "and I had the Master's
own room made up for you; was that right?"

Not right, thought Danilo, but customary and to be
endured. He nodded acquiescence at the old woman
and stood up, taking a candle in his hand.

"I am tired, nanny, and I will go up now. Go to
your own rest now, and thank you for everything."

She came and kissed his hand, and he saw her
blinking hard as if she were about to start crying
again. "There, there, nanny, go and sleep now," he
said, and patted the old woman's cheek. She went out,
clutching her apron to her face, and Regis took an
apple from the bowl on the table and came after him.
"I like your apples here," he said. "Could your steward send me a barrel of them in Thendara?"

"Nothing is easier. Remind me to tell him tomorrow," Danilo said, and together they went toward the
stairs.

III

In the upper hallway, Danilo hesitated before the
heavy carven doors of what had been his father's room.
He had not been inside it a dozen times in his life. He
said at last, "I . . . I can't go in alone . . ." and Regis'
hand was firm on his shoulder.

"Of course you can't. She should not have expected
it of you. If you were coming back here to live it would
be different." He pushed the door and they went in
together. Danilo touched his candle to a branch of
candles that was setting on the old carven desk, and

light sprung up, gentle to the faded tapestries, the
shabby carpet; but the old furniture was well-kept and
shining with wax. The big bed listed heavily to one
side where the old man had slept in it alone all these
years; on the other side was a still high, firm, untouched bolster, in pathetic contrast to the flattened
lumpy old one which had, all these years, known the
weight of his father's graying head.

*Seventeen years now, since I was born in this bed
and my mother died there on that same day.* That
sagging, one-sided old bed struck him as unutterably
pathetic. *He lived alone here, all those years, and I left
him even more alone.*

"But you are not alone here," Regis said quietly.
"I'll stay with you, Dani."

"But I . . . you . . ." Danilo looked helplessly at
Regis, and his friend smiled a little. He said, "No,
Dani . . . we must talk about this now. Neither of us
could face it *then*, I know. But . . . we are sworn. And
you know as well as I what that means. . . ."

Danilo looked at the threadbare carpet. He said,
striking out in protest, "I thought . . . you were as . . .
as shocked, as *sickened* as I was . . . by what Dyan
wanted of me. . . ."

Regis' mobile face twisted in the candlelight, his
brows coming almost together.

"I still am . . . by force or unwillingness," he said,
"but what made me sick was Dyan's . . . insistence,
not his tastes, if you understand me. Those are . . . no
mystery to me. On the contrary. But . . . freely given
and in bond of friends. Not otherwise. I thought . . ."
as if from a very great distance, Danilo knew that his
friend's voice shook and barriered himself against the
naked outrush of that emotion, "I thought you truly
shared that—that we were as one, but that we had
simply set it aside for another time. A time when we
were not ill, nor terrified, nor in danger of death, nor
under the shadow . . . the shadow of your fear of

Dyan. And I believed no time would be better than now . . . to confirm what once we swore to one another, that we would be together. . . ."

Moving through intense embarrassment, Danilo managed to reach out to Regis, to take him into a kinsman's embrace. He kissed him shyly on the cheek. He remembered when he had done this before, that day in the orchard. He said, groping for words, "You are . . . you are my beloved brother and my lord. All that I am, all that I can give in honor . . . I cherish you. I would give my life for you. As for the rest . . . *that*, I think, it is not in me to give . . ." and he could not go on.

Regis held him hard, his hands sliding up to grip Danilo by the elbows. He stared into his eyes. He said softly, "You know I want nothing of you that you are not willing to give. Not ever. What I do not understand is why you are not willing. Dani, do you still believe that what I want of you is . . . is shameful, or that I want you . . ." No less than Danilo, the younger boy knew, Regis was groping blindly through a forest of uprushing words, avoiding the deeper touch of *laran*. "Do you think I want you for pride, or to show my power over you, or . . . or any of those things? You said, once, that you knew I was not like Dyan, and that you were not afraid of me . . ." But he sighed and let Danilo go.

"Truly, his shadow lies heavy on us both. I cannot bear that he should still come between us this way." He turned a little, and Danilo felt cold, aching at the distance between them. But it was better this way.

"Well, you should rest, Danilo," Regis said quietly, "but if you do not want to stay here alone, I will stay with you, or you can come and share the guest-room with me. Look, your father kept your picture here beside . . . I suppose that is your mother?"

Danilo picked up the two small paintings; he had seen them here beside this bed ever since he could remember. "This is my mother," he said, "but this cannot be my picture; it has been here since I was old enough to remember."

"But surely it is you," said Regis, studying the painted face. Two young men stared at one another, their hands clasped, and Danilo realized, bewildered, who it must be.

"It is my brother Rafael," he said, "Rakhal, they called him."

Regis said in a whisper, "Then this must be *my* father. His name was Rafael too, and if they had their pictures painted together, this way, they, too, must have sworn the oath of *bredin* . . ."

They were both named Rafael; they were sworn to one another and they died trying to shield one another, and they are buried in one grave on the field of Kilghairlie. The old story had brought them together as children; for a moment they stood together beneath the old shifting lights of the Guard-hall barracks, children in their first Cadet year, caught up for a moment in the old tragedy. Time seemed to fold in upon itself and return, and Regis remembered the father whose face he had never seen, the moment when Danilo had somehow *touched* him, awakening the *laran* he had never believed he had. . . .

"I never saw my father's face," he said at last, "Grandfather had a picture . . . I never thought; it must have been the other copy of this; but he could never bring himself to show it to me, but my sister had seen it. She, of course, can remember our father and our mother, and she said, once, that Dom Rakhal Syrtis had been kind to her. . . ."

"Strange," Danilo said in a whisper, turning the little portrait in his hand, "that my father, who so much resented the Hasturs, since they had taken from him first my brother, then myself, should keep this here at his side for all these years, so that both their faces were before him always. . . ."

"Not so surprising," Regis said gently. "No doubt all he remembered at the end was that they had loved each other. It might even be, at the last, that he was glad you, too, had found a friend . . ." he looked again, with an abstracted smile, at his father's face. "No, I am not really much like him, but there is a resemblance, after all; I wonder if that was why my grandfather could hardly bear to look on my face for so many years." He laid the picture gently back on the table. "Perhaps, Danilo, when it has been for years beside you, you will understand . . . come, my brother, you must rest; it is late and you are weary. You waited upon me like a body-servant at Aldaran; let me do as much for you."

He pushed Danilo into a chair and bent to tug off his boots. Danilo, embarrassed, made a gesture to prevent him.

"My lord, it is not fitting!"

"A paxman's oath goes both ways, my brother," Regis said, kneeling and looking into his face. He moved his head slightly to indicate the picture, and Danilo could see the face of the first Regis-Rafael smiling into the eyes of Rafael-Felix Syrtis. "I doubt it not . . . if he had lived, your brother would have been a second father to me as well . . . and I should have had a different life altogether, even if my father had died."

"If he had lived," Danilo said, with a bitterness he had never known was in him, "I should never have been born. My father took a second wife when most men are content to rock their grandchildren on their knees, because he would not leave his House without an Heir."

"I am not so sure." Regis' hands closed over his again, "The Gods might have sent you to your brother as a son, to grow up beside my father's son . . . and we should have been *bredin* as it was foreordained.

Do you not see the hand of destiny in this, Dani, that we should be *bredin* as *they* were?"

"I know not whether I can believe that," Danilo said, but he let his hand remain in his friend's.

"It seems to me that they are smiling at us," Regis said, and then he reached forward, holding out his arms to Danilo. He burst out, "Oh, Dani, all the Gods forbid I should try to persuade you to anything you felt was wrong, but are we to live in the shadow of Dyan forever? I know he wronged you, but that is past, and will you always make me suffer for what he tried to do? Why, then, your fear of him is stronger than your oath to me. . . ."

Danilo wanted to cry. He said, shaking, "I am a *cristoforo*. You know what they believe. My father believed, and that is enough for me, and before he is cold in his grave you would have me here, even in that very bed where he slept alone all these years. . . ."

"I do not think it would matter to him," Regis said very softly, "Because for all these years he kept beside him the faces of his son and the one to whom his son had given his heart. Would he do so if he hated the very face of a Hastur? There are portrait painters enough who could have copied his own son's picture so that he could have consigned the face of the Hastur prince who had taken his son from him, to the fires of this chamber, or to those of Hell! As for what he believed . . . I would not care for a God who spent his powers in trying to take away joy and love from a world where there is such a lack of either. Of my Divine forefather I know nothing, save that he lived and loved as other men, and it is written that when he lost the one he loved, then he grieved as do other men. But nowhere in my sacred books is it written that he feared to love. . . ."

I said myself that I could never fear Regis. What, then, has cast this long shadow between us? Is it truly Dyan, after all? Our hearts are given to one another; I hated Dyan then because he sought to impose his will on me. Yet am I not also hurting Regis this way? Am I free then of Dyan's taint?

Or is it only that I wish to think that what I feel for Regis is pure and without taint, that I am somehow better than Dyan and that what I feel for Regis has no shadow of what he flaunts with Julian?

I have hurt Regis. And worse . . . the knowledge flooded suddenly into him. *I have hurt Dyan because I do not trust him; he has accepted me as a son and found another lover, and I have been unwilling to trust him enough to accept a father's kindness from him. I have kept feeling myself superior, accepting what Dyan gives grudgingly, as if I were a better man and conferred a favor upon him by accepting it,* as if I wished him to court my favors. . . .

And as I cannot accept Dyan when he wishes to show me a father's love, so I have refused to accept Regis for what he is, to accept the need in him for love . . . he is not the kind of man who could ever seek for that love casually. It would require trust, and affection . . . something that leapt from my heart to his when I touched him, and wakened his laran. But giving with one hand I took back with the other; I accepted his devotion and his love, but for fear of idle tongues I would give no more of myself.

Regis was still holding his hand; Danilo leaned forward and embraced him again, not formally this time. He felt overwhelmingly humble. *I have been given so much and I am willing to give so little.*

"If my father kept their pictures all these years beside him, then," he said, "and if he let me go from his own hands into yours, my brother . . . why, then, the Law of Life is that we should share one another's burdens. All that I am and all that is mine is forever yours, my brother. Stay here with me tonight . . ." he smiled deliberately at Regis and spoke the word for

the first time with the inflection used only between
lovers, "*Bredu*."

Regis reached out to him, whispering, "Who knows?
Perhaps they have truly returned in us, that one day
we may renew their oath . . ." and as he pulled Danilo
close, the picture overturned and fell rattling to the
floor. Regis reached for it; so did Danilo, and their
hands met on the frame. It seemed to Danilo that
Regis' smile tore at his heart, there was so much in it
of acceptance and love and joy. There was, for an
instant, something like a struggle as each tried to take
the picture and set it aside; then Regis laughed and let
Danilo set it on the little table next to the bed.

"Tomorrow," Danilo said, "I must go through my
father's personal things; who knows what else we shall
find?"

"If we find nothing else," Regis said, holding Danilo's
hands tightly, his words coming breathless, "we have
found already the greatest treasure, *bredhyu*."

IV

"The Master had your message," said Dyan's steward, "and he asks, if the journey was not too fatiguing,
you would join him for a little in the Music room."

*Why, he, too, is glad to see me home. I have made a
place for myself here.* Danilo thanked the man and let
him take his traveling cloak, and went toward the
Music room. Inside he could hear the small sound of a
rryl, and then Dyan's deep and musical voice.

"No, my dear, try fingering it like this . . ." and as
he stepped inside he saw Lord Ardais, his hands laid
over Julian's, arranging his fingers on the strings. "See,
you can strike the chord and go on at once to pick out
the melody . . ." he broke off, and they both looked
up; the light was on Dyan's face, but Julian's face was
still in shadow, and Danilo thought, *He is content to be
in Dyan's shadow. I never understood that. I thought*

that he sought favors from Dyan as a barragana *gives her body for rich presents . . . but now I know it is more than this.* Dyan nodded at Danilo, but his attention was still on Julian. He said, "Let me hear you play it again properly this time," and as the boy repeated the phrase, he smiled, his rare smile, and said, "You see, that is better; one can hear both melody and harmony so. We need both." He stood up and came to Danilo in the entrance of the library.

Danilo thought, with a curious intuition, *he knows.* But it was no secret, nor did he shrink from it now in shame or fear. What he and Regis had shared, what they would, he knew now, continue to share for most of their lives to come; it was not after all so different from what Dyan and Julian shared, but now he was not ashamed of the similarity.

If I am no better than he, I am no worse. And that is not . . . he thought, remembering Dyan's hand gently guiding Julian's on the strings of the harp, *entirely a bad thing. I thought because I would never acknowledge that likeness, that somehow I was a better man than Dyan. Or Julian. It is a strange brotherhood we share. But nevertheless it is brotherhood.*

He took Dyan into a kinsman's embrace. "Greetings, foster-father," he said, and even managed to smile hesitantly at Julian. "Good evening, kinsman."

"I trust you have set everything in order at your home?"

"Yes," said Danilo, "I have indeed set everything in order. There was . . . a great deal of unfinished business. And the Lord Hastur sent you his respects and greetings."

Dyan bowed, formally acknowledging the words. "I am grateful. And I am glad to see you returned safely, foster-son."

"I am glad to be here, foster-father," he said. And for the first time the words were spoken unguarded. *I have lost my father; but losing him, I found I had*

*another father, and he means me well. I never believed
that before, nor trusted him.*

"Julian," Dyan said, "pour our kinsman a drink.
There is hot wine; it will be good after long riding in
the cold."

Danilo took the mug between his fingers, warming
his hands on it, and sipped. "Thank you."

"*Chiyu*," Dyan said to Julian, in that tone which
was half deprecating, half affectionate, "play for us on
the *rryl* while I talk to Danilo. . . ."

Julian's face was sullen. "Dani plays better than I
do."

"But my hands are cold with riding," said Danilo,
"and I cannot play at all. So please go on." He smiled
at Julian. They were both young. Each had his own
place in Dyan's home and affections. *And there is
another brotherhood, too. My heart is given wholly to
my lord. And so is his.* "I would be grateful to you
kinsman, if you would play for us."

As the notes of the *rryl* rose in the room, he took a
seat beside his foster-father, preparing to catch up
with his neglected duties. Tomorrow, perhaps, he would
show Dyan the painting he had brought from Syrtis;
Dyan had known Regis' father, when they were boys
together. Perhaps he had known Danilo's elder brother,
too, and perhaps Dyan could talk of him without pain,
as his own father had never been able to do.

He relaxed in the heat of the fire, knowing that he
was home again, that he had stepped out of Dyan's
shadow and taken his rightful place at his side.

Coils

by Patricia Shaw Mathews

In general, dragons have not been much featured in the Darkover stories; although I have always thought of Darkover as the sort of place of which one might say "Here there be dragons." We know there are dragons on Darkover because a well-known proverb states that "It is ill done to chain a dragon for roasting your meat."

I once mentioned them flippantly in comment as, "I might dream them up sitting on the walls of Nevarsin singing Gregorian chant" which made it into a filk song (my own dumb fault), and the ballad of the death of the last dragon was sung in TWO TO CONQUER by Master Gareth, and its content described, though not quoted.

Well, Pat Mathews is another of those writers who legitimately seem to dwell on Darkover; several of her stories are regarded by Darkover fans as canonical, authentic Darkover, especially "There is Always an Alternative" in THE KEEPER'S PRICE, and "Camilla" in SWORD OF CHAOS, as well as the rowdy and funny "Girls Will Be Girls" in FREE AMAZONS OF DARKOVER, which gives Pat a three out of three record in Darkover anthologies. She also created the Sisterhood of the Sword, which appeared in both the

Ages of Chaos novels TWO TO CONQUER and HAWKMISTRESS.

As a matter of fact, this was not intended as a Darkover story at all; it was actually submitted to a different anthology, but I felt it had the authentic feel of Darkover—in addition to being one of the very few dragon stories that wasn't a ripoff of Anne McCaffrey's "Pern" dragons. So I asked Pat if I could use this for the new Darkover anthology. She wasn't thrilled, since she didn't think it read like Darkover; but I did, and after a little arm-twisting—excuse me, I mean, of course, polite persuasion—I won her consent.

Pat lives in Albuquerque, New Mexico, is an accountant (shudder! Well, better her than me!), has two daughters, both in college, and is a secretary (?) of the local chapter of NOW.

I couldn't have let this one get away; it's delightful, and gives us a look at the mountain society where women are more independent and autonomous than in the lowlands.

"How do you burp a baby dragon? Very, very carefully."

I should also add that she is NOT by any means— and is no way to be confused with—the Patricia Mathews who writes syrupy romances such as LOVE'S TEN-DER FURY. (MZB)

Roevna rode into High Rolls at the head of a richly laden but short-handed trade caravan, horse bells ringing proudly. A solidly built woman in her thirties, well dressed in heavy embroidered wool tunic and long culottes, she had an unaccustomed worried look.

Of horse-handlers and wagon drivers, guards and traders—flamboyant, bearded men and whipcord-lean women—she had plenty. But her second in command and Trademistress had left that winter at Temora Seaport to follow a sea captain who promised even greater riches. Her Sensitive, Dame Peliel, was old and ailing, and only rode with them as far as Feather River Retreat, to which she would retire for life. It was said the women of High Rolls had the Sensitive's Gift, but latent in most cases; certainly they had a gift for making wealth. Either way, Roevna could use a new hand from this Holding.

The lands of High Rolls looked subtly wrong, however. Even this high in the mountains, with a winter chill still in the air and patches of unmelted snow along the trails, spring should be on its way. They'd had a fabulous harvest last fall, when Roevna had come through on her way to her winter holdings. The orchards had borne richly and the livestock were fat and strong.

Why were the fields still barren now? Why were the fuzzy yellow-green forerunners not out on the trees? Where were the silver kitten-buds, the early-blooming goldenflower? Where were the northward-bound birds, the newborn animals? It was far too late to be only an unusually cold or late spring. No, the land was still bound to the dead days of Midwinter!

Frightened, Roevna quickened the pace of her lead horse and rode on into her kindred's oddly frozen lands.

Smoke rose from the big stone chimney above the log and stone house. Neatly cut wood was stacked on the front porch under the roof of the eaves. A large, sturdy dog with his long blue-white winter fur still on him slept peacefully by the gates in the man-high log walls. Then suddenly Dame Peliel cried out in alarm.

Roevna's head snapped back from the peaceful scene to the lead wagon where the aged Sensitive rode, back upright against a wagon rib, legs stretched out under a thick robe of fur, wrinkled face knotted in concentration. "Dame Peliel?" the trader asked carefully.

"The dragon," the old Sensitive said impatiently. "Don't you feel it? Something's badly wrong."

Her employer shook her dark red head. The Sensitive nodded toward the snowcapped mountain to the left, its crater cold, without a plume. "Dragonhome," she said, in the resigned voice of one who continually expects others to see what she does, and fails. "The mountain was steaming last fall. It's big; he'd be an old one, long in the tooth."

"What happens when a dragon dies?" Roevna asked. "Or do they?"

"Mostly, they just petrify," Peliel said, looking around at the valley. "And some of these boulders are eggs that never came to hatch."

Roevna shivered. "This land's in the grip of something, all right. A dead dragon's coils?" A cat raced across the yard on feline business and the dog slept on, undisturbed. Perhaps the animals should have been. "To the gates," Roevna decided. "Keep your eyes and ears open; especially you, Dame Peliel."

The two ladies of High Rolls were very plainly mother and daughter. Doro, who greeted them first, was sleek and plump. A seven-months' pregnancy swelled the front of the long, full skirts of the mountain land-owner. Her auburn hair was combed and pinned back into the elaborate knot that signified her rank; and not one strand escaped its neat white cap. A generous apron shielded her fine woolen gown from spatters of the food it was her duty and her joy to provide for her people. The keys, which should have hung from her belt, rested on a ring hung from her wrist.

Ana had lost her own plumpness of a few years back, and now was as lean and rangy as any of Roevna's riders. Her ginger hair was pulled back into a heavy plait down her back, tied by a thong; her only sign of ladyhood was a single gold earring. Her shirt and divided skirt were of fine High Rolls make and probably of her own weaving; but she wore boots, belt, and jerkin of equally fine leather. She looked ready to ride out.

The High Rolls people crowded around the traders as if to find some good news in their coming. The talk over a solid but unimaginative dinner, served by an edgily defensive Doro, had an undertone of worry and uncertainty. Worst of all, Roevna saw, was Doro's husband Charlot, a stranger to the land, with no idea what had happened to it, though determined he was to mend it.

After the last course had been cleared and wine served, Roevna set down her cup and sighed. "I had hoped to find someone here to ride with me, as Sensitive or Trademaster or both, but I see your troubles overwhelm you."

"I would gladly ride out," Ana said then, "and it is long past time." She sounded, not happy, but wistful.

"You cannot," Doro said sharply, sounding like a frightened child. "With the land in a blight and I with child, you cannot leave while we need you!"

Ana looked over Doro's head as if to appeal to the sky. "The health of the land is in the health of the Lady, Doro! And you are Lady and need no other woman to rule you. Twenty years I have served and been bound to house and land, children and cookpot, and that was well while you needed me. But children grow up, Doro."

Bewildered, Doro asked, "How can you even think of exchanging everything so dear for a cold bed on a strange road?"

Ana sighed. "You at your time of life think mainly of bed and babies, house and land, and this is proper— for you. But I at my time of life should be free, and—women age and children grow!" she repeated.

Then the ground beneath them rumbled and Doro stared wide-eyed. Decisively, Ana said, "Arm yourselves, all who bear arms. I need a third of you to guard the house and your Lady, who bears the Heir; the rest of us be ready. It came from the mountain, and may be no mortal thing, but magic. Cousin Roevna, is your Sensitive strong enough to deal with magic, still?"

"I am," Peliel said in a harsh, aged voice. "Can Doro take the reins while you give orders to her men?"

"Well, someone must, as she would not," Ana snapped. "Three of you and the Sensitive, come with me to the door, and let us look out to see what we see."

It was significant to the caravaners that she was instantly obeyed, while the mistress of High Rolls wrung her hands and wailed. Even Charlot obeyed Ana, not his Lady.

It was cold underneath the mountain. Once Mother's warmth had kept the little dragon warm, but Mother had slowly cooled as the fall wore on into winter and winter into this unnamed season. He was cold, lonely, and a little frightened. He knew he should have flame, and once he had managed a feeble flicker. But he had forgotten how to sustain it, and Mother's explanations were as dim in his unformed mind as the life in her fast-petrifying body.

Awkwardly he rose and shook off the last of the shells of his egg. His wings still damp and furled close to his body, he waddled to the dim source of light before him. There he stood for a long time, breathing the sharp, cold air, trying to understand what he saw.

There was light, and light was flame, and flame he must have. There were lights far above him, and he opened his new wings to see if he could fly to them. The air currents at his cave mouth would carry him over the valley, but not, he soon decided, as high as the little lights above. The ones below were closer. Carefully, he tested the currents, stepped back as far as he could, waddled to the cave mouth as fast as he could, and launched himself onto the current like a soaring bird. He rode the currents with relief and delight, as if of a necessary and dangerous task mastered. He followed them to the nearest of the lights, then dropped under his own power, circling the log cabin in the valley.

He could feel the heat. Delighted, he swooped closer and breathed deeply. The thatch from the cottage roof went into his nostrils and tickled. He sneezed mightily and much of the roof blew off. There was flame inside, under the roof! He put his head down. A high-pitched screaming inside the cabin hurt his newborn ears sorely, but he opened his mouth to take a big bite. He felt a faint sting on his hide, and withdrew, to find a small arrow stuck in one scale.

The fire had tasted good, even if these firemakers stung a little bit. Hopefully, he felt his firebox. Nothing. It had been a good meal, but had not ignited a thing. Mournfully, he moved on to the next felt source of heat. Perhaps these flamekeepers would not bite.

The Sensitive stood by the door, sniffing. Ana, as fully armed as the men behind her, watched over her shoulder. "I don't see it—yes, I do sense something," she said at last. "It reminds me of the Fire Giant my mother used to tell me lived in that mountain. Remember?" she appealed to Doro. "He brought the gifts of fire to mortals, and for that was chained under the hills. The story always used to make me cry."

Doro sniffed. "And you used to terrify me with tales of how the Earth Giant, who carries the burdens of mortals, would one day stir and shake them all off, and give them back to us. And He is stirring now!"

Ana turned back to stare at Doro. "Serve us right if He did," she said without pity. "Well, we both sense it. Let's go, people."

Doro turned back to her kitchen, a handful of women by her side, three men following her. They stood watch at the door while she carefully ladled the leavings from supper into a covered crock and set it on a

high shelf. She counted her eggs and her cheese, her
bread and butter and milk, and her dried fruits. The
earth rumbled again and she tried to ignore it, wondering in outrage why Ana had hinted that the Earth
Giant might fail in his duty to those who depended on
him. Well, let her elders and betters desert those who
needed them! She, Doro, would not!

The earth rumbled again, and Doro heard a faint
roar with an oddly plaintive undercurrent. Then the
roof began to move.

Ana went quietly out into the night, her people and
Roevna's riders close behind her, following the mind-
trace her intuition had picked up. The night was very
dark, the stars like tiny hearth fires overhead. Hearth
fires! There were none in the valley; and even low and
banked for the night, some glow should be visible. She
stopped suddenly; Doro's husband Charlot pushed himself to the forefront of her confused people and said,
"What is it, Landmother?"

The noise should alert anything they tracked. Sig-
naling for silence, she indicated several of her followers and pointed to the village highroad. "See what ails
the cottagers," she said in a very soft tone. "Then have
someone rejoin Doro, and myself, and if they need
you, have some stay, all as you see fit, but it seems we
must split three ways after all." The look of
admiration Charlot gave her suddenly annoyed her.
Landmother, indeed! Hadn't he outgrown the wooden
sword before he married Doro? "Move!" she ordered,
and then, alone with three followers, tried to pick up
the dragon scent again.

Old? Long in the tooth? The flavor she found was
babyish; her annoyance at Doro and Charlot must be
leaking through. Trying to clear her mind, she shielded
her lantern and moved carefully toward the mountain.

This late at night, this dark, the terrain was more
menacing than any beasts. There would be no moon-
rise till later. Small holes, unnoticed in the daytime,

tripped her up. The path did not go quite where she remembered. Setting her lantern aside, she watched the ground and tried to attune her eyes to the starlight and by the sense which guided her upward. It was very slow and treacherous going.

At last she came to a sheer cliff face, and brought her lantern high enough on the end of a stick to see a cave high in the hillside.

To climb at night was folly. If Doro had ever tried it, Ana would have kept her indoors for a week. Not that Doro had ever been so venturesome, Ana thought, the old disappointment flooding back. Once again she must now clear her mind, or lose the dragon scent forever. If her thoughts concerning Doro were interfering with this quest, what else had they interfered with? It was an unwelcome and disturbing thought.

They waited at the base of the cliff, how long, she did not know, until the full light of Liriel rose over the eastern hills. Now they could climb! The moon's light flooded the cliffside, not with the sharp relief that sunlight would show, but with a wash of light and shadow that only an experienced night hunter could make any sense of. And how often had Ana's own mother kept her within doors, sewing, for such foolhardiness! Ana sensed the dragon's spoor again, and nodded.

A man behind her held out a coil of rope, with a whispered, "I'm the strongest climber of us all, ma'am."

"Then you take anchor spot; you two in the middle," she agreed, looping one end of the rope through the ring at her belt. "Mark our trail well; I don't want to wait for daylight up there." She set one booted foot upon the nearest rock—unhatched dragon egg?—and began climbing.

The way was long and arduous, for even moonlight and lantern light made poor seeing; they only made it possible, and then, only by Ana's other senses. Nor would she waste the lives of her people, however

reckless her nature, and they dared not imperil her, so
they went more cautiously than if each had been alone.

The little moon was high in the sky and the climbers
exhausted when they reached the cave mouth. If anything attacked them now, it would have easy prey.
Dry-mouthed and sore, they rested in the cave mouth,
nibbled on the rations strapped to their belts, and
stared around by lantern light. The cave was fully big
enough for them to walk upright, and the dragon scent
was strong. Yes, it was a scent of extreme old age,
dignified and dying, if not dead already. Ana rinsed
her mouth with water once more before standing up
and whispering to the other three to stand guard.
Knife in her other hand, she raised the lantern high.

There to her left was a great rock formation that
could almost once have had a dragon's shape. Hulking
before her, it rested, its immobile tail stretching on
back into the cave; its shapeless head facing the fresh
air and starlight as if craving it in death.

It was easy to believe this had once been a dragon
of great power. Ana stopped to touch the petrified
head respectfully, then followed the body and tail
back into the cave for a quarter of a mile, sometimes
crawling as the cave grew small; then standing again as
she came into a chamber deep in the mountain's rock.

Huge rocks lay scattered around, water-worn ovoids
she did not expect to see this far into the mountain.
There were other, large, curved fragments; some looked
as if a giant could use them to mow her fields. Tentatively she touched one, and a sharp pain lanced her
palm. A tiny fragment of rock jutted from it. Setting
the lantern down, she tried to pull the rock shard forth
with her other hand, got most of it, then wrapped her
pocket rag around the wound. Staring upward where
the lantern now threw unexpected light, her mouth
dropped open in sudden recognition.

She had tended the High Rolls henhouse for too
many years. She knew a nest of eggs when she saw

one; knew, too, she had a fragment of a dragon's egg in her right hand. A broken eggshell. An egg the hatchling had patiently chipped its way out of, and then fled. Carefully she made her way back, favoring her wounded hand, until she felt the strong hand of her last man on the rope help her through the last tight spot, and she stood in the cave mouth again.

"Doro will need help, and so will everyone in the dragon's path," she said, "for he is new-hatched and nearly mindless. We dare not wait; let's go."

They looked at the descent dubiously, all of them mountaineer enough to know it would be harder than the climb up, and the night was still dark. They no longer had Ana's dragon scent to guide them, for it was behind them.

Still, Ana thought as she painfully felt her way down the rock face, she had not enjoyed anything as much as this night for years; she would not be bound to Doro's apron strings any more for all her pleadings! Doro was old enough to look after herself; woman enough to turn to Charlot for help. There were men and maids and kindred of the land enough that Doro would not be alone. And if she did not hatch, Ana thought suddenly, she would petrify even as these boulders in the dragon's lair had done.

Over the eastern hills, the sky slowly turned violet-gray.

The roof of the kitchen wing slowly lifted from the rafters. Doro screamed as a huge green-bronze head looked down through the beams and slowly turned toward the great hearth, tongue lashing from the great mouth in delight. The head came closer and closer to the fire, and suddenly Doro saw one of her big sweet cakes in its path, about to be crushed. She snatched it out from under him indignantly; he made a plaintive, low-voiced sound. Where were her defenders?

The bulging eyes turned toward her, and though no

tears ran, it almost seemed to her the giant beast was crying. The scaly neck suddenly jerked and the beast looked at Doro reproachfully, emitting a small yelp. One huge claw came up to scratch at the neck exactly as a dog does for fleas; several arrows fell away and landed in the stewpot. Above her on the roof, her defenders milled around with pike and spear, lance and sword, trying for some place on the dragon's hide that would not blunt their weapons beyond recognition. The dragon's face came closer to the fire.

Heart pounding, Doro tried to reach one of the many sharp knives and cleavers any cook must have, but the massive reptile's head was between them and her hand. Wildly cursing her impotent defenders, the cryptic old Sensitive who could smell trouble but not cure it, her absent mother, and her vagrant husband, she slowly retreated to the hearth. Fascinated, the dragon's head followed her.

She reached behind her for the fireplace shovel and scooped up a large mass of hot, glowing coals, shoving it in his face. There! That should scorch his hide for him!

Delighted, the baby dragon opened his mouth wide, swiveled around to be in the proper position, and closed his mouth around the scoop. Doro, faced with the loss of her only weapon and an expensive piece of kitchenware to boot, twisted the handle. Hurt, the dragon released the scoop and hung its head, looking up at her with eyes bigger than her head. He gulped and swallowed the coals, opened his mouth, and eeped. More?

Doro, since this was the only thing she could think of to do at this time, took up another scoopful and again shoved it down the dragon's gaping maw. As the warm stuff went down in a blaze of joy, he crooned, swallowed the coals more slowly and politely this time, and purred. He opened his mouth again.

The fireplace would run out of coals at this rate.

Doro retreated to the woodpile and laid more logs on the fire. Awkward in her advanced pregnancy, she began to pump the bellows. A defender leaned down through the rafters and called out "Madam?"

"Help me with this fire," she called back, "for the poor thing's half-starved, and gobbling it up worse than a baby bird! There, there," she turned and crooned to the dragon, whose cries were becoming more and more insistent. "Over the teeth and through the gums," she assured him, scooping up another load, this one still aflame, "look out, tummy, here it comes!"

The baby dragon took it in his mouth, swallowed it hastily, and whooshed. Hot air raced through his system. Experimentally he clicked his firebox. There was a small response, not quite enough. He turned his head toward her and purred, opening wide in the security that he was being fed.

"There, boy, nice boy," she crooned as she shoveled the coals in one after the other, and then almost laughed in hysterics to realize what she was doing. But if he was like most babies who were spoon-fed, he had been ravaging the countryside in a simple, hungry temper tantrum, and once full, he would sleep. But—

—how do you burp a dragon?

Then his third eyelid slowly closed over his huge eyes. His other two eyelids drooped and came together gently. Purring, he closed his mouth against the last scoopful and laid his great head down on the stone mantel. Contentedly, he slept.

"Now what do we do with him?" Doro asked Peliel, showing her the great beast draped in full-fed contentment over her ruined kitchen roof. "How long do they sleep? An immortal beast like this may sleep for years!"

"It was only a little snack," Ana put it. "He should only need a little nap."

Doro ignored that and turned to the Sensitive. "Well?" she demanded.

"Light his fire and show him the way out," Dame Peliel said in her aged voice. "Or would you keep him chained to our kitchen?"

Ana opened her mouth, then subsided as Doro said simply, "Neither gods nor dragons are my kitchen drudges, Wise Mother. So I shall do." As Ana started to speak, Doro said sharply, "Mother, do not interfere! I am Mistress here!"

"Yes, dear," Ana said meekly, picked up her bedroll and saddlebags and went to join Roevna's caravan. Behind her, Dragon stirred and stretched. Doro thrust a long torch down his throat, then stepped back. He clicked his firebox a few times, huffed experimentally, raised his head, and a great gout of flame poured into the sky. Slowly the snow began to melt.

He rose into the air, spread his wings, and soared. Behind him, an apron of Doro's that had been caught in his wing spurs fell to earth, severed at the apron string. Where it landed, the fields filled with new buds. By the time he reached his mountain, and Ana the gates, spring had returned to the land.

The Promise

by Mary Fenoglio

Mary Fenoglio's "The Promise" comes very close to being a full-fledged "Free Amazon story" but, as always, when a story has a situation or a character which really "grabs" me, I will break all my own self-imposed rules to share it with other Darkover fans. I fell quickly in love with the characters in this one.

Mary Fenoglio states that she is "forty-eight, whether I like it or not" (Well, Mary, you're still a spring chicken—I just figured out that I've been active in science fiction for forty years!), has been married to a psychologist for thirty years, and has two grown children "who, thanks be, have turned out very well so far." (Yes, with God's help they do *grow human in time!) She adds that she has won, over the years, various competitions, "mostly for poetry," but that "real life has a way of crowding out writing time."*

Doesn't it always! (MZB)

Calla swung down from her horse directly into a hole full of water; the icy stuff flooded her boot and did nothing to improve her temper. She turned to glare at her companion, ready to nip laughter short, but her expression changed from disgust to concern at the sight of the pale face. Big blue eyes gazed at her dully,

247

great dark circles around them emphasizing the delicate face's pallor. Calla moved quickly to the side of
the other horse and lifted her arms to the young rider.

"Come down, Ari," she said gently, ignoring the
stinging rain pelting her upturned face. She smiled as
reassuringly as she could. "We'll get you inside where
it's warm and dry, get you something warm to drink.
That'll be good, won't it? You'll feel much better
then. No, don't worry about the horses," for the girl
had laid her small hand on the streaming neck of her
mount. "I'll see to them, if this inn has no stableboy."

Gently, Calla led the younger girl into the great
room of the inn. Her foot squished in the cold boot
most uncomfortably, but she ignored it, as well as
muscles screaming with fatigue and eyes burning from
lack of sleep. She was strong and lithe, accustomed to
riding long distances as a courier. If she felt the effects
of their journey so desperately, she could only imagine
how her young companion must feel. Ariel had led a
quiet and protected life, sheltered from physical discomfort and emotional distress as much as possible.
Both had been suddenly thrust upon her, but the eyes
she turned to Calla were as trusting as ever.

Few heads turned when they entered the room;
miserable travelers were hardly a novelty at this time
of year, when the weather was interminably nasty.
Calla found them a table in the corner of the room
nearest the fire roaring in the great fireplace. Heads
did turn when she helped Ari remove her sodden
cloak; as the hood came off and the firelight struck her
golden hair and limned her delicate face with a rosy
glow she did not at the moment really possess, a
stillness came over the men in the room.

Calla noticed it; she had been prepared for it. She
herself was sturdy and dark, her hair cut short to
facilitate the wearing of the courier's cap. Her features
were regular, her eyes dark and lustrous, her body
graceful and well-made, but she paled to invisibility

next to Ari's classic golden beauty. She didn't care about that, since she herself had little use for men at this point in her life and preferred Ari's company—or her own solitary self—to the company of any man she had so far met. What disturbed her was the attitude of men toward Ariel; they took on a watchful, predatory manner. Calla despised them for it.

Ari, of course, never noticed it. She was as sweetly trusting of one person as of another. When men discovered that she was childlike and innocent, they seemed doubly excited by her, and Calla was doubly repelled by them. Ari had never spoken; from babyhood she had been sweet and silent, biddable and easily led, without much will of her own. Dainty and fastidious in her daily habits, she nevertheless required constant watchful care and attention. In return, she gave undemanding and unlimited love and affection. Calla loved her dearly, but even if she had not, she would have cared for her as faithfully. It was a debt she felt she owed; a responsibility she had shouldered gladly.

She straightened now and glared at the men in the room who were noticing Ari so intently. Shrugging off her weariness, she strode with almost a soldier's manner to the rough bar at one side of the room and pounded on it. A maid appeared in response, and soon Calla was carrying mugs of steaming broth back to the table. Ari sat limp, eyes closed, soaking up the warmth from the fire. Her eyes opened, great blue orbs that looked at Calla gratefully when she thrust the hot mug into the cold little hand.

"Drink," Calla commanded with a smile that belied the tone in her voice. "No, don't sniff it; it'll put you off for sure. Just drink it." She sat down herself, longing to take off her cold, wet boots. "A boy is seeing to the horses," she told Ari comfortably, "and we've a room to go to as soon as we've eaten. No, we are going to eat first; you've had nothing all day," she insisted, for Ari's look had told her that she much preferred just to go to their room now. "By the gods," Calla said irritably, "I don't think you'd ever eat if I didn't see to it! My stomach is growling like a mountain cat right now; I'd never be able to sleep. We'll go to our room directly."

"You can go to my room right now, poppet," rasped a voice behind Calla. She turned in her chair to glare at a big man dressed in the rough jerkin and leather breeches of a soldier. He was bearded, his eyes glittering and greedy as they stared at Ari. He put a beefy hand on the back of Calla's chair and she brushed it off; he reeked of ale. Undaunted, he leaned closer to Ari, who looked at him wonderingly and unafraid. Calla put her hand inside her jerkin and felt the smooth haft of her knife come into her palm.

"What say, you pretty, pretty thing?" the man wheedled. "I've got some things to show you, upstairs." And he looked invitingly toward the stairs disappearing up into darkness. He put his hand heavily on the back of Calla's chair again and gave a sudden yelp as blood spurted from the knife slash across the back of it. The chair overturned as Calla leaped to her feet and faced him, head lowered slightly and eyes gleaming. The knife shone in her hand, and she stood in the defensive posture of a fighter.

The big man stepped back a pace, cradling his wounded hand in his good one. Another man joined him; this one was not drunk, and his eyes were intent and intelligent. Calla instantly marked him as the one to watch, her heart racing with anticipation. A quick glance around the room showed her no friendly face; she was alone, then. Well, she'd been alone before; her jaw tightened as the two men advanced toward her.

"You outweigh her considerably, gentlemen," came a dry voice from the doorway. "and I use the term gentlemen loosely."

Calla glanced at the door and saw a tall, cloaked figure there; the face was hidden in the deep folds of the hood, but the body was impressive. The cloak had been swung back over one shoulder; a gloved hand rested casually on the haft of a sword in a manner suggestive of one who knew how to use it. As Calla stared, the other hand pushed the hood down, and she looked into the lean, chiseled features and sharp, fearless eyes of one of the Sisterhood. The hair was auburn, cropped as closely as her own, the deepset green eyes glowing now with the anticipation of combat.

"Are these two disturbing you and your companion, my friend?" the warrior asked in her dry and pleasant voice. "If so—" But the two men had begun to back away; they were not true warriors themselves, and neither felt a woman, no matter how beautiful, to be worth their own skins. The woman in the doorway smiled thinly and stepped into the room. Everyone in the inn suddenly had someplace else to look rather than at her.

"Will you join us?" asked Calla gratefully as she sheathed her knife. "I was in a tight spot. If you hadn't come in—"

"I think you would have managed," smiled the tall woman as she took the seat Calla offered. "Though you might have been the worse for wear. I'd hate to face you, with that look on your face." She was looking at Ari as she spoke, with open curiosity on her face. Her eyes were warm and sympathetic when she looked back at Calla. "My name is Linzel," she offered quietly. "and you two are—?"

A mug of ale and a greasy supper later, Linzel knew as much about the two young travelers as Calla was willing to share just then. She climbed the stairs with them, saw how tenderly Calla put the drooping, exhausted Ariel to bed, and then retired to her own room next door. As she left, she turned and smiled at Calla, sitting on the side of the bed tiredly.

"Don't worry. You can sleep soundly. They know, down there, that I'm up here. Believe me, no one will try your door tonight." She closed the door softly and went into her own room. She did not, however, go to bed at once. She stood for a long while, gazing out her window into the streaming darkness.

Calla, meanwhile, had at last removed her sodden boots. Pulling off her outer clothes, she lay down next to Ari, who already slept deeply, and relaxed. Just before she went to sleep, she got up and pulled her knife out of the mound of damp clothes on the floor. She trusted Linzel, but she felt better with the sharp-edged blade under her pillow.

Brisk rapping on the door brought her up abruptly out of her exhausted sleep. Heart pounding, she stared wildly around the room for a moment until she remembered where she was. Ari still slept, though the room was flooded with sunlight. Calla took the knife in her hand and called out for the person knocking to enter. The door swung slowly open and the maid gasped fearfully as she saw the wicked blade in Calla's hand. Calla grinned sheepishly as she saw the tray in the maid's hands; steam curled gently from the mugs on it, and there was a plate with thick slices of bread and a jug of jam.

"Come in," she said as she slid the knife back under the pillow. "Many thanks."

"Don't thank me," replied the maid tartly, put off by facing a knife so early in the morning. "Thank herself; she's the one sent me." She set the tray down on the small table and left the room with a sniff. While Calla was sipping the mug of hot morning drink, a soft rap at the door was followed by Linzel's face round the edge of it.

"Come in," said Calla warmly. "Many thanks for your thoughtfulness. Join me, won't you? Ari will sleep for awhile longer; she wears out so easily." She frowned anxiously at the slight figure under the bedclothes.

Linzel entered the room and sat down across from Calla. Her warm green eyes studied the younger woman unabashedly. She had spent much of the night thinking, and had come to a decision; it was evident in her forthright manner as she spoke to Calla.

"I have a proposition for you. As you have no definite destination in mind, and no one to help you care for Ariel, perhaps you would be interested in coming to our Guild House. I can guarantee you safety there, and friendship. You are an unusual young woman, accustomed to being independent and on your own. Just the sort we are always looking for."

"Are you recruiting me?" asked Calla mildly.

"I wouldn't exactly call it that," Linzel said, smiling. "But once you got to know us, understood us a litle better, saw what we had to offer—"

"As you said, I've always been on my own," Calla said slowly. "For a long time, at least. I like it that way. Depending on others has always led to disappointment for me. I'm grateful for your help last night, but—"

"There were no strings on that," Linzel said quickly, firmly.

"Still, I am grateful. But there are some things you don't know, that perhaps would change your mind about wanting us."

"I have time to listen," Linzel said affably.

"Ari has a younger brother, Alyn. He has control of our home, Blaumtarken, because Ari is—the way she is—and their lady mother, who was my father's sister, is dead. My own brother and I came to Blaumtarken after our parents were killed in a bandit raid; Ari's mother took us in. When she died, Alyn wanted to put Ari away somewhere—permanently."

"I don't understand," said Linzel, puzzled. "She's hardly any threat to her brother—"

"Ah, but she is. As the eldest child, she inherits the estate, and there is no law in our district that prevents—someone like her—from inheriting. The estate is a large one, and Alyn is greedy. He wants it all for his own. If Ari should marry—and believe me, that's not as stupid as it sounds, for one lord has already kidnapped her with exactly that intention, only we rescued her in time—then Alyn loses everything. He'd kill her first, to prevent that."

"So you took her away."

"Yes. I promised her lady mother on her deathbed to look after her, and I know Alyn is looking for us. We're not safe anywhere, and it would go hard for anyone found to be sheltering us. Alyn is a powerful man."

Linzel was silent, considering. When she looked into Calla's eyes, her own were hard and bright.

"We of the Guild do not fear any man," she said quietly. "My offer stands."

Calla's eyes were as bright, her voice as determined, as she offered her hand to Linzel.

"Then we accept, Ari and I, with thanks."

"She has a way with flowers, the little one," said the sister pleasantly to Calla as they watched Ari digging happily among the flowerbeds. Calla smiled.

"Yes, she always loved flowers and herbs. She can make anything grow, believe me. Once, just after we left Blaumtarken, our home, I was thrown from a horse and had my leg broken. Some good sisters in a convent near the town where I was injured took us in, and Ari was a great favorite with them. They loved her gaiety and gentleness, and her way with growing things. They wanted me to leave her with them, but I couldn't do that." Her expression darkened, remembering.

"And why not?" asked the other woman gently.

"I'm certain she would have been well treated, if they loved her.'

"I had no doubt of that, and she seemed happy there, but I gave my promise. I don't do that lightly. I promised to look after Ari."

"But surely there is more than one way of fulfilling a promise—"

"For me there's only one way," Calla interrupted. "My way. Forgive me, you've been very kind, and I don't mean to give offense, but—"

"I understand," replied the woman quietly. "You must love Ari very much, as well as whomever you gave your promise to."

"Yes," said Calla gratefully, "I do."

"We'll speak of it no more," the woman said. "Now I must help Ari with the spading, and Linzel has asked to see you in her room before she goes."

"Goes?" Calla's voice was distressed; she and Linzel had become close in the past weeks, and she was dismayed to think her friend would leave without telling her first.

"Yes, the request for her services came just this morning. She will be gone for awhile, I should think. You'd better hurry if you want to see her."

Calla walked quickly into the great main hall and mounted the curving staircase two steps at a time. The Guild House was not so grand as Blaumtarken, but it was a sizable and very comfortable place, willed to the Sisterhood by a lady who stood much in their debt. In it there was room for any who had need of its shelter, and on its lands grew everything the inhabitants could need, making them independent except for taxes and other small necessities. The money for these was earned by members who went into the service of others as bodyguards, escorts, or warriors where a male would not do as well. Jealous husbands, sending their women on a journey, much preferred the company of female guards for their women. Certainly the members of the

Guild were as formidable as any man could be, and as effective in deterring bandits and highwaymen.

Calla admired them tremendously. She especially admired the women who served as couriers; theirs was a unique and exciting occupation, combining the things Calla most loved: riding good horses and long stretches of solitude. She had been a courier on the outside; she had begun to think that if she could ride for the Guild, she and Ari would join. Her deepening companionship with Linzel added incentive for her decision. For the first time, she had a friend, someone she felt she could trust, who cared and understood.

At the top of the stairs that friend waited for her, trying to compose her thoughts into a persuasive argument that would not alienate the fiercely independent Calla. So much was at stake for all concerned; the subject was so delicate, the auburn-haired warrior was doubly anxious as to how to approach her young friend.

Linzel looked up as Calla entered the room, her face lighting as always when she saw the dark, intense face of her friend. She had become very attached to the younger woman, attracted by the fierce loyalty and strength of will she felt in Calla. She reached within herself now, searching for the right words to say, words that would not bring out the stubborn defiance she knew lay just beneath Calla's calm exterior.

Calla's face was distressed; plainly, she had just heard that Linzel was going away.

"Sit down, Calla," Linzel invited warmly. *Careful, careful, she's like a skittish colt where Ari is concerned.*

"You're going away?" Calla asked as she sat down.

"Yes, but don't look so doleful. I do this often; frankly, I'm surprised I haven't had a summons before now. It's necessary, you know; helps pay the bills." She smiled, and Calla nodded unhappily.

"It's just—I'll miss you."

"Of course, and I'll miss you. But I'll be back, and you'll be busy in the meantime. Very busy, I hope."

"What do you mean?"

"I want you to think about joining the Guild. It makes such good sense, Calla. You have no one—except Ari, of course," she added quickly, seeing the protest coming. "And we need you. I know you've been thinking of becoming a courier for us, and it's a good choice. I've never seen a rider who could get more out of a mount and harm it less. Think of it, Calla, a family at last, always there for you. Demanding from you, yes, but giving to you, too."

"I have thought of it, Linzel, and I think I want it. I know I want it, very much. I know the vows, and there's nothing in them that's a problem for me. But Ari—she cannot take your vows, the little one. She doesn't understand."

"That won't be a problem." Linzel's hands were suddenly very busy among the clothes in her pack, her eyes intent on what she was doing. A wave of relief surged through Calla.

"Oh, I'm so glad!" she cried. "I thought—that's what's held me back, all this time. I thought that only those who could swear your vows could become members of the Sisterhood."

"That's right." *Gently, now, Linzel, carefully. You can lose her in a heartbeat.* Linzel looked up into Calla's puzzled eyes.

"But you just said—no problem—she can stay with me, even though she—"

"For a time of course." Linzel turned to face Calla fully, squaring her shoulders determinedly. "She can remain with you for a time. But she can't ever be independent, Calla, you know that better than anyone. What about the times you're gone, and there's no one with the time to look after her? Suppose she wandered away, or got hurt? What then? Calla, you've got so much potential, and Ari—she's dear, and I know you love her, but— "

"But she doesn't fit in? Is that what you're getting

at?" Calla asked coldly. Her dark eyes were brilliant and hard as obsidian, gleaming with hostility.

"Calla, I know a place where Ari can go, where she'll be cared for gently. She can have her flowers, and you can see her whenever you like. You'll have your freedom—no, listen to me!" For Calla had turned away, hands balling into fists at her sides, shoulders stiff, body rigid with the shock of her disappointment. The vision of safe haven and happy, useful life receded into the bog of bitterness she knew so well, and her stomach cramped with the old desperation. Nothing Linzel could say would matter. It all meant separation from Ari.

"Ari loves me," she said distantly, without turning. "She trusts me. I won't betray her. I've seen those places you speak of, those snake pits! Do you think I'd choose that for her? Gods, that's what set us on the road, to save her from that! I'd kill her first, with my own hands!" She whirled to face Linzel and spat out the words.

"Calla, Calla, try to be calm and listen, think, try to understand—"

"I understand, Linzel, only too well. Betrayal is easy to understand."

"Calla, there's no betrayal here, only the desire to help—"

"If you really want to help us, then leave us alone! We'll go our own way, as we always have. It was a mistake to trust you. I just thought—I hoped—"

"Calla, the time always comes when you have to trust someone," Linzel said sadly. She looked at the younger woman with deep distress.

"I trust myself. It's always been enough."

"None of us can live like that forever. Eventually the burden is too geat. We need one another—"

"I have Ari. I don't need anyone else," Calla said stubbornly. Her eyes bored into Linzel's defiantly for a moment; she turned on her heel and was gone.

I didn't handle that at all well, thought Linzel miserably. *It meant so much to me. Damn that girl's pride! Why must she always learn the hard way! And this time the lesson may cost her more than she can pay.*

Linzel returned to her packing. She had been summoned; she had to go, for the honor of the House. What miserable timing!

Calla, meanwhile, had found Ari and pulled her away from her happy puttering among her herbs. Her great blue eyes watched Calla intently as the dark girl's capable hands swiftly packed their belongings. They had little enough, and when Ari realized what Calla was about, she began to bring her things to be included. When she handed her a silver-backed brush which Linzel had given her, and with which she loved to brush her long, golden hair by the hour, Calla startled her by throwing the brush against the wall with a curse.

"We don't want that! No, no, we don't want it, I say!" for Ari had retrieved it and held it out with an aggrieved look. "Oh, all right! I haven't time to argue!" And she threw the brush into the pack. Carrying the two heavy packs and leaving the traveling cloaks to Ari, she led her swiftly down the back stairs to the stableyard. As she saddled their horses, noting with disapproval how fat they had both become in the last weeks, she heard the clatter of shod hooves coming in the side gate. Something made her lead Ari and the horses inside the stable quickly; the hooves sounded in too big a hurry to suit her. As she peered back out, she thanked whatever gods had directed her.

The rider was one of Alyn's men. He pulled up and spoke imperiously to the young woman who ran out to take his horse, demanding to see the person in charge of the Guild House. As he mounted the steps to the side entrance and disappeared, Calla got Ari mounted, the packs secured, and they rode out as quietly and quickly as possible.

Calla's mind was spinning. How had Alyn found out where they were? Would Linzel tell him, in an effort to rid herself of Ari and so free Calla to join the Guild? No, angry as she was, Calla could never believe that. Perhaps he didn't know, but had sent men out searching. In that case, would they tell him, at the House, that she and Ari were there? They were fearless of outside influence, and did not lie.

Please, she thought desperately, *let them lie just a little. Just enough to give us time to put some distance between us.* She urged Ari to a faster pace, but Ari didn't really like to ride, and wasn't very good at it. Alone, Calla would have had no trouble outdistancing or eluding any followers, but with Ari—

She had to get them to a place of safety, where Alyn wouldn't think to look.

It was late afternoon when they left the Guild House; they rode all night and sunrise found them at the mouth of a valley lying in some low hills. Calla was tired; she knew Ari must be exhausted. Perhaps there would be some sheltering place in the valley to rest. She slowed their pace, her eyes searching the slopes sharply until she saw what she wanted. In a tumble of rocks and tangled brush, Calla caught a glimpse of darkness; they were past it almost as she saw it, and she backtracked to check it out. It was indeed a cave; not deep, it was sheltered on three sides by steep rock and with a little work the mouth could be so disguised as to be invisible from the road.

In a few minutes it was done, and Calla led a drooping Ari inside. For once she didn't try to get her to eat; Ari dropped onto the pallet of blankets and was instantly asleep. Calla tethered the horses, feeling the pang of thirst and cursing herself for her unthinking haste when they left. Food they could do without, but water they could not. Well, one problem at a time.

She set herself to watch the road below, every nerve strung tight. There was no fear of her going to sleep, not with Alyn behind them.

But she was more tired than she'd thought, and even the fear of discovery didn't keep her from sleep. She woke with a start to find that darkness had fallen. Her throat was parched and her tongue felt swollen; she was glad that Ari still slept. Looking at the little one, Calla realized how fragile she truly was; she slept like a child, heavily, her hair damp on her brow and her eyes like dark bruises in her unblemished face. If Alyn found them—

Calla gasped when she straightened and looked down the valley. There was a camp, and not a small one. The watchfires ringing it blazed brightly and she saw the men around them. She knew the camp was Alyn's. They were between her and freedom; going back was impossible. She was certain he had men waiting at the Guild House in case they returned, and she would not drag the sisters into this. It was her fight. If only Ari were not along—and then she laughed, realizing the absurdity of the thought. If Ari were not along, Alyn wouldn't be after them.

"Don't worry, little one," she said softly, looking at the sleeping girl. "He won't have you, I promise you that." She sighed. Always promises. She hoped she could keep them.

Just before dawn she saddled the horses and roused Ari.

"It's time to go," she said softly, "and we must go quietly. There are men down there who wish us harm." Ari's wide eyes followed the direction of Calla's pointing finger and she looked frightened. "No, no, there's nothing to fear. I'm here, aren't I? Don't I always take care of you? Don't I?" Ari nodded solemnly, but she had seen the size of the camp, and her eyes didn't lose their fear. "Well, and so I shall this time, too. Just do as I say and we'll be fine."

Calla saw Ari mounted, and swung up herself. She kept hold of Ari's horse, just in case, and they moved off up the slope. She was afraid to stay in the cave; with sunrise she knew Alyn would have men out combing the hills, looking for signs of them. Their only hope was to climb above the camp and go around, but the slopes grew steeper and the horses struggled with the uncertain footing. Calla dismounted and led the uneasy horses, reassuring Ari as best she could, but Ari's horse began to fidget and try to pull away. As he danced backward, his foot struck a rock that rolled, giving way, and with a terrified snort, the horse fell and rolled partway down the slope. Calla stood horrified, watching as Ari rolled free and lay still while the horse struggled up and stood quivering.

She dared not cry out; they'd made enough noise to wake sleeping gods already. But she couldn't help a little cry of relief when Ari climbed shakily to her feet and looked up at her, white-faced. Calla motioned to her to climb up the slope quickly, and as Ari struggled to do so, Calla looked down anxiously at the camp. All was as before; it was just waking. Perhaps they yet had a chance, though with one horse—

"Ari!" she whispered as she pulled the girl the last few steps up. "Ari, are you all right? Damn that stupid horse! Oh, Ari, when I saw him falling, and you going under him—here, sweet. Come over here, let me look at you." She felt the girl trembling uncontrollably as she led her to a rock and sat her down. In the growing light she examined her; cuts and bruises, but no broken bones, thanks be.

"We have to go on," Calla said urgently. "It'll be light soon, and Alyn will be out looking. Here, get on my horse; he's as sure-footed as a mule. He won't fall with you. Come, Ari, we must go!"

She led the horse up the precarious slope and breathed at last when they reached the top. As they crested the slope and started down the other side,

Calla heard voices. She froze; they were deep, male, very near. The horse raised his head and before she could stop him he let out a ringing neigh, welcoming a horse he recognized from his old stable. Instantly pandemonium broke loose. Men and horses exploded from the surrounding rocks and trees; Calla made a dash for a cleft in the rocks where she might at least have protection for her back, and Ari fainted silently. Ari rolled off the horse and into the cleft as neatly as if Calla had intended it; the horse broke loose and was gone, leaving Calla standing in the mouth of the cleft with only her knife between her and several hard-faced men.

"What do you mean, frightening two women almost to death?" she demanded, drawing her traveling cloak close about her. Perhaps they wouldn't recognize her, though she knew several of them.

"We ask your pardon, my lady," spoke a young man obviously in charge. Calla did not know him. "We seek two young women traveling alone. It's strange you'd be up here on the slopes, when the road runs down the floor of the valley."

"We saw your camp," replied Calla smoothly, "and not knowing who you were, we chose not to confront you. One can't be too careful. As for whom you seek—"

"It's you, Calla," spoke up one of the older men. "You know us; you know what we want. Give us the girl and you can go your way, I swear it. You know my word is good."

"And what of Ariel, Oberlon?" Calla asked, facing the speaker boldly. "Can you make such a promise for her, that she will come to no harm?"

"That's Lord Alyn's affair, and none of mine. As for me, I wish the poor lass no harm at all. But I make no promises I can't keep."

"Then the devil take you!" hissed Calla, and drew her knife. A few men in the group snickered, but those who knew her did not. They hung back, not wishing to harm her, and let the others press in. Calla was well shielded by the rocks; only one man could come against her at a time, and while she had plenty of room to slash with her knife, the heavier swords the men carried were too large to be of use in such close quarters. Calla was faster, lighter, more determined than her adversaries; after three of them had reteated from the cleft yelping and spurting blood, the one called Oberlon sighed and said, "Well, then, and I must take ye, lass. I have no pleasure in the task."

"Oberlon, I warn you," she panted, facing him squarely, "I will do what I must."

"Aye, lass, as will I," said the older man, and started forward.

"Hold there!" a voice rapped out, and all eyes turned to the speaker. The sun burst over the crest of the hill at that moment and fell on the golden hair and slender, erect form of Alyn of Blaumtarken, his blue eyes shining with triumph. His startling resemblance to Ari always took Calla by surprise; his nature was so different from hers.

They confronted one another, Alyn moving slowly but deliberately toward Calla, who watied defiantly. She wiped her sweaty face with a grimy hand on which blood had already dried. She was weary; for a crazy moment she hoped he would let them go. If she explained that she was taking Ari away, that he would never see either of them again, and he could have all of Blaumtarken and its holdings, that Ari wanted nothing—Calla forced herself to meet his eyes squarely; his attention was focused elsewhere, on something behind her. She half-turned and saw Ari crouching against the rock face, trying to make herself smaller and smaller inside her traveling cloak. Her dirty little face was streaked with tears and blanched with terror and fatigue; wisps of her golden hair escaped her hood and framed its paleness. Her blue eyes were huge and terrified, like the eyes of a small animal that hears the hunter's step and cannot flee.

Calla looked back at Alyn and all hope died at the look in his eyes. Triumph, hatred, murder glistened there, soul-deep.

Alyn moved forward, lifting his sword as if he would just step past Calla and fall upon Ari with no resistance. A surge of strength burst through Calla, propelled on a red wave of rage. Did he suppose she would stand idly by and see her dear one murdered? He might yet kill them both, but he would not do so easily!

"Alyn!" she rapped out, her voice resonating among the rocks. He stopped and seemed to see her for the first time.

"Calla, don't get in my way. I warn you, stand clear."

"Alyn! Stay back! Keep away from her! She's no threat to you." Calla's voice rose in desperation. "Take Blaumtarken. She doesn't care! Have it all—only let us go our way!"

"I can't do that." His terrible eyes shifted to Ari, who stared at him hopelessly. "Look at her. Vacant. A stupid sheep of a girl who can't even speak. A blot on the family name that I intend to remove!" He lunged forward, blade upraised, and Calla braced herself, her knife gripped firmly in both hands. She hoped he would come in close, too furious and overconfident to be careful, and she could get one swift, deep blow into his body.

It didn't happen that way.

The fury of his attack drove her back a few steps; the loose footing gave way under her and she fell backward, the knife flying from her hands. Alyn made one swift almost careless thrust that sliced her jerkin and opened a gash along her ribs. She gasped with the shock of it and doubled over involuntarily, feeling the warm stickiness of her own blood flowing between her fingers. Alyn drove over her for Ari, and she knew in bleak despair she could do nothing; he would kill Ari and then turn on her. Behind her she heard a sharp cry, a scuffle, a sudden grunt of surprise and pain, and silence. Fighting nausea and faintness, she struggled up and turned to look, dreading what she would see but wanting to face Alyn as he came for her.

Alyn stood with his back to her, his sword arm hanging at his side, the blade trailing on the ground. Just beyond him Calla saw a disheveled Ari standing, her face, twisted with terror and streaked with tears, staring up at Alyn. As Calla watched, Ari released the haft of Calla's knife and stepped back a pace or two; Alyn half-turned and Calla saw the knife handle protruding from just beneath his ribs. Ari had driven it in as deep as it would go; his own weight as he lunged had helped her. His face held only immense surprise; as Calla watched, even that faded to the vacant look of death and he fell at her feet. She fell beside him, insensible.

Calla woke to warmth, and softness, and the ache of sore muscles. She moved and let out a squawk; fire ran along her side with every breath. Looking around, she saw Linzel hurrying toward the bed where she lay, concern lining her face.

"Ari?" Calla croaked, not daring to move again. Linzel grinned.

"Now, how did I know that would be your first question?" she asked wryly. "Ari is fine. She's down in the herb garden with Maurita, though how she's keeping her away from you I don't know. She's haunted this room, and carried water and broth and I don't know what all up here every hour. These are from her." And Linzel gestured to the flowers sitting on the bedside table.

"Alyn?"

"Dead. His men were so shocked to see how he

died that they made no move to take you. One of them—Oberlon, his name was— said it was a sign that you and 'the poor lass' were in the right, and he'd not raise his hand against you. He brought you here, and I arrived two days later."

"Two days? But how long have I—"

"Almost a sevenday. We had begun to think—but then, I said, she's strong and stubborn. No matter how much blood she lost, she'll not die so easily. At least, not until she finds out what happened to Ariel."

"Well, you'll be pleased to know that I don't feel in the least like dying. But I don't feel much like moving, either. I'm awfully thirsty, though, and maybe some food—"

"You're better, that's for sure, when you start demanding things," said Linzel happily. "I'll see to your supper, and then we'll have Ari in to see you. But there's something I want to tell you first. I think you're strong enough. In fact, I think it might do you good to hear this."

"Well, what is it? I'm getting weaker, just waiting."

"We had a meeting of the Guild House members, when Oberlon brought you in and told your tale. There you were, all pale and wounded, dying, for all we knew. And there was Ari by your side, silent as always but guarding you with her life. And you maybe had already given yours for her."

Linzel stopped, remembering that awful afternoon. Her voice thickened.

"Your brother came, as soon as he heard what had happened. He's next in line to inherit Blaumtarken, now that Alyn is dead, if Ari doesn't go back there. He seems a good man, and fond of you both; he wouldn't stand in her way. We took a vote, we members of the Guild, and if you still want to join the Guild House, you're welcome and wanted. And Ari, too. Maybe she can't take the vows, but she understands what we're about. She's proven that. And anyway, no one can grow flowers like she can. She brightens our lives in many ways. As do you, Calla."

Linzel walked to the door and turned. She looked at Calla, whose eyes shone with tears of weakness and joy.

"You needn't answer now, of course," she said. "After all, you may get a better offer."

Smiling, she closed the door, and Calla closed her eyes, hearing the dear, familiar sounds of home around her, easing her into sleep.

The Dare

by Marny Whiteaker

Marny Whiteaker began writing with a Darkover story—but, unlike others in this anthology, it wasn't a winner. In short, it made no impression upon me at all—for I can't remember anything about it.

However, in submitting "The Dare," she wrote that I had stated in rejecting her story, "This is very well written. Learn to plot."

I can well believe it; because I'm always looking, not so much for good writing—"good writing" is turned out every year in freshman Composition classes in every college, and if the young writer can somehow escape those turners-out of mediocrity and purple prose called "Creative Writing" classes, the good young writer might someday be a creditable writer of stories. In general I am not much impressed by "good writing"; I much prefer good storytelling, and that means plot.

Plot, and likable characters in plenty, this story certainly has. I'm pleased that Marny Whiteaker rose out of the nothingness of "good writing" to tell a good story.

I always wind up an anthology with regrets for the characters and stories I had to trim out at the last minute; two or three stories I gave up with infinite regret, and I am always wondering if I made a mistake;

I am sure that at least half a dozen of the stories I rejected (at the last minute and only because of the inelasticity of typeface) would have pleased my readers at least as much as the ones I printed. Maybe some of them will come back next year . . . since my publishers have graciously agreed that there will be another such anthology.

But that is another story—or a whole lot of stories.

Long live Darkover, then, because Darkover itself is the real hero of the series, not me, or any of us. (MZB)

Rhys turned away from the windowpane and the great silver flakes of snow fluttering silently against the glass. The weather disgusted him. In reality it terrified him.

Kimri, Lady of Arilinn, was out in that morbid whiteness. After leaving Armida she had never reached the Tower and none of the telepaths on Darkover could find her. Assured, however, that she was still alive, search parties had been organized. Men and some Free Amazons shuffled below in the audience hall, cursing worsening conditions and eating stew to calm their nerves. Their voices carried through the upstairs hallway and found a way to his ears. From the sound of it they were discouraged. No signs, no tracks, only the patient insistence of the telepaths that she was still alive.

The search was in its third dreary day. Payne, Rhys' older brother, had arrived earlier that day from Thendara to direct the madness in the masses assembled below. His freemate, Allira, and her fifteen-year-old nedestro son, Diego, had come the week before upon hearing of her mother-in-law's collapse.

Rhys yawned, unfolded his long legs, and freed himself from the narrow window seat in which he had lodged. The firelight threw a long thin shadow on the opposite wall. Its black image startled him until he recognized it as a distortion, strange and eerie, of his own gangly body. He shivered.

This was all his fault, of course. Zandru! If he'd been older, someone would have listened to him, someone would have recognized him as the head of the Alton household while his brother was away. But no, not even Kimri of Arilinn would listen when, in one desperate attempt, he begged her to wait out the clouds.

She had smiled and said no. Apparently the summons was too urgent for common sense. She placed the starstone nestled in its pouch around his neck and promised she would inform the Circle of his acceptance. Until then he was to remain at Armida and watch over his mother's recuperation. And above all, he was not to use his *laran*.

Damnation! She'd admonished him like a child—as if he didn't know trouble when he saw it. He knew there was danger in the premature use of the Alton gift. He had sense enough to leave that part of his *laran* alone even though there were times when he was mightily tempted to use it.

Rhys Alton chewed at a ragged nail on his index finger, pulling his brows together in thought. If only he were older he could help—or maybe if he weren't an Alton. After all, Payne had allowed Diego to go out on the search and he was a whole year younger.

Well, that would be one way of getting rid of him, especially after the scene he'd made before Kimri's departure. He had told her he had *laran*. He had even gone as far as to say he had a Gift. Kimri let him play his little game, but Rhys knew she didn't believe him.

Diego! What did Diego Delleray (as he called himself) know about *laran* or the Gifts? That line had been purged ages ago. When they went against the Council, allying themselves with Aldaran, they forfeited any right to *laran*. It was bad enough the two boys were now related. It was bad enough that Payne sought to establish Diego as his son before the Council in order that Diego could receive all the privileges of the Comyn. At this point Payne would probably go out of his way to prove Diego had *laran*. Rhys might have learned how to say "cousin" without contempt but not now after that little stunt. How could he do such a thing, and before Kimri, his future Keeper?

The very memory of it made Rhys squirm before the flames. The last thing he needed was that shadow trailing him around the Tower. Better a Delleray lost than an Alton if it came down to that.

Rhys sighed and threw a heavy, knotted log on the fire. The flames spun upward like hornets from a nest, crackling and popping. Mesmerized by the sound, he didn't hear the door open.

"I knocked three times, Rhys. Didn't you hear me? May I come in?"

Rhys peered over his shoulder. Diego stuck his head around the doorway. Though his clothes were dry, his red hair was wet. Beads of melting snow trickled down the sides of his red cheeks. He looked cold.

"What are you doing back?" Rhys asked.

"Armida's my home, too, remember?" came the younger boy's sharp retort. His cheeks turned a deeper red, reminding Rhys of the sun. He looked back at the fire.

Seeing his frown, Diego gave a hasty explanation, "I'd go to my room, but Payne's stuffed seven Free Amazons in there. He told me to sleep in here tonight."

Rhys thought of the cluttered attic room where Diego slept, picturing seven Free Amazons crawling over each other like beetles in an overcrowded hole. He made no attempt to stifle the sigh escaping from his lips.

"Come on," he shrugged. "Get over to the fire. You look great." It was not a compliment.

At the invitation Diego hurried to the hearth. He rubbed his hands together, shifting back and forth on his feet, his voice jerking with each lunge.

"I just got back from leading the third group out to

the camp at Mariposa. The snow's falling in blankets out there! The wind about ripped my ears off."

Diego was exaggerating, of course. He always did when he was excited or nervous. Rhys rose and began to pace. Diego's hopping was giving him a headache.

"I suppose Payne let you go because you're used to snow like this up there in the Hellers," he grumbled, still mad at Payne for not allowing him to have any responsibility. How could his older brother favor the son of some other man over his own family?

As if Diego had read his thoughts, the boy said, "He didn't do me a favor, Rhys. It would be real easy to get lost out there. And you'd probably like that."

Rhys stopped pacing and swung around on his bootheels. The hairs on the back of his neck stood on end. He opened his mouth to protest but Diego continued before he could speak.

"No, I know how you feel about me. If I got lost that would be one less Delleray your Council would have to deal with. Gads! You Comyn are so smug; it makes me sick."

He turned away from Rhys and held his hands out to the fire. Diego's throat hurt with the pent-up anger he had built up in his mumbling, bitter ride back to Armida, in snow so deep he'd spent the last league dragging his terrified mare behind him. Every head in the hall downstairs had turned when he'd entered. Payne even stood speechless after Diego had reported on the weather conditions.

He had only wanted to help; instead he had managed to do one more thing his cousin found offensive. Perhaps trying to befriend Rhys Alton was like trying to put a chick back in its egg. He couldn't pretend to be Rhys' equal, even *laran* couldn't help there. Rhys didn't believe him anyway. Why try? What should it matter that Rhys and most of the Alton clan wanted to be rid of him? The tight pain in Diego's chest insisted that it mattered.

"You're a liar, Diego Delleray. No one wants that and you know it," Rhys tugged on Diego's tunic, forcing him to turn around.

"It's true, Rhys Alton, and you know it!" Diego answered. "Admit it. If I got lost out there, your Council wouldn't have to worry about what to do with me now that Payne has called me his son and wants me to receive cadet training. What you fools don't realize is that a Delleray can't ever get lost!"

The moment those words were out of his mouth, Diego regretted them. He moaned, clamping a cold hand over his lips. Around him the room began to tilt and Rhys' face went out of focus. What had possessed him to say that? That was for the ears of Kimri of Arilinn; no one else would have understood.

"Just what do you mean by that?" Rhys shook him.

Diego jerked out of his grip.

"Nothing," he mumbled, hoping to keep the bile in his stomach where it belonged. All he needed was to make a mess on the floor in front of his cousin. He would never hear the end of it. Rhys, however, was persistent.

"What do you mean, a Delleray can't get lost?" The jarring words made Diego's head pound.

"I feel sick," he managed to say, putting a hand to his head.

"Oh, no, you don't! You're not so special. I could always make you tell me whether you wanted to or not."

Diego stumbled away from Rhys' threat. All his life he had heard about the Alton Gift. Rhys' inherited ability to force rapport had been enough reason to accept him into Arilinn Tower.

Minutes raced past him. Rhys was still demanding to know what he meant. The words roared through the back of his brain until he thought he would go mad.

"We never get lost," Diego finally admitted just to

make the roaring stop. His voice seemed a world away. "We can't. It's part of our Gift. It's a rapport with all inanimate objects. And," he added, amazed at the foolish pride in it, "it's a lot better than having you as a friend any day!"

"I don't believe you."

"Of course you don't. That's exactly why your precious Kimri is going to die out there in that blizzard."

Rhys put his hands on his waist, eyeing Diego critically. He looked sick.

"I suppose you're saying only a Delleray can find her because of this so-called 'Gift' of yours? What would you do, ask a tree which way she went?"

"I could," replied Diego.

Rhys lifted his eyes to the ceiling. Diego apparently thought he could do anything just because he had not gotten lost outside.

"But it's not that easy. If I were trained—but no one thinks it's important to send a Delleray to a Tower."

"It's not my fault you Dellerays joined the Aldarans."

Diego's face grew red. "And must I be blamed for what my ancestors did? I haven't done anything you can hate me for, Rhys."

"Prove it," Rhys challenged, "Find Kimri with your Gift then. I dare you!"

"Yes, dare me right out into that snow again and hope this time it'll bury me," Diego replied, knowing the whole idea was insane. He wasn't trained. His forefathers had seen to that. They had made it impossible to live with *laran*. Without training one went mad, and that scared him worse than death.

"I'll go with you," Rhys said, dropping his hands from his waist, his eyes coming alive at the thought.

"As if Payne would let you. Don't make me laugh." Diego sank down on the bed.

"I'm not joking. I'll go. If Kimri dies, I'll have to wait even longer to go to Arilinn and I've had it up to here with waiting." Rhys raised his hand above his head.

Diego hardly heard Rhys. He was too busy trying to force his thoughts into some kind of order. If Kimri died, what chance did he have of any Tower accepting him? At least she had promised to test him for *laran*. None of the other Keepers would have.

"If you die out there, what chance have you of being accepted anywhere?" he asked. He might save Kimri on his own, but if Rhys went along with no snow wisdom, they might all be doomed.

Rhys chose to ignore the comment. Instead his next words came as a total surprise.

"Find her, Diego. In the name of all the gods, find her if you can, and I'll do what I can to help you get accepted by the Tower."

"Why would you do a thing like that?" The question sprang from Diego's mouth like an insult.

"Because," Rhys explained, irritated at the question. Diego sat up with a shrug.

"What will stop you from saying you found her?"

"I wouldn't say that," Rhys exploded angrily. Outside the snow bashed into the window glass in heavy thuds. Rhys was cold again.

"Sure."

"Diego, I swear it. I wouldn't do a thing like that."

"And I said sure."

Rhys swung on him, pulling his short knife from the sheath at his side. Diego's face went pale. Rhys aimed it at him for an instant, then tossed it on the bed.

"There. Let the knife be my promise." He flung his words across the tense air between them.

Speechless, Diego picked up the knife. Its silver hilt flashed streaks of light upon the ceiling. Surely Rhys was desperate. Exchanging knives was a gesture of *bredin*. If Diego gave Rhys his own blade, they would become sworn brothers, oath-bound to protect each other to the death.

"Well? Isn't that good enough?" asked Rhys impatiently. His foot tapped in time to the thud of the snowflakes.

"Do you know what you're doing?" Diego asked in a whisper of amazement.

"Yes, yes, of course, and I might live to regret it, but that's all up to you. All I can say is, you'd better not be lying."

Diego flung himself off the bed, dragging up his own knife and handing it, hilt-face to Rhys. It was light and small, insignificant against the decorative hilt of Rhys' knife, pressed hard against the palm of his other hand.

"You won't regret this," Diego promised. His voice cracked with emotion and a sudden pride, "I swear it, *bredu*. I won't let you down."

Diego pried his frozen glove off the horn of his saddle with a grunt. The deep breath he took to make the sound froze in his throat. The snow which had let up for a few hours before dawn was beginning to fall again. It pierced his skin with that needle-point sharpness that brought tears to his eyes. His cheeks were frozen, his toes were numb in spite of the fur-lined boots, and his thoughts were smoldering dangerously on the tip of his tongue.

But what could he say? Rhys was expecting him to fail. That was it. Why else would he risk his knife? Rhys could always take it back again if Diego did not live up to their promise. Why did he feel he owed Rhys Alton anything, especially a favor like this? Did he want the acceptance of his father's brother so much that he would jeopardize both their lives? Or did it go deeper? Did he value the acceptance of the Comyn so much that folly seemed braver and more honorable than life without *laran*?

They had been trudging through walls of snow for several hours now. It had been easy to sneak out of

Armida. In the sleepy masses no one noticed the two boys make their way to the kitchens and out to the stables. Diego only regretted not having time to rest or eat. At the time resting was not feasible, and the thought of food had made his stomach turn.

Now he shut his eyelids against the snowstreaks. All he could see were the blue energy patterns of the Leronis of Arilinn. They stood out in front of dull, unnamed patterns swirling in the background of his mind. His head ached. His nerves were raw from the contact he had made with the silk pouch Kimri had placed around Rhys' neck. Such a contact had established her patterns for him, but it wasn't easy to keep them in focus.

If he could match up that pattern with a similar one on an inanimate object she might have touched, he would be able to find her. Unfortunately, any time he opened his eyes, the multiple patterns of older passersby made him dizzy and nauseous. Rhys' voice and face faded out on him or came up sharply in focus as if he were only inches away. Every time Diego closed his eyes, the blue of Kimri's pattern filled the blackness. If Kimri had been anywhere they happened to cross, the blue light swirled in a multitude of others who'd come or gone before her. It helped to pull his stiff body off his horse and touch the object to make the pattern come clear.

Diego had not been trained to filter out old patterns and as a result the contact was a lengthy process of self-learned sorting. He often came out of it disoriented and incoherent. All Rhys could do was wait. He waited now.

Diego forced his eyelids up, looking through the space between the snowflakes to the blur that was his cousin. He shook his head. The gesture hurt his face like someone twisting a screw.

A most independent person, this Rhys Alton. *Bredu*, he thought, but neither had earned a reason to use the word. A boast and a dare hardly made two antagonistic young men *bredin*. *Working together like this must be awful for you,* he thought, unable to keep the strong silver-blue patterns of Rhys' energons from swirling all about. Diego clung to the saddle horn to keep himself from toppling off his mare.

He looked away, thankful for the blanketing cloud-cover. Scanning the scene around them, he sighed. The valley was filling with snow as if Zandru himself desired to make of it a tenth hell. Snow smothered the road to Syrtis. On the far rim of the valley, large irregular shapes hid boulders and overhangs. He knew them to be a rock formation called the Covey. It had once housed a certain wild hawk used in falconry. Abandoned now, because thieves of an earlier day had a passion for the red-speckled eggs, all that remained were the black eyes of shallow caves and narrow crevices.

Had anyone desired to escape this weather, the Covey provided ample protection from the elements. At that thought Diego forced the clear blue pattern of Kimri onto the snow-draped bulges. They seemed so far away, farther still because he felt so awful.

Diego leaned forward in his saddle. His shifting weight made it creak and moan beneath trembling legs.

Yellows, greens, even faded blues danced across the boulders to his right. Old and blurred and yet, like a ripple in the water, one seemed stronger than the rest. Kimri?

A blast of wind made him lose his balance, plummeting forward into the icy neck of his mare. The horse neighed, pranced nervously in little side-steps, and rocked Diego as he fought to keep his balance.

A gloved hand gathered up the reins and the jolting stopped abruptly. Another glove pushed him back to a sitting position. The grip was strong. He came up facing the dancing eyes of Rhys Alton.

"This is madness, Diego!" shouted Rhys above the wind. "Kimri wasn't headed toward Syrtis! It's way out of the way."

Diego shook his head, flinging patches of snow from his hood.

"No, Rhys. I think she's there." He pointed a shaking finger toward the highest peaks of the Covey.

"Are you crazy?"

Rhys stared at him with his mouth open. The snowflakes caught on the purple of his tongue, melting instantly. He swallowed.

"Up there? Kimri couldn't get up there. Not that high."

Diego ignored Rhys' belligerent tone and pointed again to the spot where the blue pattern danced. Rhys bent close to him and said, angrily, "Diego, I am soaked to the bone and frozen to this saddle, and there's no way you're going to get me across that valley or up there in snow like this. I'm going home."

"Rhys!" Diego cried out, fumbling for his wrist, "You've got to believe me. I saw something. She's there. I know she is." He prayed to himself, *She's got to be.*

Rhys looked down in horror at Diego's gloved hand on his wrist. The rapport came like a flood of emotions roaring out of a secret inner place, opening a channel between their misery. Rhys had heard Diego's unspoken plea. He succumbed to his uncertainty and sickness. It revolted him. He shook his hand free as if he'd scorched it on the forge. Diego moaned.

"Please, Rhys," he begged, "we're so close. Please. Just across the valley. if I can't get a clearer picture, we'll turn back. But I can't go back now, even if you do."

"You're crazy. Aldones above, why didn't you tell me you were sick? You don't know what you're doing," Rhys told him, outraged.

Diego managed to pull his shoulders back.

"I do so. Don't believe me then. Go back, you coward." Diego urged his horse past Rhys in the direction he had pointed.

"Gods!" Rhys swore, angered at the insult, angered at the part of him that dared not break the oath of *bredin*.

Fine time to prove it. He swung his horse around, no longer feeling the reins which, by this time, had frozen to his gloves.

"Diego!" he yelled until the boy looked at him. "All right. But if you fall off your horse, I'm picking you up and taking you home." He shook his head, mumbling, "Fool. I'm a fool to think any Delleray could make sense."

"I'm not lying, Rhys."

Diego had not opened his swollen lips. Rhys caught the thought clearly enough. It was strong.

"Yeah, but you're sick. Come on. Let's get up there before Zandru turns us both into icicles."

Diego rocked forward on his knees, holding his hands out to prevent himself from keeling over. His gloves went elbow-deep into the powdery snow. He could scarcely feel his fingers anymore, they were so numbed by the cold. But the energon pattern was there. He'd spotted it in one brilliant flash of familiarity. He had not been wrong. The curving blue lines of the Keeper Kimri were spread across the snow-covered boulder as if she were sitting right in front of him. They were so close. Diego blanked out the world until all he knew were the iron-hard lines of blue racing out up the cliff face.

"Diego! Diego!"

He moaned as a silver splinter of light shattered the clear blue pattern under his fingers. A voice was yelling at him. It sounded like the howling of the wind rocking him with that same insistent motion by which it shook the limbs of the distant trees.

"Diego. Come back. Come out of it." The voice was very stern. "Don't scare me like this."

"What?" Diego opened his eyes and tried to focus on the deep gray eyes of his cousin. He could feel Rhys' breath on his numb cheek. Warm! Was anything warm in this world anymore?

"What?" he asked again, surprised at the weakness in his voice.

"Stop it. Let's go back. Let someone else find her," Rhys pleaded. "They'll find her, but don't scare me anymore."

Rhys shook him again. He had no idea what Diego had seen, but the blank, dead look in his eyes was frightening.

None of this made any sense. Why hadn't he listened to Payne? Why hadn't Kimri listened to him? They were all going to die out here. He had been crazy to believe Diego. He had been desperate. Diego had *laran*, all right. Their earlier rapport had proven that. But he also had threshold sickness. He could not even tell when Diego was in rapport with the rocks or entering crisis. His channels were muddied, gray like the clouds. They had to go home. Panicked, he began to mumble.

"I'm crazy. You're not crazy. You're just sick. I dared you into this. You told me you had a rapport with rocks. Zandru's hell, Diego, that gene's been extinct for ages. If you don't stop this, you'll throw your body into crisis." Rhys shook his head wildly, "Damn it! Why didn't you tell me you were having threshold sickness."

Diego only fell forward with his chin resting uneasily on Rhys' snow-white jacket. Lazy flakes twirled in and out of the space around them.

"Rhys, I know where she is," Diego muttered, then choked, "but I . . . I can't. . . ."

Rhys squeezed Diego's limp body. "I'll get someone. They can start searching from here, but we've got to go back. They'll find her," he said into his ear.

"*No!*" The mental yell was acute. "She can't live that long. She's .fading." Suddenly Diego's fingers pressed hard into Rhys' back. "Rhys, you're an Alton, *take* it from me! I can't get it past the sickness. I can't get it into words. Rhys, please."

Rhys looked at him in horror. Where had Diego gotten such an idea? It could kill him. He took a great breath, remembering. He'd given Diego the idea himself. Pride and anger had made him declare a power Kimri told him to avoid using above all else.

How could he even think of using it? Aldones, he didn't even know how to control it. The Alton gift was the gift of forced rapport. Absolute trust was essential if one didn't want to damage the victim. Victim. Diego had always been his victim. He had never believed any Delleray worthy of his trust or friendship.

Then why did you throw him your knife? This is all your fault. You've craved responsibility all your life and now you're ready to toss it back. Grown up? Hardly. Well, grow up now. Now or never.

A meek voice popped into the storm in Rhys' head. It was clear, calm. "I trust you."

Rhys drew a sharp breath. "I could throw you into crisis. Why? Why didn't you tell me you were sick?"

As if slapped, the voice retreated. "I couldn't stand to have you laugh at me. You would have laughed at me." Stunned by the truth of it, Rhys could not speak. "There is a knife between us. I trust you because you believed me. I know where Kimri is. Hurry, take it from me before I pass out, or throw up, or die."

Rhys grabbed Diego's wrist. The trust was unworthy of him. His whole body shook. Hadn't Diego done enough to prove his friendship? Even without the knife they were brothers with *laran*. They were *bredin*.

He would try once more to discourage him.

"Diego. . . ."

"Please, *bredu*," Diego whispered.

"I could kill you."

Diego shook his head. "You still don't understand, do you? It's Kimri you kill, not I, if you don't help me now. Isn't she more important to Darkover than either of us?"

And this time it was Rhys who pulled away as if slapped, slapped with the profound truth of Diego's words. There was no arguing them and he knew it. Tenderly, he pulled Diego closer.

"You are right and I am wrong. Thank you, *bredu*."

"No thanks, just speed. Hurry."

Hurry!

Rhys scanned the cliff face. The wind hummed eerie tunes around the rocks. Kimri was up there. Would she understand? He had to use the gift. If it killed Diego, it killed them all. She'd have to understand he'd used it to save them—but he was scared. This was responsibility.

Hurry!

He placed his fingers just above Diego's forehead, and bit down hard on his bottom lip in concentration.

"Stop!"

Rhys' mind filled with the warning. He pulled himself back to consciousness and looked up. Kimri of Arilinn stood before him dressed in heavy furs and thick leather boots. Her smile was benevolent, sad.

"That will not be necessary." She bent down and covered Diego's eyes with the palm of her hand as others, members of Arilinn's Tower, came out of the snow around them.

"The boy lives," she pronounced, solemnly. "You have both done well."

"Done well?"

Rhys was stunned. The realization that the entire situation might have been planned filled his brain like a fire. He began to shake. Done well? This wasn't a performance.

"He could have died," Rhys shouted at her.

"I think not," replied a heavyset man with damp red hair. "Kimri is a good judge of men."

The keeper rose to her feet, beckoning the same man to lift Diego out of the snow. A hand at Rhys' elbow helped him off his knees. Rhys stared at the keeper unable to hide his anger.

"Even I cannot question my responsibilities, Rhys Alton. Too many other lives depend on that." She looked around at the friends before her. "Bring them," she said, and walked away.

If Rhys had not known better, he could have sworn he was sitting in the family hall at Armida and not in a cave formed by the jagged rocks of the Covey.

He sat near the fire, sipping hot spiced wine and feeling nervous. His temper was smoldering. Kimri's men had taken Diego somewhere out of sight and, though he'd been reassured that Diego would live, he could not find it in himself to believe them. The idea that he and Diego could have died out there, that innocent men and women could have died believing they sought a missing woman when in reality she knew exactly where she was, made him boil inside. She'd lied to them. How could he ever trust them, trust her, again?

"Rhys?"

He turned at the sound of his name. Payne and Kimri stood together at the mouth of the tunnel leading deep inside the cave. Rhys groaned at the thought that his brother had known all along, perhaps even designed the plan with Kimri. He slouched down in his chair. They stepped closer.

"Is Diego all right?" Rhys asked, not looking up.

"He'll be fine now," Payne replied.

Long seconds of silence followed.

"You have something to say to me?" Kimri asked.

"This wasn't fair," he mumbled. She asked him to repeat himself. "It wasn't fair."

"Few things in life are fair. I must be concerned with how one deals with injustice and so must you. Should Diego suffer for the sins of his forefathers? Would it be fair, Rhys, for a Gift long hidden to be lost because foolish men are determined to live by tradition and not see beyond their comfortable Comyn laws?"

Rhys tapped his foot nervously against the stone floor, keeping his eyes averted.

Kimri made sense. He had been on the verge of breaking tradition himself before she came upon them. He would have used the Alton Gift before he had been prepared.

"Well?" Payne asked.

"No, it wouldn't have been fair."

"Then maybe someday you will find it in your heart to judge me fairly. You are both welcome at Arilinn," she said. When he did not reply, she added, "I will send Diego in."

"He is my son, even if not of my body. I couldn't let him die," Payne told Rhys after Kimri had disappeared.

"You came pretty close."

"I had faith in you, Rhys."

Rhys stared at his older brother.

"Armida will be yours one day. I know now I will leave it in good hands."

"Armida?"

"I will have no more sons, Rhys. It was crucial to know what you both would do. We had to be sure."

"But Diego . . ."

"Does not have the Alton Gift, the sign of inheritance. I must give Diego what I can, but Armida will be yours. I am confident that you will use your Gift wisely. Ah, here is Diego."

With that pronouncement, Payne left the room while Diego entered. A silent greeting passed between father and son before Payne disappeared.

Diego looked tired, but there was more color in his cheeks and the fire's reflection danced in his green eyes. He held something in his left hand.

"I didn't know, Rhys. Honestly. She said she'd test me for *laran*, but I never dreamed she would do it that way."

Rhys didn't know what to say. He believed Diego, but still didn't know if he could forgive Kimri.

"Here," Diego said, holding the knife out to Rhys, "you probably want this back."

"Don't you dare give that knife back to me, Diego," he said, resting his hand on his brother's to push the knife away.

Their rapport was instant, strong, and clear. They both knew they had earned the right to call other other *bredin*. They both had learned that friendship was not easily given or taken away. Relieved, they took each other into a bear hug as their laughter filled the room.

DAW PRESENTS THESE BESTSELLERS BY
MARION ZIMMER BRADLEY

THE DARKOVER NOVELS

The Founding

☐ DARKOVER LANDFALL UE2234—$3.95

The Ages of Chaos

☐ HAWKMISTRESS! UE2064—$3.95
☐ STORMQUEEN! UE2092—$3.95

The Hundred Kingdoms

☐ TWO TO CONQUER UE2174—$3.50

The Renunciates (Free Amazons)

☐ THE SHATTERED CHAIN UE1961—$3.50
☐ THENDARA HOUSE UE2119—$3.95
☐ CITY OF SORCERY UE2122—$3.95

Against the Terrans: The First Age

☐ THE SPELL SWORD UE2091—$2.50
☐ THE FORBIDDEN TOWER UE2235—$3.95

Against the Terrans: The Second Age

☐ THE HERITAGE OF HASTUR UE2079—$3.95
☐ SHARRA'S EXILE UE1988—$3.95

THE DARKOVER ANTHOLOGIES
with The Friends of Darkover

☐ THE KEEPER'S PRICE UE2236—$3.95
☐ SWORD OF CHAOS UE2172—$3.50
☐ FREE AMAZONS OF DARKOVER UE2096—$3.50
☐ THE OTHER SIDE OF THE MIRROR UE2185—$3.50
☐ RED SUN OF DARKOVER UE2230—$3.95